George B. Douglas

Contemporary Scottish Verse

George B. Douglas

Contemporary Scottish Verse

ISBN/EAN: 9783337238414

Printed in Europe, USA, Canada, Australia, Japan

Cover: Foto ©Andreas Hilbeck / pixelio.de

More available books at **www.hansebooks.com**

The Canterbury Poets.

Edited by William Sharp.

SCOTTISH VERSE.

 CONTEMPORARY SCOTTISH
VERSE: EDITED, WITH AN
INTRODUCTION, BY SIR GEORGE
DOUGLAS, BART., AUTHOR OF
"THE NEW BORDER TALES."

LONDON:
WALTER SCOTT, LIMITED,
24 WARWICK LANE.
NEW YORK: 3 EAST FOURTEENTH STREET.

AUTHORS AND TITLES.

vi   *AUTHORS AND TITLES.*

INTRODUCTORY NOTE.

THE editor does not for one moment claim for this little book that it represents all that is good, or even all that is best, in the Scottish poetry of the period. Had he intended it to do this, a much larger number of writers must have been laid under contribution. But, in dealing with writers who are still, so to speak, more or less upon trial, he has judged it most satisfactory to represent each one *substantially*, rather than by one or two poems merely, —thus enabling readers to form an opinion of the scope and character of each; a course which has necessarily reduced to a very few the number of names which could be included in so small a volume. He wishes it, then, to be understood that he presents his book as a sample, rather than as the highly concentrated essence, of the Scottish verse of to-day and yesterday; whilst for further "Specimens" of Modern Scottish Poets, he would refer his readers to the comprehensive work of Mr. Edwards, of Brechin, the fifteenth and final volume of which has recently issued from the press.

A word as to the manner in which the selections have

been made.   Except in the cases of the deceased poets
and of three of the living ones—Dr. George MacDonald,
Mr. Andrew Lang, and Mr. R. L. Stevenson—the
editor has had the advantage of suggestions from the
poets themselves.   These suggestions have in some cases
been slight ; but in several cases the selection from his
own work has literally been made by the poet in person.
The question may perhaps be asked, Is this method of
selection a desirable one ? for has it not often been main-
tained that the poet is the worst judge in the world of
his own poetry?   It may be answered that, in an age
like the present, when the critical so much preponderates
over the creative faculty, this dictum probably contains
even less of truth than at other times.   Again, among
the writers here represented, not a few are professed
critics as well as poets ; whilst in all cases those of his
own productions which a writer prizes most highly must
possess at the least a special interest for the student.
The editor, then, desires to return his best thanks not
only for the permission which has been so generously
granted to him by the poets to make selections from
their works, but also for the assistance which in many
cases has been afforded him in making these selections.
At the same time he is enabled to feel that a certain
share of responsibility as to some of the pieces selected
is shifted from his shoulders.

If we now turn to the poems themselves, they will be
found to include some very beautiful, and many highly

interesting and characteristic pieces. It will, no doubt, be matter of surprise and of unfeigned regret to some readers that the most distinctive form of Scottish poetical composition—the vernacular song—is almost unrepresented. Alone, perhaps, in the native melody of "Surfaceman" is the ancient genius of Scottish poetry heard once more. And to "Surfaceman"—to Mr. Alexander Anderson— belongs a further distinction of a peculiarly winning character. He has written the ideal poem of the nursery. His *Cuddle Doon* has just that touch of tenderness which—with all their wonderful and delightful reconstruction of child-life—we miss from the nursery poems of William Miller and of Mr. R. L. Stevenson. And though the author is as yet but in middle life, Scotland has already made his masterpiece quite her own —as much her own, indeed, as she has made Burns's songs. For I should suppose that there is scarcely a cottage—in the southern half of the country at least— where *Cuddle Doon* is not a "household word,"—an item in the little hoard of things of beauty, of humour, and of tenderness, spontaneously treasured by the Scottish peasant for his almost unconscious delectation. Surely to have achieved so much is to have achieved immortality —not, indeed, in its grandest, but in one of its fairest forms. Neither must we omit a word of praise for the kindly humour, and the admirable moral lesson, so soundly inculcated amid such sunny laughter, in the author's *Big Fittie Jock*.

Next among writers of the vernacular come "Hugh

Haliburton" and Mr. R. L. Stevenson. Their use of the Scottish dialect is quite peculiar, and to a Scotsman highly interesting and delightful. They employ the language of the peasant in the manner of the scholar, and they are the first, I believe, who have so employed it. Of course there have been men of letters, men of learning, before now who have used the dialect; but when they did so they had no aim but to speak as like peasants as they could. With Mr. Robertson and Mr. Stevenson, especially the former, the aim, unless I am mistaken, is wholly different. They are "stylists" in the language of the unlettered. Their classic elegance, their *curiosa felicitas*, keeps step with their command of, with their erudition in the Doric. Is this yet another augury that our native tongue is soon to be ranked among the dead ones? If it be, it is the only happy augury of that sad consummation of which I have ever heard; for in this case death carries within it the germ of a new life. And it is to Mr. Robertson and Mr. Stevenson, and to the followers—for I think there will be followers—in the movement which they have inaugurated, that we must look for a revival of poetry written in the Scottish dialect.

But the gallant muse of Mr. Stevenson has already played many parts in literature. Even here, in the course of a page or two, we have had occasion to refer to the author of *Treasure Island* as a writer of nursery, and of dialect, poetry. His best verse, his most distinctive metrical compositions, must be classed under yet another heading. His Polynesian *Ballads* are too long to be quoted here in full, and they do not lend themselves to the extract. But, in spite of one noticeable and regrettable falling away, it is in these ballads that the author's finest and most characteristic poetry is to be found. There is a passage in his latest novel—the novel in which, as seems to me, his genius stands for the first time fully developed—which, unconsciously, beneath a figure, exactly sets forth his own position in the literature of our time. He is speaking in the person of one of his characters, who is looking westward over the sea from San Francisco. "I stood there," says he, "on the extreme shore of the West and of to-day. Seventeen hundred years ago, and seven thousand miles to the east, a legionary stood, perhaps, upon the wall of Antoninus, and looked northward toward the mountains of the Picts. For all the interval of time and space I, when I looked from the cliff-house on the broad Pacific, was that man's heir and analogue: each of us standing on the verge of the Roman empire (or, as we now call it, Western civilization), each of us gazing onward into zones unromanized." And, so, it is Mr. Stevenson's especial distinction,—a lofty one truly—that he has left behind him the old world, with its old and somewhat worn scenes and characters, and set forth—a literary pioneer equipped *cap-à-pie*—toward the new worlds which yet remain to conquer and to reclaim. In this he is true to the enterprize and to the roving genius of his countrymen. For us he is the Homer—and a truly Homeric Homer—of the Islands of the Pacific.

It is, however, no part of my intention to claim for each or all of the writers here represented a distinctively Scottish character. Without descending to over-refinement, or to artificiality, I could not do so if I would. For, to state a sufficiently obvious fact, the narrowly national character which, during well-nigh four centuries, so plainly distinguished the best of Scottish poetry has in this century entirely passed away. The poets, then, who figure in the present volume are there grouped together almost solely for the sake of convenience. They have the accident of a Scottish parentage, a birth upon Scottish soil, in common, and but little if anything more. Indeed it is by the variety and individuality, rather than by the similarity or community, of their enterprize and their inspiration that the reader of the following pages is likely to be impressed. A few brief notes, dealing in the most general fashion with the scope and character of each writer's work, must, therefore, here take the place of any more comprehensive critical considerations.

Mr. William Bell Scott is the only Scottish Pre-Raphaelite of whose existence I am aware; yet Rossetti in his writings was as much a Scotsman as he. Mr. Bell Scott's finest poetry is to be found among his sonnets, which—though too often marred by faulty rhymes—will probably be remembered for their grace, their depth, and their meditative passion, as among the finest produced in an age peculiarly prolific in sonnets.

The City of Dreadful Night is the despair of a maker of selections. It is the work by which its author's reputation must stand or fall, and from it alone can he be represented ; yet to convey by means of quotation any adequate idea of its sombre and terrifying imaginative grandeur would be impossible. The poem owes its effect to the admirable art by which a powerful and peculiar impression, produced at the commencement, is unflaggingly sustained and continually heightened until the close. Examined in detail, the workmanship is by no means of an absolute perfection—the verse inclines to halt, minor flaws disfigure the surface. But if the poem be viewed broadly, as a whole, these flaws will be lost sight of; and, as I have already indicated, it is only as a whole that the Epic of Pessimism can be fairly judged. Necessity has somewhat narrowly limited my quotations from it ; but if these should serve the purpose of sending new readers to the book itself their end will be attained. Next after *The City of Dreadful Night,* the peculiar genius of James Thomson is perhaps seen to best advantage in the highly imaginative, though somewhat too diffuse and fluid, poem entitled *In the Room.*

In the high spirits, the sturdy prejudices, and the aggressively outspoken opinion of the veteran Professor Blackie, Scotsmen will recognise well-marked character- istics of a certain type of Scotsman; and the Professor also treats by preference themes which are national.

Verse, if one may hazard a guess, has been with him rather a relaxation than a pursuit ; but, whether in verse or prose, everything that he does is essentially *sui generis.* And, in Scotland at least, his appeal seldom fails of a response. Personally I might have wished that he had written oftener whilst in the vein which.produced lines so truly Shakespearian in sentiment as these :

> " What live we for but this,
> Into the sour to breathe the soul of sweetness,
> The stunted growth to rear to fair completeness,
> Drown sneers in smiles, kill hatred with a kiss,
> And to the sandy waste bequeath the fame
> That the grass grew behind us where we came! "

Probably no man living knows the Border Country, its history and traditions, better than does Professor Veitch, the study of whose verse may well be supplemented by a reading of his *History and Poetry of the Scottish Border.*

There is nothing Scottish about Professor Nichol's work. Learning, weight of thought, condensation of language without obscurity : these qualities—in general more essentially distinctive of the finer Roman, than of English, writers—are the characteristics of his two published volumes of verse. Such a poem, too, as the most purely personal of its author's utterances, the fine and austere *Donna Vera,* seems also to disclose a Roman temper of mind in the writer. Lovers of literature will await with interest the publication of a promised Second Part of his *Hannibal.*

The names of Dr. Walter Smith and Dr. George

MacDonald are naturally mentioned together. The former has rendered into easy verse much of the thought which forms the current coin of the contemporary Broad Church pulpit. He is a voluminous writer, and many of his poems have passed through several editions. His poetry belongs for the most part to the school of Browning; which is to be regretted, for though the author of *Sordello* may be a fine poet he is a dangerous model. The scene from *Kildrostan* extracted in the text contains a masterly dramatic exposition of the gospel according to a certain brilliant living writer who shall here be nameless. But the dramatist fails in humour as well as in justice when he takes Tremain so seriously. The twinkle never absent from the poet's eye, the innocent delight in speculation and in eloquence run mad, the love of paradox for its own sake, remain unindicated in the picture. On the other hand the inconceivable moral cowardice displayed by Sir Diarmid at a later period in the play—whilst completely shattering our early vision of him as a simple young Highland chieftain, *sans peur et sans reproche*—imparts, upon a retrospect, rather an unpleasant flavour to his present single-minded censures. *Kildrostan*, nevertheless, appears to me to remain the most successful of its author's works, and the play the form most favourable to the display of his talents. The great mass of Dr. MacDonald's poetry is of a religious character, and is probably most widely in demand among readers who turn to it for qualities which are not primarily poetic. In its union of pure devotional feeling with quaintness and simplicity of illustration and expression, it often reminds us of George Herbert's verse. As a poet, however, the author is seen to best advantage in his ballads and Scots pieces ; and it is from these that our extracts, necessarily narrowly limited, have for the most part been drawn.

On its first publication, if I am rightly informed, Lord Southesk's *Pigworm and Dixie* met with very rough usage at the hands of certain of the critics. But, viewed in due relation to the author's aim, to me it appears to be nothing less than a masterpiece. The self-delineation of the speaker, Joey Peggram, is as life-like (need I point out that I don't say as beautiful or as dignified?) as a portrait by Moroni, and is dashed in with the spirit and the ease of a Frans Hals. The verse employed by the author is doggerel, it is true; but it is the one medium in which his effect could have been produced. Then the poem is brimful of wit, and the triumph of the whole achievement is that, notwithstanding our categorical detestation of every trait revealed by the uncompromising candour of the blackleg, our feelings towards him in the end are very far from unkindly. We have been parenthetically informed by honest Ben Dixie in another poem, his Confession, that his discarded crony "had some heart"; and this, I suppose, must be the explanation of the singular anomaly. The delightful little piece entitled *The Flitch of Dunmow*—so thoroughly English, not Scottish, in its character—almost seems to recapture once more the lost charm of the classic nursery rhyme, or of one of those Songs of the People whose words are remembered though their authors are forgotten; and, in an age so starved of animal spirits—at least in its literature—as the present, it can scarcely be too highly prized. These two poems seem to me to suffice of themselves to support a poetical reputation.

To revert to poets of a younger generation, Mr. Robert Buchanan's work is altogether too multifarious and fills too large a space in the public eye to be summed up in a few lines, whilst it is of course much too well known to render any attempt at so summing it up desirable. Something of the versatility of the author's talent may be gathered from the specimens in the text. In *The Wake of O'Hara*, an every-day occurrence of humble life—the unpicturesque humble life, too, of a city—detailed in the plainest verse, becomes the perfect means of a revelation of the author's "gift of tears." In *The Vision of the Man Accurst*, on the other hand, the greatest difficulties of ideal presentment and environment are surmounted with a success no less entire. In the Coruisken Sonnets, again, the author appears in person as the poet, contemplative and inspired, of Nature's most repellent fastnesses. Our extracts are based upon the poet's own published selections from his works, with the addition, suggested by himself, of the fine *Confessio Amantis*, in the impassioned verse of which some of his most dearly-cherished beliefs seem to find utterance.

From Mr. Buchanan we turn to the tender feeling,

the classic grace, the "golden line" of Mr. Andrew Lang—a poet, alas ! too prone to "trifle" with the Muse. As a translator from the classical poets, Mr. Lang's perfect art has probably never been equalled in our literature. Circumstances have unfortunately circumscribed our selections from his work.

In the work of Mr. William Sharp—as the writer of the Introduction to an American edition of his works has pointed out—the streams of a northern and a southern inspiration—of Yarrow and of Helicon—flow freely and untroubled side by side. He has imported the warmth and colour of Italian landscape into his "impressionist" pictures of Rome and the Campagna, whilst the grey, fateful, low-impending heaven of his native shores closes above the weird of Michael Scott. Whether the writer's aim is perfectly legitimate or not, I do not undertake to decide ; but if we would match the splendour of colour in the little poem entitled *The Swimmer of Nemi*, we should have to turn, I think, from poetry to painting, and in painting to the work of Etty.

In presuming to appear in person in the company of his elders and betters, the editor relies on the indulgence of his readers; and, finally, in the author of *Scaramouch in Naxos*, he hails in a luxuriant spring the promise of a rich poetic harvest.

GEORGE DOUGLAS.

LONDON, *September* 1893.

NOTE.

The Editor desires to record his thanks to the living poets represented in this volume for leave to print extracts from their writings, and to the late Professor Minto, literary executor to the late Mr. William Bell Scott, for leave to print extracts from the writings of that gentleman. The Editor also desires to make the due acknowledgments to publishers—particularly to the following :—to Messrs. Reeves & Turner, publishers of *The City of Dreadful Night;* to Messrs. Chatto & Windus, publishers of Dr. MacDonald's poems, and of Mr. Stevenson's *Underwoods* and *Ballads;* to Messrs. Maclehose, publishers of Dr. Walter Smith's poems; Messrs. Longmans, publishers of Mr. Andrew Lang's poems, and of Mr. Stevenson's *Child's Garden of Verse;* and Messrs. Paterson, publishers of Mr. J. Logie Robertson's poems.

Contemporary Scottish Verse.

WILLIAM BELL SCOTT.

MUSIC OF THE SPHERES.

(1837 ; REVISED 1872.)

"All things were created by numbers, and again it must be so."
—PLATO.

THE Angel of Death through the dry earth slid,
Like a mole to the Dervish Yan,
Lying beneath the turf six feet,
Till he reached the coffin and smote its lid
With his hammer that wakes the Mosleman ;
And whispered thus through board and sheet,
    " Arise, that thy closed eye and ear
    The things that Are may see and hear !"
The Dervish turned him round, and rose
On his knees at the sound of the three dread blows:
He was alive and a man again,
Yet he felt no earth, nor of it thought,
But rose without a strain.

I

Friends wept aloud for the Dervish Yan,
And a wife she wept for a Christian man,
A long train of mutes had but lately laid
Under the sward in the cool green shade
Of a sanctified wall whose stones divide
The earth where heretic corses hide,
From that set apart for the faithful alone,
And over him carved his name on a stone ;
But the dead man laughed as he woke below,
For he rejoiced at wakening so,—
  " I am awake, awake and well ;
  Am I myself indeed, and where ?—
  Here is no light, here is no air,
  Here is neither heaven nor hell."
The Angel of Death stooping clasped his hand,
And silenced him, whispering, " I command
The power whose song shall answer thee,—
As it hath been, so shall it be."

Beneath the head
When the Jew is dead
Is a clod of quick clay kneaden :
And as the mourners backward go,
Three turfs, green turfs, to the grave they throw,
Saying, " Thou shalt like these green turfs grow,
May thy soul be buried in Eden."
Thus in the Levites' vault was laid
A Rabbi, thus were the last rites paid,
At the same time that the Summoner
Made the two Gentile corses stir,
And with a writhe like theirs, his eyes
The Rabbi opening, tried to rise.
" Have the demons power o'er me ?" he cries,
Dragging himself with painful toil

From the mould which is the earth-worm's spoil,
And trembled to hear the words " Follow thou too,
Within the sphere of the melody
That re-createth those who die !"

And thus have these three mortals passed,
Being dead, into the formless vast,
Which we in life, expectant, still
By creeds and myths and fancies, fill
With hopes and fears like life on earth,—
Things for the days 'tween death and birth,
For which we care not any more
Down upon the further shore.

" By what uncertain sense we're led,
Born thus again—the body dead
Our mother—the grave our nursing bed !

" Haunted still with hearth and home,
Hammer in hand, sword, pen, and tome,
Sun and moon and starry dome.

" Morn till evening toil-in-vain,
Market loss and market gain,
Restless sea and wheaten plain.

" Down the darkness go we still,
Go we without choice of will ;
From Gentile's scoff and scorner's rail,
From worm and asp, from kiss and wail ;
From master's whip, Muezzim's cry,
Camel and rice, and blank white sky.

"Carried or driven, through sea, through air,
Carried sheer down by cloud or stair,
Are we or are we not—whither away?
Phantoms of life's fever-day.
Can we not return again,
As leaves come after spring-time's rain?
The trumpet cannot call the dead,
Yet I hear it overhead;
A madman's sleep is thick and brief;
The dawn would give us all relief!—
Ah, 'tis gone, and thou, the dearest!
Thou with moonlike light appearest;
Thou, mine own, beside the hearth,
Assiduous with childish mirth—
Dreams, only dreams! the past doth cry,
In the throes of dissolving memory.
O brother spectres who have come
Out of yourselves,—oh, can ye tell,
Rise we or sink—to heaven or hell?
But even now with my own old eyes
I saw the ghost of myself arise;
And then forthwith I was beguiled
To think myself again a child.
But what, alas! are those below
That to and fro
Pass like men walking fast, and then
Pass the very same again?
Alike they are, even every one,
Not as men beneath the sun;—
Now they stalk our heads above,
Now beneath our feet they move,
Now they pass through us quite, as though
Shadows with like shadows blent,
Shadows from some real things sent,
We their shadows cannot know!

Gone, gone, gone ! a fiery wind
Severs the vision, and mountain or flood,
City or temple, or cedar-wood,
Or rock-walls with their multitude
Of caverns void and blind,
Fragments of this baseless world,
About us are flashed out and furled ;
And phantoms without number vast,
Interlace the insane dream,
Hurtle together, and never get past :
And a leprous light, a light and breath,
Like the phosphor in the eyes of Death,
Follows each phantom ; down they stream,
Wingless, from above descending,
Straight and stiff ; nor is the hair
On their rigid shoulders pending
Stirred by any fitful air.
Together they rush now, from near and far,
As if around a central war,
And now in circles whirl, while we—
We cleave the whirlpool steadily.
If any god still hears our wail,
For an hour again
Let us be men,
Or now cease utterly and fail
To know ourselves, to think and be !

" Hath our prayer been heard ?   Ah, no ;
Spectres that have never trod
Earth with man or heaven with God
Rise stark and slow ;
Rings of gold
About their corded locks are rolled,
Dreadful symbols of dead creeds,

And dripping brands
Are in their hands ;—
Naked giants ! how they hold
By the nostrils monstrous steeds !
They meet, they rush together : now
The furies of battle are over all,
And some struggle upwards in pain, some fall
Sheer through the seething gulf below ;—
Allah el Allah, how are we
In this collapsing death-strife free ?
Oh, that we could dissolve at once
To nothingness ;—advance,
Ye barbed giants ! smoke and fire
Lap us round till we expire,—
Expire, cease utterly and fail
To retract ourselves, to think and be ! ”

Thus the dead men from the grave
Wailed as they went ; but who can say
How to paint the unknown way
Within the wondrous door of death ?
Or what the mysteries are that pave
The path to New Life, when the breath
And senses cease to be, as now,
The guardians of our souls?   The plough
Casts up bones where warriors trod,
Belted, plumed, and iron-shod ;
Those shreds the plough exhumes, I deem,
Little like the warriors seem.

Two lights, two haloed lights appear,
Round like the moon at the fall of the year,
When the sky is mantled o’er
With a fleece of mist, and of all the store

Of stars, not one can penetrate
To the traveller's eye till the night be late.
Two haloes slowly and steadily
Advancing like a double day,
Increasing in beauty more and more ;—
Behold ! they are the tires of light
On the heads of gods, and a golden sound,
Swooning and recreating, wound
From those two haloes, passed right round
The dead men's hearts with a painful might.
Would I could say
Whose voices or whose harps were they,
That had such vital force divine,
Holy Spirit, like to thine !
But what was the song
That bore along
These weary ghosts with a power so strong ?
If we could repeat that lay
In the light of upper day,
It might unravel warp and woof
Of this prisoned conscious Life
Tear all sensuous ties aloof ;
Of good and ill unwind the strife :
Interweave it with amaranth again,
Die it with nepenthe bloom,
That we no more knew sin or pain,
Nor feared the darks beyond the tomb !

But what was the song
That bore along
Those dead hearts with a power so strong ?
Would I could repeat the lay
In the dull light of this cold day ;
Wean the soul from the thirst to know,

By wisdom be as gods, that so
The slave unmanacle his hand,
The ploughshare rest upon the land.

When the sound of the wires
Of those holy lyres
Had the dead men's lives remade,
Did their shadows remain in the world of shade,
Their flesh in the earth
That gave it birth ?
Then in what were they arrayed ?
But the child just born forgetteth quite
Its ante-natal garments ; night
And utter change doth interpose,
And when this life over the body doth close,
And the freed Soul hears without ears the hymn,
Sphere-music of God's cherubim,
And sees the haloed powers below,—
Utterly changeth it also ;
And after the new birth again
Forget the ante-natal gain ?
We cannot know.

THE WITCH'S BALLAD.

O, I HAE come from far away,
    From a warm land far away,
A southern land across the sea,
With sailor-lads about the mast,
Merry and canny, and kind to me.

And I hae been to yon town,
　　To try my luck in yon town ;
Nort, and Mysie, Elspie too.
Right braw we were to pass the gate,
Wi' gowden clasps on girdles blue.

Mysie smiled wi' miminy mouth,
　　Innocent mouth, miminy mouth
Elspie wore her scarlet gown,
Nort's grey eyes were unco gleg,
My Castile comb was like a crown.

We walked abreast all up the street,
　　Into the market up the street ;
Our hair with marygolds was wound,
Our bodices with love-knots laced,
Our merchandise with tansy bound.

Nort had chickens, I had cocks,
　　Gamesome cocks, loud-crowing cocks ;
Mysie ducks, and Elspie drakes,—
For a wee groat or a pound :
We lost nae time wi' gives and takes.

Lost nae time, for well we knew,
　　In our sleeves full well we knew,
When the gloaming came that night,
Duck nor drake nor hen nor cock
Would be found by candle-light.

And when our chaffering all was done,
    All was paid for, sold and done,
We drew a glove on ilka hand,
We sweetly curtsied each to each,
And deftly danced a saraband.

The market lasses looked and laughed,
    Left their gear and looked and laughed ;
They made as they would join the game,
But soon their mithers, wild and wud,
With whack and screech they stopped the same.

Sae loud the tongues o' randies grew,
    The flitin' and the skirlin' grew,
At all the windows in the place,
Wi' spoons or knives, wi' needle or awl,
Was thrust out every hand and face.

And down each stair they thronged anon,
    Gentle, semple, thronged anon ;
Souter and tailor, frowsy Nan,
The ancient widow young again,
Simpering behind her fan.

Without a choice, against their will,
    Doited, dazed, against their will,
The market lassie and her mither,
The farmer and his husbandman,
Hand in hand dance a' thegether.

Slow at first, but faster soon,
    Still increasing wild and fast,
Hoods and mantles, hats and hose,
Blindly doffed and cast away,
Left them naked, heads and toes.

They would have torn us limb from limb,
    Dainty limb from dainty limb ;
But never one of them could win
Across the line that I had drawn
With bleeding thumb a-widdershin.

But there was Jeff the provost's son,
    Jeff the provost's only son ;
There was Father Auld himsel',
The Lombard frae the hostelry,
And the lawyer Peter Fell.

All goodly men we singled out,
    Waled them well, and singled out,
And drew them by the left hand in ;
Mysie the priest, and Elspie won
The Lombard, Nort the lawyer carle,
I mysel' the provost's son.

Then, with cantrip kisses seven,
    Three times round with kisses seven,
Warped and woven there spun we,
Arms and legs and flaming hair,
Like a whirlwind on the sea.

Like the wind that sucks the sea,
　　Over and in and on the sea,
Good sooth it was a mad delight ;
And every man of all the four
Shut his eyes and laughed outright.

Laughed as long as they had breath,
　　Laughed while they had sense or breath ;
And close about us coiled a mist
Of gnats and midges, wasps and flies,
Like the whirlwind shaft it rist.

Drawn up I was right off my feet,
　　Into the mist and off my feet ;
And, dancing on each chimney-top,
I saw a thousand darling imps
Keeping time with skip and hop.

And on the provost's brave ridge-tile,
　　On the provost's grand ridge-tile,
The Blackamoor first to master me
I saw,—I saw that winsome smile,
The mouth that did my heart beguile,
And spoke the great Word over me,
In the land beyond the sea.

I called his name, I called aloud,
　　Alas ! I called on him aloud ;
And then he filled his hand with stour,
And threw it towards me in the air ;
My mouse flew out, I lost my pow'r !

My lusty strength, my power, were gone ;
    Power was gone, and all was gone.
He will not let me love him more !
Of bell and whip and horse's tail
He cares not if I find a store.

But I am proud if he is fierce !
    I am as proud as he is fierce ;
I'll turn about and backward go,
If I meet again that Blackamoor,
And he'll help us then, for he shall know
I seek another paramour.

And we'll gang once more to yon town,
    Wi' better luck to yon town ;
We'll walk in silk and cramoisie,
And I shall wed the provost's son ;
My-lady of the town I'll be !

For I was born a crowned king's child,
    Born and nursed a king's child,
King o' a land ayont the sea,
Where the Blackamoor kissed me first,
And taught me art and glamourie.

Each one in her wame shall hide
    Her hairy mouse, her wary mouse,
Fed on madwort and agramie,—
Wear amber beads between her breasts,
And blind-worm's skin about her knee.

The Lombard shall be Elspie's man,
    Elspie's gowden husband-man ;
Nort shall take the lawyer's hand ;
The priest shall swear another vow :
We'll dance again the saraband !

LOVE'S CALENDAR.

THAT gusty spring, each afternoon
    By the ivied cot I passed,
And noted at that lattice soon
    Her fair face downward cast ;
Still in the same place seated there,
So diligent, so very fair.

Oft-times I said I knew her not,
    Yet that way round would go,
Until, when evenings lengthened out,
    And bloomed the may-hedge row,
I met her by the wayside well,
Whose waters, maybe, broke the spell.

For, leaning on her pail she prayed
    I'd lift it to her head,
So did I ; but I'm much afraid
    Some wasteful drops were shed,
And that we blushed, as face to face
Needs must we stand the shortest space.

Then when the sunset mellowed through
  The ears of rustling grain,
When lattices wide open flew,
  When ash-leaves fell like rain,
As well as I she knew the hour
At morn or eve I neared her bower.

And now that snow o'erlays the thatch,
  Each starlit eve within
The door she waits, I raise the latch,
  And kiss her lifted chin ;
Nor do I think we've blushed again,
For Love hath made but one of twain.

From "OUTSIDE THE TEMPLE."

I.

HOPE DEFERRED.

COURAGE of heart and hand, Faith first of all :
  Such is the prayer of the perplexèd man,
As the storm-scattered blossoms round him fall,
  And shrinking from the rod and from the ban
Of starless chance.   Prayer prompted by desires
  For mastery and godhead sense denies,
And by sky-pointing mediæval spires,
  Symbols of creeds the beaten hound still tries
To shelter under in this pilgrimage,
  Passing from birth to death.   But let us hear

What Nature, cruel mother ! says so sage,—
  Still listening if perchance gods interfere—
"Gain faith and courage through self-harmony,
And live your lives, nor only live to die."

II.

CONTENTMENT IN THE DARK.

WE asked not to be born : 'tis not by will
  That we are here beneath the battle-smoke,
Without escape ; by good things as by ill,
  By facts and mysteries enchained : no cloak
Of an Elijah, no stairs whereupon
  Angels ascending and descending shine
Over the head here pillowed on a stone,
  Anywhere found ;—so say they who repine.
But each year hath its harvest, every hour
  Some melody, child-laughter, strengthening strife,
For mother Earth still gives her child his dower,
  And loves like doves sit on the boughs of life.

ONENESS OF ALL.

(PEBBLES IN THE STREAM.)

UPON this rustic bridge on this warm day
  We rest from our too-thoughtful devious walk ;
  Over our shadows its melodious talk
The stream continues, while oft-times a stray

Dry leaf drops down where these bright waters play
  In endless eddies, through whose clear brown deep
  The gorgeous pebbles quiver in their sleep ;
The stream still flows, but cannot flow away.

Could I but find the words that would reveal
  The unity in multiplicity,
And the profound strange harmony I feel
  With these dead things, God's garments of to-day ;
The listener's soul with mine they would anneal,
And make us one within eternity.

A SYMBOL.

AT early morn I watched, scarce consciously,
  Through the half-opened casement the high screen
  Of our trees touched now by the bright'ning sheen
Of the ascending sun : the room was grey
And dim, with old things filled this many a day,
  Closing me in, but those thick folds of trees
  Shone in the fresh light, trembled in the breeze :
A shadow crossed them on its arrowy way
  Cast by a flying bird I could not see ;
Then called a voice far off that seemed to say,
  Come, we are here ! Such might or might not be
  What the voice called, but then methought I knew
I was a soul new-born in death's dark clay,
  Awakening to another life more true.

From " Parted Love."

I.

MORNING.

Last night,—it must have been a ghost at best,—
  I did believe the lost one's slumbering head
  Filled the white hollows of the curtained bed,
And happily sank again to sound sweet rest,
As in times past with sleep my nightly guest,
  A guest that left me only when the day
  Showed me a fairer than Euphrosyne,—
Day that now shows me but the unfilled nest.

O night ! thou wert our mother at the first,
  Thy silent chambers are our homes at last ;
  And even now thou art our bath of life.
Come back ! the hot sun makes our lips athirst ;
  Come back ! thy dreams may recreate the past ;
  Come back ! and smooth again this heart's long strife.

II.

EVENING.

As in a glass at evening, dusky-grey,
  The faces of those passing through the room
  Seem like ghost-transits thwart reflected gloom,
Thus, darling image ! thou, so long away,
Visitest sometimes my darkening day :
  Other friends come ; the toy of life turns round,
  The glittering beads change with their tinkling sound,
Whilst thou in endless youth sit'st silently.

How vain to call time back, to think these arms
  Again may touch, may shield, those shoulders soft
  And solid, never more my eyes can see :
But yet, perchance—(*speak low*)—beyond all harms,
  I may walk with thee in God's other croft,
  When this world shall the darkling mirror be.

From "The Old Scotch House."

I.

THE BOWER.

In the old house there is a chamber high,
  Diapered with wind-scattered plane-tree leaves ;
  And o'er one corbelled window that receives
The sunrise we've inscribed right daintily,
"Come, O fair Morn, fulfilling prophecy!"
  Over another, western watch doth keep,
  Is writ, "O Eve, bring thou the nursling Sleep !"
Adorning the old walls as best we may.

For up this bower-stair, in long-vanished years,
  The bridegroom brought his bride and shut the door;
Here, too, closed weary eyes with kindred tears,
  While mourners' feet were hushed upon the floor :
And still It seems these old trees and brown hills
Remember also our past joys and ills.

II.

A SPRING MORNING.

VAGUELY at dawn within the temperate clime
  Of glimmering half-sleep, in this chamber high,
  I heard the jackdaws in their loopholes nigh,
Fitfully stir: as yet it scarce was time
Of dawning, but the nestlings' hungry chime
  Awoke me, and the old birds soon had flown;
  Then was a perfect lull, and I went down
Into deep slumber beneath dreams or rhyme.

But, suddenly renewed, the clamouring grows,
  The callow beaklings clamouring every one,
    The grey-heads had returned with worm and fly;
I looked up and the room was like a rose,
  Above the hill-top was the brave young sun,
    The world was still as in an ecstasy.

III.

BELOW THE OLD HOUSE.

BENEATH those buttressed walls with lichens grey,
  Beneath the slopes of trees whose flickering shade
  Darkens the pools by dun green velvetted,
The stream leaps like a living thing at play,—
In haste it seems; it cannot, cannot stay!
  The great boughs changing there from year to year,
  And the high jackdaw-haunted caves, still hear
The burden of the rivulet—Passing away!

And some time certainly that oak no more
  Will keep the winds in check ; his breadth of beam
Will go to rib some ship for some far shore ;
  Those quoins and eaves will crumble, while that stream
Will still run whispering, whispering night and day,
That over-song of father Time—Passing away !

ON THE INSCRIPTION, KEATS' TOMBSTONE.

(ENGLISH CEMETERY, ROME.)

From "SONNETS ON LITERARY SUBJECTS."

COULD we but see the Future ere it comes,
  As gods must see effects in causes hid,—
  How calmly could we wait till we were bid !
Heroes would hear their triumph's far-off drums,
Would see Fame's splendours ere the threads and
      thrums
  Had formed them in to-morrow's living loom ;
  Would feel the honours round the future tomb,
Across the sunless fosse where life succumbs.

If it were so !   But wiser fates conspire
  That each shall bear his own lamp through the
      night,
  Showing but short way round its blood-red light,
    And find, by it alone, the herb that springs
Fast by the wells of fathomless desire ;
  And of this healing herb the poet sings.

THE EPITAPH OF HUBERT VAN EYCK.

(CARVED ON THE SHIELD HELD BY A MARBLE SKELETON, CATHEDRAL OF ST. BAVON, GHENT.)

WHOE'ER thou art who walkest overhead,
Behold thyself in stone : for I yestreen
Was seemly and alert like thee : now dead,
Nailed up and earthed, and for the last time green,
(The first spring greenness and the last decay,)
Am hidden here for ever from the day.
I, Hubert Van Eyck, whom all Bruges hailed
Worthy of lauds, am now with worms engrailed.[1]
My soul with many pangs by God constrained
Fled in September when the corn is wained,
Just fourteen hundred years and twenty-six
Since Christ Himself was our first crucifix.
Lovers of Art, pray for me that I gain
God's grace, nor find I've worked and lived in vain.

SANDRART'S INSCRIPTION,

ON ALBERT DÜRER'S GRAVE, NÜRNBERG.

REST here, thou Prince of Painters, thou who wast better
    than great,
In many arts unequalled in the old time or the late.
Earth thou didst paint and garnish, and now, in thy new
    abode,
Thou paintest the holy things overhead in the city of God.
And we, as our patron saint, look up to thee ever will,
And crown, with a laurel crown, the dust left here with
    us still.

[1] Spotted, pitted.

JAMES THOMSON ("B. V.").

From "The City of Dreadful Night."

I.

The City is of Night; perchance of Death,
  But certainly of Night; for never there
Can come the lucid morning's fragrant breath
  After the dewy dawning's cold grey air;
The moon and stars may shine with scorn or pity;
The sun has never visited that city,
  For it dissolveth in the daylight fair.

.   .   .   .   .   .

A river girds the city west and south,
  The main north channel of a broad lagoon,
Regurging with the salt tides from the mouth;
  Waste marshes shine and glister to the moon
For leagues, then moorland black, then stony ridges;
Great piers and causeways, many noble bridges,
  Connect the town and islet suburbs strewn.

Upon an easy slope it lies at large,
  And scarcely overlaps the long curved crest
Which swells out two leagues from the river marge.
  A trackless wilderness rolls north and west,
Savannahs, savage woods, enormous mountains,
  Bleak uplands, black ravines with torrent fountains;
  And eastward rolls the shipless sea's unrest.

The city is not ruinous, although
   Great ruins of an unremembered past,
With others of a few short years ago
   More sad, are found within its precincts vast.
The street-lamps always burn ; but scarce a casement
In house or palace front from roof to basement
   Doth glow or gleam athwart the mirk air cast.

The street-lamps burn amidst the baleful glooms,
   Amidst the soundless solitudes immense
Of rangèd mansions dark and still as tombs.
   The silence which benumbs or strains the sense
Fulfils with awe the soul's despair unweeping:
Myriads of habitants are ever sleeping,
   Or dead, or fled from nameless pestilence !

Yet as in some necropolis you find
   Perchance one mourner to a thousand dead,
So there ; worn faces that look deaf and blind
   Like tragic masks of stone.   With weary tread,
Each wrapt in his own doom, they wander, wander,
Or sit foredone and desolately ponder
   Through sleepless hours with heavy drooping head.

Mature men chiefly, few in age or youth,
   A woman rarely, now and then a child :
A child !   If here the heart turns sick with ruth
   To see a little one from birth defiled,
Or lame or blind, as preordained to languish
Through youthless life, think how it bleeds with anguish
   To meet one erring in that homeless wild.

They often murmur to themselves, they speak
    To one another seldom, for their woe
Broods maddening inwardly and scorns to wreak
    Itself abroad ; and if at whiles it grow
To frenzy which must rave, none heeds the clamour,
Unless there waits some victim of like glamour,
    To rave in turn, who lends attentive show.

The City is of Night, but not of Sleep ;
    There sweet sleep is not for the weary brain ;
The pitiless hours like years and ages creep,
    A night seems termless hell. . . .

II.

It is full strange to him who hears and feels,
    When wandering there in some deserted street,
The booming and the jar of ponderous wheels,
    The trampling clash of heavy ironshod feet :
Who in this Venice of the Black Sea rideth ?
Who in this city of the stars abideth
    To buy or sell as those in daylight sweet ?

The rolling thunder seems to fill the sky
    As it comes on ; the horses snort and strain,
The harness jingles, as it passes by ;
    The hugeness of an overburthened wain :
A man sits nodding on the shaft or trudges
Three parts asleep beside his fellow-drudges :
    And so it rolls into the night again.

What merchandise ? whence, whither, and for whom ?
   Perchance it is a Fate-appointed hearse,
Bearing away to some mysterious tomb
   Or Limbo of the scornful universe
The joy, the peace, the life-hope, the abortions
Of all things good which should have been our portions,
   But have been strangled by that City's curse.

III.

Because he seemed to walk with an intent
   I followed him ; who, shadowlike and frail,
Unswervingly though slowly onward went,
   Regardless, wrapt in thought as in a veil :
Thus step for step with lonely sounding feet
We travelled many a long dim silent street.

At length he paused : a black mass in the gloom,
   A tower that merged into the heavy sky ;
Around, the huddled stones of grave and tomb :
   Some old God's-acre now corruption's sty :
He murmured to himself with dull despair,
Here Faith died, poisoned by this charnel air.

Then turning to the right went on once more,
   And travelled weary roads without suspense ;
And reached at last a low wall's open door,
   Whose villa gleamed beyond the foliage dense :
He gazed, and muttered with a hard despair,
Here Love died, stabbed by its own worshipped pair.

Then turning to the right resumed his march,
  And travelled streets and lanes with wondrous strength,
Until on stooping through a narrow arch
  We stood before a squalid house at length :
He gazed, and whispered with a cold despair,
Here Hope died, starved out in its utmost lair. . . .

IV.

The mansion stood apart in its own ground ;
  In front thereof a fragrant garden-lawn,
High trees about it, and the whole walled round :
  The massy iron gates were both withdrawn ;
And every window of its front shed light,
Portentous in that City of the Night.

But though thus lighted it was deadly still
  As all the countless bulks of solid gloom :
Perchance a congregation to fulfil
  Solemnities of silence in this doom,
Mysterious rites of dolour and despair
Permitting not a breath of chant or prayer ?

Broad steps ascended to a terrace broad
  Whereon lay still light from the open door ;
The hall was noble, and its aspect awed,
  Hung round with heavy black from dome to floor ;
And ample stairways rose to left and right
Whose balustrades were also draped with night.

I paced from room to room, from hall to hall,
    Nor any life throughout the maze discerned;
But each was hung with its funereal pall,
    And held a shrine, around which tapers burned,
With picture or with statue or with bust,
All copied from the same fair form of dust:

A woman very young and very fair;
    Beloved by bounteous life and joy and youth,
And loving these sweet lovers, so that care
    And age and death seemed not for her in sooth:
Alike as stars, all beautiful and bright,
These shapes lit up that mausoléan night.

At length I heard a murmur as of lips,
    And reached an open oratory hung
With heaviest blackness of the whole eclipse;
    Beneath the dome a fuming censer swung;
And one lay there upon a low white bed,
With tapers burning at the foot and head:

The Lady of the images: supine,
    Deathstill, lifesweet, with folded palms she lay:
And kneeling there as at a sacred shrine
    A young man wan and worn who seemed to pray:
A crucifix of dim and ghostly white
Surmounted the large altar left in night :—

The chambers of the mansion of my heart,
In every one whereof thine image dwells,
Are black with grief eternal for thy sake.

The inmost oratory of my soul,
Wherein thou ever dwellest quick or dead,
Is black with grief eternal for thy sake.

I kneel beside thee and I clasp the cross,
With eyes for ever fixed upon that face,
So beautiful and dreadful in its calm.

I kneel here patient as thou liest there ;
As patient as a statue carved in stone,
Of adoration and eternal grief.

While thou dost not awake I cannot move ;
And something tells me thou wilt never wake,
And I alive feel turning into stone.

Most beautiful were Death to end my grief,
Most hateful to destroy the sight of thee,
Dear vision better than all death or life.

But I renounce all choice of life or death,
For either shall be ever at thy side,
And thus in bliss or woe be ever well.—

He murmured thus and thus in monotone,
    Intent upon that uncorrupted face,
Entranced except his moving lips alone :
    I glided with hushed footsteps from the place.
This was the festival that filled with light
That palace in the City of the Night.

V.

I sat me weary on a pillar's base,
    And leaned against the shaft ; for broad moonlight
O'erflowed the peacefulness of cloistered space,
    A shore of shadow slanting from the right :
The great cathedral's western front stood there,
A wave-worn rock in that calm sea of air.

Before it, opposite my place of rest,
    Two figures faced each other, large, austere ;
A couchant sphinx in shadow to the breast,
    An angel standing in the moonlight clear ;
So mighty by magnificence of form,
They were not dwarfed beneath that mass enorm.

Upon the cross-hilt of a naked sword
    The angel's hands, as prompt to smite, were held ;
His vigilant, intense regard was poured
    Upon the creature placidly unquelled,
Whose front was set at level gaze which took
No heed of aught, a solemn trance-like look.

And as I pondered these opposèd shapes
    My eyelids sank in stupor, that dull swoon
Which drugs and with a leaden mantle drapes
    The outworn to worse weariness. But soon
A sharp and clashing noise the stillness broke,
And from the evil lethargy I woke.

The angel's wings had fallen, stone on stone,
  And lay there shattered; hence the sudden sound:
A warrior leaning on his sword alone
  Now watched the sphinx with that regard profound;
The sphinx unchanged looked forthright, as aware
Of nothing in the vast abyss of air.

Again I sank in that repose unsweet,
  Again a clashing noise my slumber rent;
The warrior's sword lay broken at his feet:
  An unarmed man with raised hands impotent
Now stood before the sphinx, which ever kept
Such mien as if with open eyes it slept.

My eyelids sank in spite of wonder grown;
  A louder crash upstartled me in dread:
The man had fallen forward, stone on stone,
  And lay there shattered, with his trunkless head
Between the monster's large quiescent paws,
Between its grand front changeless as life's laws.

The moon had circled westward full and bright,
  And made the temple-front a mystic dream,
And bathed the whole enclosure with its light,
  The sworded angel's wrecks, the sphinx supreme:
I pondered long that cold majestic face
Whose vision seemed of infinite void space.

VI.

Anear the centre of that northern crest
　Stands out a level upland bleak and bare,
From which the city east and south and west
　Sinks gently in long waves; and thronèd there
An Image sits, stupendous, superhuman,
The bronze colossus of a wingèd Woman,
　Upon a graded granite base foursquare.

Low-seated she leans forward massively,
　With cheek on clenched left hand, the forearm's might
Erect, its elbow on her rounded knee;
　Across a clasped book in her lap the right
Upholds a pair of compasses; she gazes
With full set eyes, but wandering in thick mazes
　Of sombre thought beholds no outward sight.

Words cannot picture her; but all men know
　That solemn sketch the pure sad artist wrought
Three centuries and threescore years ago,
　With phantasies of his peculiar thought:
The instruments of carpentry and science
Scattered about her feet, in strange alliance
　With the keen wolf-hound sleeping undistraught;

Scales, hour-glass, bell, and magic-square above;
　The grave and solid infant perched beside,
With open winglets that might bear a dove,
　Intent upon its tablets, heavy-eyed;
Her folded wings as of a mighty eagle,
But all too impotent to lift the regal
　Robustness of her earth-born strength and pride;

And with those wings, and that light wreath which seems
  To mock her grand head and the knotted frown
Of forehead charged with baleful thoughts and dreams,
  The household bunch of keys, the housewife's gown
Voluminous, indented, and yet rigid
As if a shell of burnished metal frigid,
  The feet thick-shod to tread all weakness down ;

The comet hanging o'er the waste dark seas,
  The massy rainbow curved in front of it
Beyond the village with the masts and trees ;
  The snaky imp, dog-headed, from the Pit,
Bearing upon its batlike leathern pinions
Her name unfolded in the sun's dominions,
  The "MELENCOLIA" that transcends all wit.

Thus has the artist copied her, and thus
  Surrounded to expound her form sublime,
Her fate heroic and calamitous ;
  Fronting the dreadful mysteries of Time,
Unvanquished in defeat and desolation,
Undaunted in the hopeless conflagration
  Of the day setting on her baffled prime.

Baffled and beaten back she works on still,
  Weary and sick of soul she works the more,
Sustained by her indomitable will :
  The hands shall fashion and the brain shall pore,
And all her sorrow shall be turned to labour,
Till Death the friend-foe piercing with his sabre
  That mighty heart of hearts ends bitter war.

But as if blacker night could dawn on night,
   With tenfold gloom on moonless night unstarred,
A sense more tragic than defeat and blight,
   More desperate than strife with hope debarred,
More fatal than the adamantine Never
Encompassing her passionate endeavour,
   Dawns glooming in her tenebrous regard :

The sense that every struggle brings defeat
   Because Fate holds no prize to crown success ;
That all the oracles are dumb or cheat
   Because they have no secret to express ;
That none can pierce the vast black veil uncertain
Because there is no light beyond the curtain ;
   That all is vanity and nothingness.

Titanic from her high throne in the north,
   That City's sombre Patroness and Queen,
In bronze sublimity she gazes forth
   Over her Capital of teen and threne,
Over the river with its isles and bridges,
The marsh and moorland, to the stern rock-ridges,
   Confronting them with a coëval mien.

The moving moon and stars from east to west
   Circle before her in the sea of air ;
Shadows and gleams glide round her solemn rest.
   Her subjects often gaze up to her there :
The strong to drink new strength of iron endurance,
The weak new terrors ; all, renewed assurance
   And confirmation of the old despair.

PROFESSOR BLACKIE.

THE DEATH OF COLUMBA.

From "LAYS OF THE HIGHLANDS AND ISLANDS."

SAXON stranger, thou did'st wisely,
  Sunder'd for a little space
From that motley stream of people
  Drifting by this holy place;
With the furnace and the funnel
  Through the long sea's glancing arm,
Let them hurry back to Oban,
  Where the tourist loves to swarm.
Here, upon this hump of granite,
  Sit with me a quiet while,
And I'll tell thee how Columba
  Died upon this old grey isle.

I.

'Twas in May, a breezy morning,
  When the sky was fresh and bright,
And the broad blue ocean shimmer'd
  With a thousand gems of light.
On the green and grassy Machar,
  Where the fields are spredden wide,

And the crags in quaint confusion
  Jut into the Western tide:
Here his troop of godly people,
  In stout labour's garb array'd,
Blithe their fruitful task were plying
  With the hoe and with the spade.
" I will go and bless my people,"
  Quoth the father, "ere I die,
But the strength is slow to follow
  Where the wish is swift to fly;
I am old and feeble, Diarmid,
  Yoke the oxen, be not slow,
I will go and bless my people,
  Ere from earth my spirit go."
On his ox-drawn wain he mounted,
  Faithful Diarmid by his side;
Soon they reach'd the grassy Machar,
  Soft and smooth, Iona's pride:
" I am come to bless my people,
  Faithful fraters, ere I die;
I had wish'd to die at Easter,
  But I would not mar your joy,
Now the Master plainly calls me,
  Gladly I obey his call;
I am ripe, I feel the sickle,
  Take my blessing, ere I fall."
But they heard his words with weeping,
  And their tears fell on the dew,
And their eyes were dimmed with sorrow,
  For they knew his words were true.
Then he stood up on the waggon,
  And his prayerful hands he hove,
And he spake and bless'd the people
  With the blessing of his love:
" God be with you, faithful fraters,

With you now, and evermore ;
Keep you from the touch of evil,
  On your souls his Spirit pour ;
God be with you, fellow workmen,
  And from loved Iona's shore
Keep the blighting breath of demons,
  Keep the viper's venom'd store !"
Thus he spake, and turn'd the oxen
  Townwards ; sad they went, and slow,
And the people, fix'd in sorrow,
  Stood, and saw the father go.

II.

List me further, Saxon stranger,
Note it nicely, by the causeway
  On the left hand, where thou came
With the motley tourist people,
  Stands a cross of figured fame.
Even now thine eye may see it,
  Near the nunnery, slim and grey ;—
From the waggon there Columba
  Lighted on that tearful day,
And he sat beneath the shadow
  Of that cross, upon a stone,
Brooding on his speedy passage
  To the land where grief is none ;
When, behold, the mare, the white one
  That was wont the milk to bear
From the dairy to the cloister,
  Stood before him meekly there,
Stood, and softly came up to him,
  And with move of gentlest grace
O'er the shoulder of Columba
  Thrust her piteous-pleading face,

Look'd upon him as a friend looks
  On a friend that goes away,
Sunder'd from the land that loves him
  By wide seas of briny spray :
" Fie upon thee for thy manners ! "
  Diarmid cried with lifted rod,
" Wilt thou with untimely fondness
  Vex the prayerful man of God ? "
" Not so, Diarmid," cried Columba ;
  " Dost thou see the speechful eyne
Of the fond and faithful creature
  Sorrow'd with the swelling brine ?
God hath taught the mute unreasoning
  What thou fail'st to understand,
That this day I pass for ever
  From Iona's shelly strand.
Have my blessing, gentle creature,
  God doth bless both man and beast ;
From hard yoke, when I shall leave thee,
  Be thy faithful neck released."
Thus he spoke, and quickly rising
  With what feeble strength remain'd,
Leaning on stout Diarmid's shoulder,
  A green hillock's top he gained.
There, or here where we are sitting,
  Whence his eye might measure well
Both the cloister and the chapel,
  And his pure and prayerful cell,—
There he stood, and high uplifting
  Hands whence flowed a healing grace,
Breathed his latest voice of blessing
  To protect the sacred place,—
Spake such words as prophets utter
  When the veil of flesh is rent,
And the present fades from vision,

On the germing future bent :
"God thee bless, thou loved Iona,
  Though thou art a little spot,
Though thy rocks are grey and treeless,
  Thine shall be a boastful lot ;
Thou shalt be a sign for nations ;
  Nurtured on thy sacred breast,
Thou shalt send on holy mission
  Men to teach both East and West ;
Peers and potentates shall own thee,
  Monarchs of wide-sceptre'd sway
Dying shall beseech the honour
  To be tomb'd beneath thy clay;
God's dear saints shall love to name thee,
  And from many a storied land
Men of clerkly fame shall pilgrim
  To Iona's little strand."

III.

Thus the old man spake his blessing ;
  Then, where most he loved to dwell,
Through the well-known porch he enter'd
  To his pure and prayerful cell ;
And then took the holy psalter—
  'Twas his wont when he would pray—
Bound with three stout clasps of silver,
  From the casket where it lay;
There he read with fixed devoutness,
  And with craft full fair and fine,
On the smooth and polish'd vellum
  Copied forth the sacred line,
Till he came to where the kingly
  Singer sings in faithful mood,

How the younglings of the lion
  Oft may roam in vain for food,
But who fear the Lord shall never
  Live and lack their proper good.[1]
Here he stopped, and said, "My latest
  Now is written; what remains
I bequeath to faithful Beathan
  To complete with pious pains."
Then he rose, and in the chapel
  Conned the pious vesper song
Inly to himself, for feeble
  Now the voice that once was strong;
Hence with silent step returning
  To his pure and prayerful cell,
On the round smooth stone he laid him
  Which for pallet served him well.
Here some while he lay; then rising,
  To a trusty brother said:
"Brother, take my parting message,
  Be my last words wisely weigh'd.
'Tis an age of brawl and battle;
  Men who seek not God to please,
With wild sweep of lawless passion
  Waste the land and scourge the seas.
Not like them be ye; be loving,
  Peaceful, patient, truthful, bold,
But in service of your Master
  Use no steel and seek no gold."
Thus he spake; but now there sounded
  Through the night the holy bell
That to Lord's Day matins gather'd
  Every monk from every cell.
Eager at the sound, Columba

1 Psalm xxxiv. 10.

In the way foresped the rest,
And before the altar kneeling,
  Pray'd with hands on holy breast.
Diarmid followed ; but a marvel
  Flow'd upon his wondering eyne,—
All the windows shone with glorious
  Light of angels in the shrine.
Diarmid enter'd ; all was darkness.
  "Father !" But no answer came.
"Father ! art thou here, Columba ?"
  Nothing answer'd to the name.
Soon the troop of monks came hurrying,
  Each man with a wandering light,
For great fear had come upon them,
  And a sense of strange affright.
"Diarmid ! Diarmid ! is the father
  With thee ? Art thou here alone ?"
And they turn'd their lights and found him
  On the pavement lying prone.
And with gentle hands they raised him,
  And he mildly look'd around,
And he raised his arm to bless them,
  But it dropped upon the ground ;
And his breathless body rested
  On the arms that held him dear,
And his dead face look'd upon them
  With a light serene and clear ;
And they said that holy angels
  Surely hover'd round his head,
For alive no loveliest ever
  Look'd so lovely as this dead.

Stranger, thou hast heard my story,
  Thank thee for thy patient ear ;

We are pleased to stir the sleeping
  Memory of old greatness here.
I have used no gloss, no varnish,
  To make fair things fairer look ;
As the record stands, I give it,
  In the old monk's Latin book.
Keep it in thy heart, and love it,
  Where a good thing loves to dwell ;
It may help thee in thy dying,
  If thou care to use it well.

THE SONG OF MRS. JENNY GEDDES.

(TUNE—*British Grenadiers.*)

SOME praise the fair Queen Mary, and some the good
    Queen Bess,
And some the wise Aspasia, beloved by Pericles ;
But o'er all the world's brave women, there's one that
    bears the rule,
The valiant Jenny Geddes, that flung the three-legged
    stool.
With a row-dow—at them now !—Jenny fling the stool !

'Twas the twenty-third of July, in the sixteen thirty-
    seven,
On Sabbath morn from high St. Giles' the solemn peal
    was given :
King Charles had sworn that Scottish men should pray
    by printed rule ;
He sent a book, but never dreamt of danger from a stool.
With a row-dow—yes, I trow !—there's danger in a stool !

The Council and the Judges, with ermined pomp elate,
The Provost and the Bailies in gold and crimson state,
Fair silken-vested ladies, grave Doctors of the school,
Were there to please the King, and learn the virtue of a
    stool.
With a row-dow—yes, I trow!—there's virtue in a stool!

The Bishop and the Dean came in wi' mickle gravity,
Right smooth and sleek, but lordly pride was lurking in
    their e'e ;
Their full lawn sleeves were blown and big, like seals in
    briny pool ;
They bore a book, but little thought they soon should
    feel a stool.
With a row-dow—yes, I trow!—they'll feel a three-legged
    stool!

The Dean he to the altar went, and, with a solemn look,
He cast his eyes to heaven, and read the curious-printed
    book :
In Jenny's heart the blood upwelled with bitter anguish
    full ;
Sudden she started to her legs, and stoutly grasped the
    stool !
With a row-dow—at them now! firmly grasp the stool!

As when a mountain wild-cat springs on a rabbit small,
So Jenny on the Dean springs, with gush of holy gall ;
Will thou say the mass at my lug, thou Popish-puling
    fool ?

No! no! she said, and at his head she flung the three-
    legged stool.
With a row-dow—at them now!—Jenny fling the stool!

A bump, a thump! a smash, a crash! now gentle folks
    beware!
Stool after stool, like rattling hail, came tirling through
    the air,
With, Well done, Jenny! bravo, Jenny! that's the
    proper tool!
When the Deil will out, and shows his snout, just meet
    him with a stool!
*With a row-dow—at them now!—there's nothing like a
    stool!*

The Council and the Judges were smitten with strange
    fear,
The ladies and the Bailies their seats did deftly clear,
The Bishop and the Dean went, in sorrow and in dool,
And all the Popish flummery fled, when Jenny showed
    the stool!
With a row-dow—at them now! Jenny show the stool!

And thus a mighty deed was done by Jenny's valiant
    hand,
Black Prelacy and Popery she drave from Scottish land;
King Charles he was a shuffling knave, priest Laud a
    meddling fool,
But Jenny was a woman wise, who beat them with a
    stool!
*With a row-dow—yes, I trow!—she conquered by the
    stool!*

THE WORKING MAN'S SONG.

I AM no gentleman, not I !
  No bowing, scraping thing !
I bear my head more free and high
  Than titled count or king.
I am no gentleman, not I !
    No, no, no !
And only to one Lord on high
    My head I bow.

I am no gentleman, not I !
  No vain and varnished thing !
And from my heart without a die,
  My honest thoughts I fling.
I am no gentleman, not I !
    No, no, no !
Our stout John Knox was none—and why
    Should I be so ?

I am no gentleman, not I !
  No mincing, modish thing !
In gay saloon a butterfly,
  Some wax-doll Miss to wing.
I am no gentleman, not I !
    No, no, no !
No moth, to sport in fashion's eye,
    A Bond Street beau !

I am no gentleman, not I !
 No bully, braggart thing !
With jockeys on the course to vie,
 With bull-dogs in the ring.
I am no gentleman, not I !
  No, no, no !
The working man might sooner die
  Than sink so low !

I am no gentleman, not I !
 No star-bedizened thing !
My fathers filched no dignity,
 By fawning to a king.
I am no gentleman, not I !
  No, no, no !
And to the wage of honesty
  My rank I owe !

I am no gentleman, not I !
 No bowing, scraping thing !
I bear my head more free and high
 Than titled count or king.
I am no gentleman, not I !
  No, no, no !
And thank the blessed God on high,
  Who made me so !

A SONG OF GEOLOGY.

From "MUSA BURSCHICOSA."

I'LL sing you a ditty that needs no apology—
  Attend, and keep watch in the gates of your ears !—
Of the famous new science which men call Geology,
  And gods call the story of millions of years.
    Millions, millions—did I say millions ?
      Billions and trillions are more like the fact !
    Millions, billions, trillions, quadrillions,
      Make the long sum of creation exact !

Confusion and Chaos, with wavering pinion,
  First swayed o'er the weltering ferment of things,
When all over all held alternate dominion,
  And the slaves of to-day were to-morrow the kings.
    Chaos, Chaos, infinite wonder !
      Wheeling and reeling on wavering wings ;
    Whence issued the world, which some think a
        blunder,
      A rumble and tumble and jumble of things !

The minim of being, the dot of creation,
  The germ of Sire Adam, of you and of me,
In the folds of the gneiss in Laurentian station,
  Far west from the roots of Cape Wrath you may see.
    Minims of being, budding and bursting,
      All on the floor of the measureless sea !
    Small, but for mighty development thirsting,
      With throbs of the future, like you, Sir, and me !

The waters, now big with a novel sensation,
  Brought corals and buckies and bivalves to view,
Who dwell in shell houses, a soft-bodied nation ;
  But fishes with fins were yet none in the blue.
    Buckies and bivalves, a numberless nation !
      Buckies, and bivalves, and trilobites too !
    These you will find in Silurian station,
      When Ramsay and Murchison sharpen your view.

Then fins were invented ; when Queen Amphitrite
  Stirred up her force from Devonian beds,
The race of the fishes in ocean grew mighty,
  Queer-looking fishes with bucklers for heads.
    Fishes, fishes—small greedy fishes !
      With wings on their shoulders and horns on their
        heads,
      With scales bright and shiny, that shoot through the
        briny
      Cerulean halls on Devonian beds !

God bless the fishes !—but now on the dry land,
  In days when the sun shone benign on the poles,
Forests of ferns in the low and the high land
  Spread their huge fans, soon to change into coals !
    Forests of ferns—a wonderful verity !
      Rising like palm-trees beneath the North Pole ;
    And all to prepare for the golden prosperity
      Of John Bull reposing on iron and coal.

Now Nature the eye of the gazer entrances
  With wonder on wonder from teeming abodes ;
From the gills of the fish to true lungs she advances,
  And bursts into blossoms of tadpoles and toads.

Strange Batrachian people, Triassic all,
  Like hippopotamus huge on the roads !
You may call them ungainly, uncouth, and un-
    classical,
  But great in the reign of the Trias were Toads !

Behold, a strange monster our wonder engages,
  If dolphin or lizard your wit may defy, .
Some thirty feet long on the shore of Lyme-Regis,
  With a saw for a jaw, and a big staring eye.
    A fish or a lizard ? an ichthyosaurus,
      With a big goggle eye, and a very small brain,
    And paddles like mill-wheels in clattering chorus,
      Smiting tremendous the dread-sounding main !

And here comes another ! can shape more absurd be,
  The strangest and oddest of vertebrate things ?
Who knows if this creature a beast or a bird be,
  A fowl without feathers, a serpent with wings ?
    A beast or a bird—an equivocal monster !
      A crow or a crocodile, who can declare ?
    A greedy, voracious, long-necked monster,
      Skimming the billow, and ploughing the air.

Next rises to view the great four-footed nation,
  Hyenas and tapirs, a singular race,
You may pick up their wreck from the great Paris basin,
  At the word of command every bone finds its place.
    Palæothere, very singular creature !
      A horse or a tapir, or both can you say ?
    Showing his grave pachydermatous feature,
      Just where the Frenchman now sips his café.

And now the life-temple grows vaster and vaster,
  Only the pediment fails to the plan ;
The winged and the wingless are waiting their master,
  The Mammoth is howling a welcome to Man.
    Mammoth, Mammoth ! mighty old Mammoth !
      Strike with your hatchet and cut a good slice ;
    The bones you will find, and the hide of the
        mammoth,
      Packed in stiff cakes of Siberian ice.

At last the great biped, the crown of the mammals,
  Sire Adam, majestic, comes treading the sod,
A measureless animal, free without trammels
  To swing all the space from an ape to a god.
    Wonderful biped, erect and featherless !
      Sport of two destinies, treading the sod,
    With the perilous licence, unbridled and tetherless,
      To sink to a devil or rise to a god.

And thus was completed—miraculous wonder !
  The world, this mighty mysterious thing ;
I believe it is more than a beautiful blunder,
  And worship, and pray, and adore, while I sing.
    Wonder and miracle !—God made the wonder ;
      Come, happy creatures, and worship with me !
    I know it is more than a beautiful blunder,
      And I hope Tait, and Tyndall, and Huxley agree.

THE SONG OF THE HIGHLAND RIVER.

DEW-FED am I
With drops from the sky,
Where the white cloud rests on the old grey hill ;
Slowly I creep
Down the precipice steep,
Where the snow through the summer lies freezingly still ;
Where the wreck of the storm
Lies shattered enorm,
I steal 'neath the stone with a tremulous rill ;
My low-trickling flow
You may hear, as I go
Down the sharp-furrowed brow of the old grey hill,
Or drink from my well,
Grass-grown where I dwell,
In the clear granite cell of the old grey hill.

In the hollow of the hill
With my waters I fill
The little black tarn where the thin mist floats ;
The deep old moss
Slow-oozing I cross,
When the lapwing cries with its long-shrill notes ;
Then fiercely I rush to the sharp granite edge,
And leap with a bound o'er the old grey ledge ;
Like snow in the gale,
I drive down the vale,
Lashing the rock with my foamy flail ;
Where the black crags frown,
I pour sheer down,

Into the caldron boiling and brown ;
Whirling and eddying there I lie,
Where the old hawk wheels, and the blast howls by.

From the treeless brae
All green and grey,
To the wooded ravine I wind my way,
Dashing, and foaming, and leaping with glee,
The child of the mountain wild and free.
Under the crag where the stone-crop grows,
Fringing with gold my shelvy bed,
Where over my head
Its fruitage of red,
The rock-rooted rowan tree blushfully shows,
I wind, till I find
A way to my mind,
While hazel, and oak, and the light ash tree,
Weave a green awning of leafage for me.
Fitfully, fitfully, on I go,
Leaping, or running, or winding slow,
Till I come to the linn where my waters rush,
Eagerly down with a broad-faced gush,
Foamingly, foamingly, white as the snow,
On to the soft green turf below ;
Where I sleep with the lake as it sleeps in the glen,
'Neath the far-stretching base of the high-peaked Ben.

Slowly and smoothly my winding I make,
Round the dark-wooded islets that stud the clear lake;
The green hills sleep
With their beauty in me,
Their shadows the light clouds
Fling as they flee,

While in my pure waters pictured I glass
The light-plumed birches that nod as I pass.
   Slowly and silently on I wend,
   With many a bay and many a bend,
Luminous seen like a silvery line,
Shimmering bright in the fair sunshine,
Till I come to the pass, where the steep red scaur
Gleams like a watch-fire seen from afar,
   Then out I ride,
   With a full-rolling pride,
While my floods like the amber shine ;
   Where the salmon rejoice
   To hear my voice,
And the angler trims his line.

Gentlier now, with a kindly slope,
The green hills lie to the bright blue cope,
And wider the patches of green are spread,
Which Time hath won from my shifting bed.
   And many a broad and sunny spot,
   Where my waters wend,
   With a larger bend,
Shows the white-fronted brown-thatched cot,
Where the labouring man with sweatful care,
Hath trimmed him a garden green and fair,
   From the wreck of the granite bare.

And many a hamlet, peopled well
With hard-faced workmen, smokes from the dell ;
   Cunning to work with axe and hammer,
   Cunning to shear the fleecy flock,

Cunning, with blast and nitrous clamour,
To split the useful rock.
And many a rural church far-seen
Stands on the knolls of grassy green,
Where my swirling current flows;
And, with its spire high-pointed, shows
How man, that treads the earthy sod,
Claims fatherhood from God.

Now broader and broader my rich bed grows,
And deeper and deeper my full tide flows;
And, while onward I sail,
Like a ship to the gale,
With my big flood rolling amain,
The glen spreads out to a leafy vale,
And the vale spreads out to a plain.
And many a princely mansion good
Looks from the old thick-tufted wood,
On my clear far-winding line.
And many a farm, with acres spread,
Slopes gently to my fattening bed,
The farm, whose broad and portly lord
Loads with rich fare the liberal board,
And quaffs the ruby wine.
And richly, richly, round and round,
With green and golden pride, the ground
Swells undulant, gardened o'er and o'er
With beauty's bloom, and plenty's store;
And many a sheaf of yellow corn,
The farmer's healthful gain,
Up my soft-shaded banks is borne,
On the huge slow-labouring wain.

And many a yard well stacked with hay,
And many a dairy's trim array,
And many a high-piled barn I see,
And many a dance of rustic glee,
     Where sweats the jocund swain.
And many a town thick-sown with steeples
With various wealth my border peoples,
     And studs my sweeping line;
While frequent the bridge of well-hewn stone,
Arch after arch, is proudly thrown,
     My busy banks to join;
Thus through the plain I wend my fruitful way,
To meet the sounding sea, and swell the briny bay.

     The briny bay! how fair it lies
     Beneath the azure skies!
With its wide sweep of pebbly shore,
And the low far-murmuring roar
Of wave and wavelet sparkling bright
With a thousand points in the dancing light.
     There round the promontory's base,
     Bluff bulwark of the bay,
Free ranging with a lordly grace,
     I wind my surging way,
  To mingle with the main.   Where wide
This way and that my turbid tide
Is spread, behold in pennoned pride
Strong Neptune's white-winged couriers ride!
     From east to west,
     Upon my breast,
Rich bales they bear, to swell the stores
Of merchant kings, who on my shores
Pile their proud palaces. Busily plying,

And with fleet wings in fleetness vying,
The fire-fed steam-consuming boat
Casts from its high-reared iron throat,
The many-volumed smoke, while heaves
Beneath the boiling track it leaves
My furrowed flood.   Line upon line,
The ships that crossed the fretful brine,
Far-stretching o'er my spacious strand,
A myriad-masted army stand ;
While many a pier, and many a mole,
Breaks my strong current as I roll ;
And block and bolt, and bar and chain,
With giant-gates my flood detain,
To serve the seaman's need.   Around,
Thick as a forest, from the ground
Street upon street, the city rears
Its pride, in strangely-clambering tiers
Of various-fashioned stone, while domes,
And spires, and pinnacles, and towers,
And wealthy tradesmen's terraced bowers
          Nod o'er my troubled bed,
And Labour's many-chambered homes,
          In straggling vastness, spread
Their smoking lines.   Thus, where I flow,
The stream of being, growing as I grow,
Floods to a tumult, and much-labouring man,
Who, with my small beginnings, small began,
Ends where I end, and crowns his swelling plan.

CHINESE GORDON.

SOME men live near to God, as my right arm
   Is near to me; and thus they walk about
Mailed in full proof of faith, and bear a charm
   That mocks at fear, and bars the door on doubt,
And dares the impossible. So Gordon, thou,
   Through the hot stir of this distracted time,
Dost hold thy course, a flaming witness how
   To do and dare, and make our lives sublime
As God's campaigners. What live we for but this,
   Into the sour to breathe the soul of sweetness,
   The stunted growth to rear to fair completeness,
Drown sneers in smiles, kill hatred with a kiss,
   And to the sandy waste bequeath the fame
   That the grass grew behind us where we came!

DR. GEORGE MACDONALD.

I WOULD I WERE A CHILD.

From "ORGAN SONGS."

I WOULD I were a child,
That I might look, and laugh, and say, My Father !
And follow thee with running feet, or rather
  Be led through dark and wild !

IIow I would hold thy hand,
My glad eyes often to thy glory lifting !
Should darkness 'twixt thy face and mine come drifting,
  My heart would but expand.

If an ill thing came near,
I would but creep within thy mantle's folding,
Shut my eyes close, thy hand yet faster holding,
  And soon forget my fear.

O soul, O soul, rejoice !
Thou art God's child indeed, for all thy sinning ;
A poor weak child, yet his, and worth the winning
  With saviour eyes and voice.

Who spake the words? Didst Thou?
They are too good, even for such a giver :
Such water drinking once, I should feel ever
    As I had drunk but now.

Yet sure the Word said so,
Teaching our lips to cry with his, Our Father !
Telling the tale of him who once did gather
    His goods to him, and go !

Ah, thou dost lead me, God !
But it is dark and starless, the way dreary
Almost I sleep, I am so very weary
    Upon this rough hill-road.

Almost! Nay, I *do* sleep;
There is no darkness save in this my dreaming;
Thy fatherhood above, around, is beaming;
    Thy hand my hand doth keep.

With sighs my soul doth teem ;
I have no knowledge but that I am sleeping ;
Haunted with lies, my life will fail in weeping ;
    Wake me from this my dream.

How long shall heavy night
Deny the day? How long shall this dull sorrow
Say in my heart that never any morrow
    Will bring the friendly light ?

Lord, art thou in the room ?
Come near my bed ; oh, draw aside the curtain !
A child's heart would say *Father*, were it certain
  That it would not presume.

But if this dreary sleep
May not be broken, help thy helpless sleeper
To rest in thee ; so shall his sleep grow deeper—
  For evil dreams too deep.

Father ! I dare at length ;
My childhood sure will hold me free from blaming :
Sinful yet hoping, I to thee come, claiming
  Thy tenderness, my strength.

——

BABY.

WHERE did you come from, baby dear ?
Out of the everywhere into here.

Where did you get those eyes so blue ?
Out of the sky as I came through.

What makes the light in them sparkle and spin ?
Some of the starry twinkles left in.

Where did you get that little tear?
I found it waiting when I got here.

What makes your forehead so smooth and high?
A soft hand stroked it as I went by.

What makes your cheek like a warm white rose?
I saw something better than any one knows.

Whence that three-cornered smile of bliss?
Three angels gave me at once a kiss.

Where did you get this pearly ear?
God spoke, and it came out to hear.

Where did you get those arms and hands?
Love made itself into bonds and bands.

Feet, whence did you come, you darling things?
From the same box as the cherubs' wings.

How did they all just come to be you?
God thought about me, and so I grew.

But how did you come to us, you dear?
God thought about you, and so I am here.

LEGEND OF THE CORRIEVRECHAN.

Prince Breacan of Denmark was lord of the strand
  And lord of the billowy sea ;
Lord of the sea and lord of the land,
  He might have let maidens be !

A maiden he met with locks of gold,
  Straying beside the sea :
Maidens listened in days of old,
  And repented grievously.

Wiser he left her in evil wiles,
  Went sailing over the sea ;
Came to the lord of the Western Isles :
  Give me thy daughter, said he.

The lord of the Isles he laughed, and said :
  Only a king of the sea
May think the Maid of the Isles to wed,
  And such, men call not thee !

Hold thine own three nights and days
  In yon whirlpool of the sea,
Or turn thy prow and go thy ways
  And let the isle-maiden be.

Prince Breacan he turned his dragon prow
  To Denmark over the sea :
Wise women, he said, now tell me how
  In yon whirlpool to anchor me.

Make a cable of hemp and a cable of wool
    And a cable of maidens' hair,
And hie thee back to the roaring pool
    And anchor in safety there.

The smiths of Greydule, on the eve of Yule,
    Will forge three anchors rare ;
The hemp thou shalt pull, thou shalt shear the wool,
    And the maidens will bring their hair.

Of the hair that is brown thou shalt twist one strand,
    Of the hair that is raven another ;
Of the golden hair thou shalt twine a band
    To bind the one to the other !

The smiths of Greydule, on the eve of Yule,
    They forged three anchors rare ;
The hemp he did pull, and he shore the wool,
    And the maidens brought their hair.

He twisted the brown hair for one strand,
    The raven hair for another ;
He twined the golden hair in a band
    To bind the one to the other.

He took the cables of hemp and wool,
    He took the cable of hair,
He hied him back to the roaring pool,
    He cast the three anchors there.

The whirlpool roared, and the day went by,
    And night came down on the sea;
But or ever the morning broke the sky
    The hemp was broken in three.

The night it came down, the whirlpool it ran,
    The wind it fiercely blew;
And or ever the second morning began
    The wool it parted in two.

The storm it roared all day the third,
    The whirlpool wallowed about,
The night came down like a wild black bird,
    But the cable of hair held out.

Round and round with a giddy swing
    Went the sea-king through the dark;
Round went the rope in the swivel-ring,
    Round reeled the straining bark.

Prince Breacan he stood on his dragon prow,
    A lantern in his hand:
Blest be the maidens of Denmark now,
    By them shall Denmark stand!

He watched the rope through the tempest black,
    A lantern in his hold:
Out, out, alack! one strand will crack!
    It is the strand of gold!

The third morn clear and calm came out :
No anchored ship was there !
The golden strand in the cable stout
Was not all of maidens' hair.

THE YERL O' WATERYDECK.

THE wind it blew, and the ship it flew,
  And it was " Hey for hame !"
But up an' cried the skipper til his crew,
  " Haud her oot ower the saut sea faem."

Syne up an' spak the angry king :
  " Haud on for Dumferline !"
Quo' the skipper, " My lord, this maunna be—
  I'm king on this boat o' mine !"

He tuik the helm intil his han',
  He left the shore un'er the lee ;
Syne croodit sail, an', east an' south,
  Stude awa richt oot to sea.

Quo' the king, " Leise-majesty, I trow !
  Here lies some ill-set plan !
'Bout ship !" Quo' the skipper, " Yer grace forgets
  Ye are king but o' the lan' !"

Oot he heild to the open sea
   Quhill the north wind flaughtered an' fell ;
Syne the east had a bitter word to say
   That waukent a watery hell.

He turnt her heid intil the north :
   Quo' the nobles, " He's droon, by the mass ! "
Quo' the skipper, " Haud aff yer lady-han's
   Or ye'll never see the Bass."

The king creepit down the cabin-stair
   To drink the gude French wine ;
An' up cam his dochter, the princess fair,
   An' luikit ower the brine.

She turnt her face to the drivin snaw,
   To the snaw but and the weet ;
It claucht her snood, an' awa like a clud
   Her hair drave oot i' the sleet.

She turnt her face frae the drivin win'—
   " Quhat's that aheid ? " quo' she.
The skipper he threw himsel frae the win'
   An' he brayt the helm alee.

" Put to yer han', my lady fair !
   Haud up her heid ! " quo' he ;
" Gien she dinna face the win' a wee mair
   It's faurweel to you an' me ! "

To the tiller the lady she laid her han',
  An' the ship brayt her cheek to the blast ;
They joukit the berg, but her quarter scraped,
  An' they luikit at ither aghast.

Quo' the skipper, " Ye are a lady fair,
  An' a princess gran' to see,
But war ye a beggar, a man wud sail
  To the hell i' yer company !"

She liftit a pale an' a queenly face,
  Her een flashed, an' syne they swam :
" An' what for no to the hevin ?" she says,
  An' she turnt awa frae him.

Bot she tuik na her han' frae the gude ship's helm
  'Till the day begouth to daw ;
An' the skipper he spak, but what was said
  It was said atween them twa.

An' syne the gude ship she lay to,
  Wi' Scotlan' hyne un'er the lee ;
An' the king cam up the cabin-stair
  Wi' wan face an' bluidshot ee.

Laigh loutit the skipper upo' the deck ;
  "Stan' up, stan' up," quo' the king ;
" Ye're an honest loun—an' beg me a boon
  Quhan ye gie me back this ring."

Lowne blew the win'; the stars cam oot;
  The ship turnt frae the north ;
An' or ever the sun was up an' aboot
  They war intil the firth o' Forth.

Quhan the gude ship lay at the pier-heid,
  And the king stude steady o' the lan',—
"Doon wi' ye, skipper—doon !" he said,
  "Hoo daur ye afore me stan' !"

The skipper he loutit on his knee ;
  The king his blade he drew :
Quo' the king, " Noo mynt ye to contre me !
  I'm aboord *my* vessel noo !

" Gien I hadna been yer verra gude lord
  I wud hae thrawn yer neck !
Bot—ye wha loutit Skipper o' Doon,
  Rise up Yerl o' Waterydeck."

The skipper he rasena : " Yer Grace is great,
  Yer wull it can heize or ding :
Wi' ae wee word ye hae made me a yerl—
  Wi' anither mak me a king."

" I canna mak ye a king," quo' he,
  " The Lord alane can do that !
I snowk leise-majesty, my man !
  Quhat the Sathan wad ye be at ?"

Glowert at the skipper the doutsum king
  Jalousin aneth his croon ;
Quo' the skipper, " Here is yer Grace's ring—
  An' yer dochter is my boon ! "

The black blude shot intil the king's face—
  He wasna bonny to see :
" The rascal skipper ! he lichtlies oor grace !—
  Gar hang him heigh on yon tree."

Up sprang the skipper an' aboord his ship,
  Cleikit up a bytin blade
An' hackit at the cable that held her to the pier,
  An' thoucht it 'maist ower weel made.

The king he blew shill in a siller whustle ;
  An' tramp, tramp, doon the pier
Cam twenty men on twenty horses,
  Clankin wi' spur an' spear.

At the king's fute fell his dochter fair :
  " His life ye wadna spill ! "
" Ye daur stan' twixt my hert an' my hate ? "
  " I daur, wi' a richt gude will ! "

" Ye was aye to yer faither a thrawart bairn,
  But, my lady, here stan's the king !
Luikna *him* i' the angry face—
  A monarch's anither thing ! "

"I lout to my father for his grace
  Low on my bendit knee ;
But I stan' an' luik the king i' the face,
  For the skipper is king o' me ! "

She turnt, she sprang upo' the deck,
  The cable splashed i' the Forth,
Her wings sae braid the gude ship spread
  And flew east, an' syne flew north.

Now was not this a king's dochter—
  A lady that feared no skaith ?
A woman wi' quhilk a man micht sail
  Prood intil the Port o' Death ?

———

THE MERMAID.

Up cam the tide wi' a burst and a whush,
  And back gaed the stanes wi' a whurr ;
The king's son walkit i' the evenin hush,
  To hear the sea murmur and murr.

Straucht ower the water slade frae the mune
  A glimmer o' cauld weet licht ;
Ane o' her horns rase the water abune,
  And lampit across the nicht.

Quhat's that, and that, far oot i' the gray,
    The laich mune bobbin afore?
It's the bonny sea-maidens at their play—
    Haud awa, king's son, frae the shore.

Ae rock stude up like an auld aik-root,
    The king's son he steppit ahin';
The bonny sea-maidens cam gambolin oot,
    Kaimin their hair to the win'.

O merry their lauch whan they fan the warm san',
    For the lichtsome reel sae meet!
Ilk ane flang her kaim frae her pearly han',
    And tuik til her pearly feet.

But ane, wha's beauty was dream and spell,
    Her kaim on the rock she cuist;
Her back was scarce turnt whan the munelicht shell
    Was lyin i' the prince's breist!

The cluds grew grim as he watched their game,
    Th' win' blew up an angry tune;
Ane efter ane tuik up her kaim,
    And seaward gaed dancin doon.

But ane, wi' hair like the mune in a clud,
    Was left by the rock her lane;
Wi' flittin han's, like a priest's, she stude,
    'Maist veiled in a rush o' rain.

She spied the prince, she sank at his feet,
  And lay like a wreath o' snaw
Meltin awa i' the win' and weet
  O' a wastin wastlin thaw.

He liftit her, trimlin wi' houp and dreid,
  And hame wi' his prize he gaed,
And laid her doon, like a witherin weed,
  Saft on a gowden bed.

A' that nicht, and a' day the neist,
  She never liftit heid;
Quaiet lay the sea, and quaiet lay her breist,
  And quaiet lay the kirkyard-deid.

But quhan at the gloamin a sea-breeze keen
  Blew intil the glimsome room,
Like twa settin stars she opened her een,
  And the sea-flooer began to bloom.

And she saw the prince kneelin at her bed,
  And afore the mune was new,
Careless and cauld she was wooed and wed—
  But a winsome wife she grew.

And a' gaed weel till their bairn was born,
  And syne she cudna sleep;
She wud rise at midnicht, and wan'er till morn,
  Hark-harkin the sough o' the deep.

Ae nicht whan the win' gaed ravin aboot,
　And the winnocks war speckled wi' faem,
Frae room to room she strayt in and oot,
　And she spied her pearly kaim.

She twined up her hair wi' eager han's,
　And in wi' the rainbow kaim !
She's oot, and she's aff ower the shinin san's
　And awa til her moanin hame !

The prince he startit whaur he lay,
　He waukit, and was himlane !
He soucht far intil the mornin gray,
　But his bonny sea-wife was gane !

And ever and aye, i' the mirk or the mune,
　Whan the win' blew saft frae the sea,
The sad shore up and the sad shore doon
　By the lanely rock paced he.

But never again on the sands to play
　Cam the maids o' the merry, cauld sea ;
He heard them lauch far oot i' the bay,
　But hert-alane gaed he.

THE WAESOME CARL.

THERE cam a man to oor toon-en',
  And a waesome carl was he,
Snipie-nebbit, and crookit-mou'd,
  And gleyt o' a blinterin ee.
Muckle he spied, and muckle he spak,
  But the owercome o' his sang,
Whatever it said, was aye the same :—
    There's nane o' ye a' but's wrang !
      Ye're a' wrang, and a' wrang,
      And a'thegither a' wrang ;
      There's no a man aboot the toon
      But's a'thegither a' wrang.

That's no the gait to fire the breid,
  Nor yet to brew the yill ;
That's no the gait to haud the pleuch,
  Nor yet to ca the mill ;
That's no the gait to milk the coo,
  Nor yet to spean the calf,
Nor yet to tramp the girnel-meal—
  Ye kenna yer wark by half !
    Ye're a' wrang, etc.

The minister wasna fit to pray
  And lat alane to preach ;
He nowther had the gift o' grace
  Nor yet the gift o' speech !
He mind't him o' Balaäm's ass,
  Wi' a differ we micht ken :
The Lord he opened the ass's mou,
  The minister opened's ain !

He was a' wrang, and a' wrang,
And a'thegither a' wrang ;
There wasna a man aboot the toon
But was a'thegither a' wrang !

The puir precentor couldna sing,
  He gruntit like a swine ;
The verra elders couldna pass
  The ladles til his min'.
And for the rulin' elder's grace
  It wasna worth a horn;
He didna half uncurse the meat,
  Nor pray for mair the morn !
     He was a' wrang, etc.

And aye he gied his nose a thraw,
  And aye he crook't his mou ;
And aye he cockit up his ee
  And said, Tak tent the noo !
We snichert hint oor hoof, my man,
  But never said him nay ;
As gien he had been a prophet, man,
  We loot him say his say :
     Ye're a' wrang, etc.

Quo oor gudeman : The crater's daft !
  Heard ye ever sic a claik ?
Lat's see gien he can turn a han',
  Or only luik and craik !
It's true we maunna lippin til him—
  He's fairly crack wi' pride,

But he maun live—we canna kill him !
    Gien he can work, he s' bide.
        He was a' wrang, and a' wrang,
        And a'thegither a' wrang ;
        There, troth, the gudeman o' the toon
        Was a'thegither a' wrang !

Quo he, It's but a laddie's turn,
    But best the first be a sma' thing :
There's a' thae weyds to gether and burn,
    And he's the man for a' thing !—
We yokit for the far hill-moss,
    There was peats to cast and ca ;
O' 's company we thoucht na loss,
    'Twas peace till gloamin-fa' !
        We war a' wrang, and a' wrang,
        And a'thegither a' wrang ;
        There wasna man aboot the toon
        But was a'thegither a' wrang !

For, losh, or it was denner-time
    The toon was in a low !
The reek rase up as it had been
    Frae Sodom-flames, I vow.
We lowst and rade like mad, for byre
    And ruck bleezt a' thegither,
As gien the deil had broucht the fire
    Frae's hell to mak anither !
        'Twas a' wrang, and a' wrang,
        And a'thegither a' wrang,
        Stick and strae aboot the place
        Was a'thegither a' wrang !

And luikin on, han's neth his tails,
  The waesome carl stude ;
To see him wagglin at thae tails
  'Maist drave 's a' fairly wud.
Ain wite ! he cried ; I tauld ye sae !
  Ye're a' wrang to the last :
What gart ye burn thae deevilich weyds
  Whan the win' blew frae the wast !
     Ye're a' wrang, and a' wrang,
     And a'thegither a' wrang,
     There's no a man i' this fule warl
     But's a'thegither a' wrang !

DR. WALTER C. SMITH.

From "OLRIG GRANGE."

I.

MATER DOMINA.

LADY ANNE DEWHURST on a crimson couch
Lay, with a rug of sable o'er her knees,
In a bright boudoir in Belgravia ;
Most perfectly arrayed in shapely robe
Of sumptuous satin, lit up here and there
With scarlet touches, and with costly lace,
Nice-fingered maidens knotted in Brabant ;
And all around her spread magnificence
Of bronzes, Sèvres vases, marquetrie,
Rare buhl, and bric-à-brac of every kind
From Rome and Paris and the centuries
Of far-off beauty.   All of goodly colour,
Or graceful form that could delight the eye,
In orderly disorder lay around,
And flowers with perfume scented the warm air.

Stately and large and beautiful was she
Spite of her sixty summers, with an eye
Trained to soft languors, that could also flash
Keen as a sword and sharp—a black bright eye,

Deep sunk beneath an arch of jet.   She had
A weary look, and yet the weariness
Seemed not so native as the worldliness
Which blended with it.   Weary and worldly, she
Had quite resigned herself to misery
In this sad vale of tears, but fully meant
To nurse her sorrow in a sumptuous fashion,
And make it an expensive luxury ;
For nothing she esteemed that nothing cost.

Beside her, on a table round, inlaid
With precious stones by Roman art designed,
Lay phials, scents, a novel and a Bible,
A pill box, and a wine glass, and a book
On the Apocalypse ; for she was much
Addicted unto physic and religion,
And her physician had prescribed for her
Jellies and wines and cheerful Literature.
The Book on the Apocalypse was writ
By her chosen pastor, and she took the novel
With the dry sherry, and the pills prescribed.
A gorgeous, pious, comfortable life
Of misery she lived ; and all the sins
Of all her house, and all the nation's sins,
And all shortcomings of the Church and State,
And all the sins of all the world beside,
Bore as her special cross, confessing them
Vicariously day by day, and then
She comforted her heart, which needed it,
With bric-à-brac and jelly and old wine.

II.

THE SQUIRE.

THE Squire was banished to a little room
That overlooked a paved court and a mews;
A small, close chamber, lined with dusty books
And dingy maps; and savage crania
Grinned from high shelves, with clubs and arrow-heads
And tools of flint, and shields of hide embossed.
There were great cobwebs on the windows dim,
Where bloated spiders watched their webs, and heard
The blue-fly knock his head against the pane,
And buzz about their snares.   And through the room,
On table and chair, were globes and glasses tall,
Retorts and crucibles, electric jars
And batteries, and microscopes and prisms
And balances, and fossil plants and shells,
Disorderly and dusty; and the floor
Was carpeted with papers and thick-dust,—
Papers and books and instruments and dust.

A grey old man sat in that dim grey room,
Wrapt in a dressing-gown of soft grey stuff,
And puzzling o'er a paper wearily
Of circles, squares and pentagons, and lines
Of logarithms, he strove to disentangle.
He was a little, brisk, bald-headed man,
With fiery eyes, and forehead narrow and high
And far-retiring: one who could have led
A regiment to the belching cannon's mouth
If wisely ordered when; or might have headed
The cheery hunt across the stubble field,

Taking the fences gallantly, nor turning
From the wide brook to seek the safer ford.
But being held in London half the year,
And with no taste for politics or fashion,
Or such religion as he came across,
He took to Science, made experiments,
Bought many nice and costly instruments,
Heard lectures, and believed he understood
Beetle-browed Science wrestling with the fact
To find its meaning clear ; but all in vain.
He thought he thought, and yet he did not think,
But only echoed still the common talk,
As might an empty room.   The forehead high
And fiery eye had no reflection in them
To brood and hatch the secret of the world.
He could but skim and dip, like restless swallow
Fly-catching on the surface of all knowledge
Anthropologic and Botanical
And Chemical, and what was last set forth
By charlatan to stun the vulgar sense.
But yet a strain of noble chivalry
Ran through his nature, and a faint crisp humour
Rippled his thought, and would have been a joy
Had life been kindlier ; but like forming dew
Seized in the night, and chilled into the spikes
And crystals of the hoar-frost, so the play
And mirth of genial nature had been changed
Into sharp prickles ; and his cheeriest smile
Verged on a sneer, and ran to mocking laughter.
Yet under all his pottering at Science,
And deeper than his feeble cynic sneer,
Lay a great love, to which he fondly clung,
For Rose, the stately daughter of his house.

SCENE FROM "KILDROSTAN."

Scene—*Kildrostan Park.*   Sir Diarmid, *a Highland Chief, and* Tremain, *a Modern Poet.*

Sir Diarmid.

So we give up our cruise, then, after all?
'Tis well; for, as it happens, it would scarce
Have suited me to go.   You'll not regret it?

Tremain.

Why should I?   'Twas a sudden fancy struck me,
And just as sudden left.

Sir Diarmid.

                    No other reason?

Tremain.

What other would you have?   Must one have reasons
To knock down fancies with—a club to beat
The vapour off, that passes with a puff?
I choose to have my whims, and let them go
E'en as I list.   It is a folly, man,
A superstition of these modern times,
To be in bonds to reason.

Sir Diarmid.

                    As you like.
But there's a nice breeze tripping on the Loch,
Tipping the waves with foam.   Have you no fancy
To ride the white steeds in a merry gale?

Tremain.

Nay, that's all past.   I hate a boisterous life.
Give me the calm of Tempe where no wind
Blows on the vine-stocks roughly, and where love
Pants in the sunshine dreamily among
The lotus' leaves and asphodels.

Sir Diarmid.

                                    What then :
Are all those pictures of the bounding sea,
And billowy roll of life there, and your skill
With sail and rope and rudder in a storm
But so much moonshine ?

Tremain.

                                Moonshine ! surely no ;
But poetry of course.   O you dull fellows,
Tied down to facts, you lose the half of life,
Missing its fancied part.   I sit and dream
Of lying in a pinnace with my love,
On a pard's skin, or carpet Eastern-dyed
Of gorgeous colours, with a cloudless sun
Inflaming every sense, as we look down,
And watch the pulsing globe, and tangled arms
Of myriad Medusæ.   Then I see
Ideal storms loom darkly, and the waves
Lashed into madness, which I master so
That by the sense of power we relish more
The soft delights of love.   But your wet ropes
And clumsy oars—faugh ! they give blisters first
And then a horny hand ; and life is lost,
By so much, when you lose a perfect sense.

'Tis needful for my Art that I should have
Nice touch and taste and smell and sight and hearing,
That through all gates may fine sensations pass,
Into my being, and enrich my life.

Sir Diarmid.

Tush ! man ; you are not so effeminate
As you affect.

Tremain.

       I never handled rope,
Nor held a tiller, nor yet mean to do :
A harp, even, blunts the finger-tips.   You think
To be effeminate is to be weak :
I hold that manhood only then is perfect,
When it has all a woman's delicate sense,
And absolute refinement, and will answer,
Like the wind-harp, in tremulous response
To every breath of fancy.

Sir Diarmid.

         How then shall you
Employ your holiday? Our ways are rough,
Nor do we fear to blunt a sense by use.

Tremain.

If I might just go on as now we do,
Bound to no method, held to no set plans,
Floating as Fancy wills, or Fate decrees !
Those hills are beautiful in the purple lights
Of evening, glassed upon the quiet Loch ;

And weird-like are the wavering morning mists,
Tinted with rainbow fragments, like the glories
Which hover in the cloudland of old times ;
And pleasant is the swaying of the boat,
And lapping of the waters ; and I think
I could write something smacking of the life
Of the young world, while yet the gods were in it,
As I look round, and see the fisherwomen
Wade through the surf i' the twilight to the boats,
Each with her husband, or her sweetheart, maybe,
Borne pick-a-back.

Sir Diarmid.

   A barbarous custom !   I
Have tried to shame the men out of these ways,
And do not wonder that you mock at them.

Tremain.

I do not mock at them.   I never felt
More tenderly to any ancient relic
Than to this fond survival.   Let it be.
Why drive your modern ploughshare over all
The fields of primitive custom, making them
As flat and commonplace as turnip fields.
Let it alone.   It is the antique symbol
Of woman's loyalty to love—a link
Uniting us with a more touching life
Of loyal service.   Had I but such a Naiad—
Only not quite so freckled and uncombed—
To plash her large limbs in the waves for me !

Sir Diarmid.

Never was such a plea for barbarism
Pleaded before.

Tremain.

>   And yet as good a one
As you shall find for worshipping a maid,
Until she is a wife to worship you.
Why is it barbarous?   Was the Greek a savage,
When the fair princess, with her laughing maidens,
Washed the white linens in the sparkling brook,
And lovers lay upon the grass, and noted
The dainty feet that splashed the shining spray?

Sir Diarmid.

Well, you may play the lawyer for the nonce,
And draw me out from murky heathen times
Precedents of authority to bar
The way of progress.   But you'll not persuade me
The custom's not degrading.

Tremain.

>   Ay, in vain
We hope to master prejudice by reason.—
But how about this Doris you should wed,
And will not, though her acres are so handy?
What ails you at her?

Sir Diarmid.

>   This; she loves me not,
As shrewdly I suspect; nor love I her,
As certainly I know.   And when we speak
Of marriage, that's a point at least.

Tremain.

                    I know not;
I'm not a marrying man, though all my life
Is love and poetry, which mostly lose
Their glory at the touch o' th' wedding-ring.
It is a quakerish thing connubial bliss,
Tame and slow-blooded, dressed in browns and greys,
And with no flash of passion in the eye,
Or flush o' the cheek.   Is she not beautiful?

Sir Diarmid.

Truly; yet with a dangerous kind of beauty,
Beauty as of a panther or a snake,
Lustrous and lithe; or so at least she shows
To me who love her not.   Her father wedded
In the far East a Hindoo girl, and so
The daughter is not, like our Highland maids
Ruddy and large with amber in their hair,
But slight and supple, and the sun has dyed
Her cheek with olive.   Yet she is most fair.

Tremain.

Ah ! now you interest me.   'Tis just the kind
Of beauty that I worship.   Helena's
Was dangerous, and the grand Egyptian Queen's
Who conquered the world's conquerors, and the sun
Had softly dusked the snow of cheek and bosom,
That chills our northern women.   There's no joy
Without the sense of danger; therefore men
Climb the precipitous mountains with a sense
Of tingling perilous gladness : and I hate
Your meek and milky girls that dare not kiss
A burning passion, clinging to your lips.

Sir Diarmid.

Doris is not a Cleopatra, nor
Helen of Troy—she's just a Highland lady
Touched with an Eastern strain.   You must not liken her
To your wild-eyed Aspasias.

Tremain.

But you said
Hers was a dangerous beauty like the serpent's,
And that is what I like above all things.
Serpents twine round you, clasp you in their folds,
And charm you with a gaze that does not flinch ;
Firing you as the many-husbanded
Helen was wont to do, till men would lose
The world for one brief rapture of her kiss.

Sir Diarmid.

I spoke too loosely: you misconstrue me,
So fancying her.

Tremain.

There's nothing else against her,
Except that dangerous beauty, which is only
The prejudice of people commonplace.
I like to play with adders.   I had one
I loved once as you love your dog, and had
Subtler communion with it, richer thoughts
From its uprearings and its wondrous eyes
Than you shall get from any noisy hound
With its rough shows of liking.

Sir Diarmid.

      Well, I'd rather
My dog should jump on me, and wheel about
Barking for joy, than have an adder twine
Slow folds about me. But tastes differ.

Tremain.

         Ay,
They differ ; yet there is a worse and better,
For taste is the true test of character :
The crown of culture is a perfect taste,
Which lacking, men are blind and cannot see
The higher wisdom. 'Tis the want of it
That floods the world with stale stupidities,
And hangs a vulgar arras round the mind
Of misbegotten fallacies. Tastes differ !
And so do faiths and policies, but yet
Their differences are not indifferent.

Sir Diarmid.

You need not rave about it, man. I used
A common phrase, as one does current coin,
Not caring to ring copper half-pennies
Upon the counter.

Tremain.

     Oh ! Yet I take leave
To doubt the taste that shrinks from such a girl
As you describe your Doris : that is all.
The kind of woman, bred of Christian cult,
Whom you call womanly, to me is watery—
A Ghost, a mist that chills you with its touch.
How changed from the grand creature Nature made
For joy, and music, and the giddy dance,

And glorious passion !   There's a story of
Pelagia, leader of the mimes at Antioch
On the Orontes; how she came one day
Up from the silvern baths with her fair troop
Of girls, all glowing with the flush of life,
And bounding with light mirth, and lures of love,
Like the young hinds what time the year reveals
The antlered stag freed from the down of his horns;
And as she came, arrayed in purple skirt
Of Tyrian, golden bracelets on her wrists,
And tinkling anklets, and the flash of gems
Upon her bosom, on her brow of flowers —
Lo ! then an anchorite, dried up and baked
With dirt of some dim cave where he had burrowed
With bats and owls, looked wistfully on her,
And craftily assailed her with regrets
That she brought not her beauty and her joy —
Another Magdalene !—to serve his Lord :
Wherewith being touched, she turns a penitent,
And comes next day, and lays aside her robes
Of splendour, and her bright and joyous ways
So winsome, and in squalid garb arrayed
Of sackcloth, visits graves and lazar houses,
Pale as a lily—a shadow called a saint.
What think you now of such a work as that
To pleasure heaven with ?   While the old gods lived,
A woman was the glory of our glad
And fruitful earth.   But now you make of her——

Sir Diarmid.

I prithee, peace, man.   If I did not know
This is but spinning moonshine for the love
Of phantasy, and framing paradox
To seem original, I could be wroth

With such trash-speaking.   Interrupt me not.
What, if your leader of the mimes had been
A chaste pure maiden, daughter of a home
Where mother-love enfolded her in customs
As sweet as lavender, and that she met
Some gay apostle of the flesh, and as
His penitent, became—— what you have known?
The world is bad enough, and false enough
Without such gloss to prove its darkness light.
The devil is up to that; and does not need
That you should make fine clothes for him to wear
When he goes masking.   Let this stuff alone;
Or weave it into verses, if you will,
For fools to read, although I used to think—
But that was in my youth's fond innocence—
That poetry should stir the best in us,
And give fit utterance also to our best
In rhythmic music.

Tremain.

That was not your thought:
'Twas but an echo you and others tossed
From mouth to mouth, and thought that you had
    thought.

Sir Diarmid.

Echo or living voice, the thought is true;
God gives us song to make us nobler men
And purer women.

Tremain.

Nay, for art is not
The stave of virtue, turning songs to sermons;
But it is free, and is its own excuse,
And finds its purpose in its exercise.

Sir Diarmid.

What do you mean?

Tremain.

       This.   Picturing truly all
Ideals—good or evil, as you call them—
Art doth fulfil her office, but comes short
Of her vocation when she aims at aught
But perfect form and colour and harmony.

Sir Diarmid.

Enough : I did not count on getting such
Art lectures from you.   Keep them for the freshmen.

Tremain.

You make a pedant and a pedagogue
Of that which is the sovranest thing in nature,
The freest and the gayest.   Out upon
The tyranny of small moralities,
Shop-keeping ethics, Pharisee respects !
As if high Art must minister to them,
Like a fair tablemaid who must not speak,
But let them prose and prose !   I hate it all.
For evil and good, yea sense and nonsense, Art,
Soaring above them in her own bright realm,
Yet lifts them up, and blends them in her charm
Of light and music and divinest vision.
But you are still in bonds to commonplace,
And cannot bear this yet.

Sir Diarmid.

Nor ever shall,
Nor ever wish to.   One might land in Bedlam
For less conceit of wisdom.

Tremain.

By the way,
There's one thing more I wish to know.   Last night,
Or rather in the gloaming, as you have it,
Upon the heights, beside the waterfall
That wavers like a tremulous white veil
Of bridal lace to hide the moss-clad rock,
I had a vision of beauty.

Sir Diarmid.

O belike,
The purple glow was on the hills.

Tremain.

Nay, but
A maiden passed me tall and beautiful,
Robed all in black.   Her step was like a queen's,
Pallas-Athene had no statelier mien,
Broad-browed, large-eyed, and with the confidence
Of strength and courage in her.   Who is she?

Sir Diarmid.

How should I know?   No matter.

Tremain.

                                    Girls like that
Can't walk about the shores incognito :
You surely know her ; think of it again.
I did but pass some pretty compliment—
Thrown at her, to be picked up if she chose,
Not spoken to her—an impromptu verse
That sprang up to my lips at such a vision
Of might and beauty delicately mixed,
When she, just pausing, gave me such a look,
As if she could have tossed me o'er the crag
Into the pool, then leisurely swept on.
Who is she ?   All the fisher folk would say
Was, It will be Miss Ina.

Sir Diarmid.

                              Ay, that was
Ever her favourite walk.   Now, if you chance
To meet her there again, best let her pass
Without impromptu verses.   You might find
They breed unpleasant consequences.
                  ●

Tremain.

                                    But
Who is she ?

Sir Diarmid.

            Well ; no matter : my kinswoman.
Her father was our pastor, lately dead—
No more of her.   When shall we visit Doris ?
She's far more to your taste.

Tremain.

O when you will.
But that dark-robed Pallas-Athene—your
Kinswoman, said you ?

Sir Diarmid.

Surely you would not
Intrude upon the sacredness of sorrow
Like hers.

Tremain.

The parson's daughter—

Sir Diarmid.

Sir, I tell you
She shall not be molested.

Tremain.

So : I see
Why Doris' beauty is so dangerous.
Pallas-Athene broad-browed, shining-eyed,
That is your style, is't ?

[*Exit.*

Sir Diarmid.

Pshaw ! why should I care
For that fool's babble ? for a fool he is
With all his genius, which is but a trick
Of stringing words together musically.

How could I ever bring him to the home
Of pious, pure-souled women.   Yet he'll serve
My purpose, if he only take to Doris,
And she to him—she is not over-nice.
But is it fair that I should plot and scheme
To save myself from a detested fate
By luring her into as dark a snare?
Nay, but I only bring these two together,
And by the mutual attraction of
Their kindred natures let them coalesce,
If so they will—and surely so they will:
Only the time is short.   Yet such folk jump
Into their loves; and if it so befell,
My path were clear, and all should yet be well.

MISS PENELOPE LEITH.

Last heiress she of many a rood,
  Where Ugie winds through Buchan braes—
A treeless land, where beeves are good,
  And men have quaint old-fashioned ways,
And every burn has ballad-lore,
  And every hamlet has its song,
And on its surf-beat rocky shore
  The eerie legend lingers long.
Old customs live there, unaware
  That they are garments cast away,
And what of light is shining there
  Is lingering light of yesterday.

Never to her the new day came,
　Or if it came she would not see ;
This world of change was still the same
　To our old-world Penelope :
New fashions rose, old fashions went,
　But still she wore the same brocade,
With lace of Valenciennes or Ghent
　More dainty by her darning made,
A little patch upon her face,
　A tinge of colour on her cheek,
A frost of powder, just to grace
　The locks that time began to streak.

A stately lady ; to the poor
　Her manner was without reproach ;
But from the Causeway she was sure
　To snub the Provost in his coach :
In pride of birth she did not seek
　Her scorn of upstarts to conceal,
But of a Bailie's wife would speak
　As if she bore the fisher's creel.
She said it kept them in their place,
　Their fathers were of low degree ;
She said the only saving grace
　Of upstarts was humility.

The quaint, old Doric still she used,
　And it came kindly from her tongue ;
And oft the " mim-folk " she abused,
　Who mincing English said or sung :
She took her claret, nothing loth,
　Her snuff that one small nostril curled ;
She might rap out a good round oath,
　But would not mince it for the world :

And yet the wild word sounded less
    In that Scotch tongue of other days;
'Twas just like her old-fashioned dress,
    And part of her old-fashioned ways.

At every fair her face was known,
    Well-skilled in kyloes and in queys;
And well she led the fiddler on
    To "wale" the best of his strathspeys;
Lightly she held the man who rose
    While the toast-hammer still could rap,
And brought her gossip to a close,
    Or spoilt her after-dinner nap;
Tea was for women, wine for men,
    And if they quarrelled o'er their cups,
They might go to the peat-moss then,
    And fight it out like stags or tups.

She loved a bishop or a dean,
    A surplice or a rocket well,
At all the Church's feasts was seen,
    And called the Kirk, Conventicle;
Was civil to the minister,
    But stiff and frigid to his wife,
And looked askance, and sniffed at her,
    As if she lived a dubious life.
But yet his sick her cellars knew,
    Well stored from Portugal or France,
And many a savoury soup and stew
    Her game-bags furnished to the Manse.

But if there was a choicer boon
    Above all else she would have missed,
It was on Sunday afternoon
    To have her quiet game at whist

Close to the window, when the Whigs
  Were gravely passing from the Kirk,
And some on foot, and some in gigs,
  Would stare at her unhallowed work :
She gloried in her " devil's books "
  That cut their sour hearts to the quick ;
Rather than miss their wrathful looks
  She would have almost lost the trick.

Her politics were of the age
  Of Claverhouse or Bolingbroke ;
Still at the Dutchman she would rage,
  And still of gallant Grahame she spoke.
She swore 'twas right that Whigs should die
  Psalm-snivelling in the wind and rain,
Though she would ne'er have harmed a fly
  For buzzing on the window pane.
And she had many a plaintive rhyme
  Of noble Charlie and his men :
For her there was no later time,
  All history had ended then.

The dear old sinner ! yet she had
  A kindly human heart, I wot,
And many a sorrow she made glad,
  And many a tender mercy wrought :
And though her way was somewhat odd,
  Yet in her way she feared the Lord,
And thought she best could worship God
  By holding Pharisees abhorred,
By being honest, fearless, true,
  And thorough both in word and deed,
And by despising what is new,
  And clinging to her old-world creed.

THE CONFESSION OF ANNAPLE GOWDIE, WITCH.

ANNIE WINNE and me
  Were both at Yester kirk ;—
She on a broom, and I on a straw,
" Horse and hattock " o'er Berwick Law
  We rode away in the mirk.

It was Fastern's Even,
  And we lichted down on a grave ;
Where an ape preached loud to a ghostly crowd,
Surpliced well with a bonny white shroud,
  And a corby sang the stave.

" The covin " all was there ;
  Thirteen of us with " the maid " ;—
She was Bessie Vicar from Kelvin side ;
And wow ! but she hotched in her unco pride—
  Deil thraw her neck for a jade.

And there was Pickle-the-wind,
  And there was Over-the-dyke,
And Ailie Nesbit, Able-and-stout,
And Elspie Gourlay, Good-at-a-bout ;
  Buzzing all like a byke.

Black Jock was in his tantrums ;
  And hech ! but he was daft !
Alick Flett with his chanter het,
Fizzing whenever his lips it met,
  Skirled away in the laft.

Oh, we were crouse and canty
  A' doon in Yester kirk,
And we supped on the toad and the hooded craw,
Daintily spread on a coffin braw,
  At midnight in the mirk.

And syne we held a session,
  And tried the lasses there ;
Twal gruesome carles were elders good,
And a black tom-cat for bethral stood,
  And the foul fiend took the chair.

And Elspie Gourlay first
  Confessed to a strangled bairn ;
And Bessie Vickar allowed that she
Whummled a boat in a quiet sea,
  With a bonny young bride in the stern,

And some had played their cantrips
  Wi' poor wives' milking kine ;
And one had made an image good,
And crucified on the holy rood,
  That the Laird's ae son micht pine.

But me and Annie Winnie,
  The foul thief kissed us baith ;
For we choked the priest on the Eucharist,
When he was glowering at Effie M'Christ,
  And speaking of holy faith.

Hech ! sirs, but we had grand fun
    Wi' the muckle black deil in the chair,
And the muckle Bible upside doon,
A' gangin' withershins roun' and roun',
    And backwards saying the prayer.

About the warlock's grave
    Withershins gangin' roun',
And kimmer and carline had for licht
The fat o' a bairn they buried that nicht,
    Unchristened beneath the moon.

And, when the red cock crew
    In the farmstead up on the hill,
And the black tom-cat began to mew,
Witch and warlock, away we flew
    In the morning grey and chill.

And my gudeman was sleeping,
    Wi' the besom at his side,
And hech ! but he kissed the bonny broom,
My braw gudeman, my auld bridegroom,
    As I lichted doon frae my ride.

And Annie Winnie and me
    Crack crouse o' Yester kirk,
And how she on the broom and I on a straw,
" Horse and hattock " o'er Berwick Law
    Rode away in the mirk.

THE SELF-EXILED.

From "HILDA AMONG THE BROKEN GODS."

THERE came a soul to the gate of Heaven
      Gliding slow—
A soul that was ransomed and forgiven,
      And white as snow :
And the angels all were silent.

A mystic light beamed from the face
      Of the radiant maid :
But there also lay on its tender grace
      A mystic shade :
And the angels all were silent.

As sunlit clouds by a zephyr borne
      Seem not to stir,
So to the golden gates of morn
      They carried her :
And the angels all were silent.

"Now open the gate, and let her in,
      And fling it wide,
For she has been cleansed from stain of sin,"
      St. Peter cried :
And the angels all were silent.

"Though I am cleansed from stain of sin,"
      She answered low,
"I came not hither to enter in,
      Nor may I go :"
And the angels all were silent.

"I come," she said, "to the pearly door,
    To see the Throne
Where sits the Lamb on the Sapphire Floor,
    With God alone : "
And the angels all were silent.

"I come to hear the new song they sing
    To Him that died,
And note where the healing waters spring
    From His pierced side : "
And the angels all were silent.

"But I may not enter there," she said,
    "For I must go
Across the gulf where the guilty dead
    Lie in their woe : "
And the angels all were silent.

"If I enter heaven I may not pass
    To where they be,
Though the wail of their bitter pain, alas !
    Tormenteth me : "
And the angels all were silent.

"If I enter heaven I may not speak
    My soul's desire
For them that are lying distraught and weak
    In flaming fire : "
And the angels all were silent.

" I had a brother, and also another
        Whom I loved well ;
What if, in anguish, they curse each other
        In the depths of hell ? "
And the angels all were silent.

"How could I touch the golden harps,
        When all my praise
Would be so wrought with grief-full warps
        Of their sad days ? "
And the angels all were silent.

" How love the loved who are sorrowing,
        And yet be glad ?
How sing the songs ye are fain to sing,
        While I am sad ? "
And the angels all were silent.

" O clear as glass is the golden street
        Of the city fair,
And the tree of life it maketh sweet
        The lightsome air : "
And the angels all were silent.

" And the white-robed saints with their crowns
        and palms
        Are good to see,
And O so grand are the sounding psalms !
        But not for me : "
And the angels all were silent.

"I come where there is no night," she said,
      "To go away,
And help, if I yet may help, the dead
      That have no day."
And the angels all were silent.

St. Peter he turned the keys about,
      And answered grim ;
"Can you love the Lord, and abide without,
      Afar from Him ?"
And the angels all were silent.

"Can you love the Lord who died for you,
      And leave the place
Where His glory is all disclosed to view,
      And tender grace ?"
And the angels all were silent.

"They go not out who come in here ;
      It were not meet :
Nothing they lack, for He is here,
      And bliss complete."
And the angels all were silent.

"Should I be nearer Christ," she said,
      "By pitying less
The sinful living or woeful dead
      In their helplessness ?"
And the angels all were silent.

"Should I be liker Christ were I
    To love no more
The loved, who in their anguish lie
    Outside the door?"
And the angels all were silent.

"Did He not hang on the cursed tree,
    And bear its shame,
And clasp to His heart, for love of me,
    My guilt and blame?"
And the angels all were silent.

"Should I be liker, nearer Him,
    Forgetting this,
Singing all day with the Seraphim,
    In selfish bliss?"
And the angels all were silent.

The Lord Himself stood by the gate,
    And heard her speak
Those tender words compassionate,
    Gentle and meek:
And the angels all were silent.

Now, pity is the touch of God
    In human hearts,
And from that way He ever trod
    He ne'er departs:
And the angels all were silent.

And He said, "Now will I go with you,
     Dear child of love,
I am weary of all this glory, too,
     In heaven above : "
And the angels all were silent.

"We will go seek and save the lost,
     If they will hear,
They who are worst but need me most,
     And all are dear : "
And the angels were not silent.

EARL OF SOUTHESK.

From "JONAS FISHER: A POEM IN BROWN AND WHITE."

[Jonas Fisher, a philosophical young shop-man, who has led a dissipated life, has been "converted," after an illness, and has taken to district-visiting. The second speaker in the dialogue is Mr. Grace, his mentor.—It may be stated here that the motive underlying the poem of *Jonas Fisher* is the exaltation in all things, and especially in religion, of "the spirit" above "the letter"; and that the extreme simplicity, at times verging upon rudeness, of the *style* of the poem is adopted as in harmony with that motive.—ED.]

My mission day is Saturday,
For then at Two shop-work is o'er,
(On Sabbath, day of rest, I go
Three times to church, and prayers before),

And all the afternoon I give
To visiting the poor indeed;
Rich people scarce could even guess
The wretched life these creatures lead.

Each house is many stories high,
Each room a family contains;
And there they breed, and breathe foul air,
Like rats inhabiting the drains.

Though, when one comes to think of it,
The rats are far more clean and sweet ;
These people neither comb nor wash,
Rats trim their fur and keep it neat.

O dear ! O dear ! the sights one sees !
In a close court the other day,
I saw some lean, large-stomached babes,
All busy at their childish play :

They dabbled in the thick black slime,
Stuck fish-heads in and drew them out,
Made pies of stuff much worse than mud,
While fat blue-bottles buzzed about.

Poor innocents ! for those who die
In early years what bliss untold,
To pass from filth and haddock-heads
To seas of glass and streets of gold !

I prayed an earnest prayer for them,
Then turned and climbed a winding stair
That smelt of cats, knocked at a door,
Half opened it, and looked in there.

Notions do differ.   Some good folk
Are to the poor quite rough behaved :
Push into rooms, hat on, and cry—
"Well, how's your soul?   Friend, are you saved?"

Attention thus they hope to draw
By sudden pain or startling noise ;
As pedlars shout to puff their wares,
Or teachers lash their careless boys.

But I have always liked to act
On "Do as you'd be done by" rule,
And show the manners that I learned
At my dear native Berkshire school.

Well, at the opening door I paused,
Stood still and just put in my chin,
Took off my hat, half bowed, and said—
"Good afternoon.   May I come in?"

An inner porch I then perceived;
The door that moment open burst,
Out rushed two angry Irish wives,
And shook their fists, and raged and cursed.

"Off with you, dirty Protestant!
You beast! you devil! get away."
(I cannot write their curious brogue,
But tell the things they meant to say.)

On hearing this I breathed a prayer—
Which helps one much, and much protects—
"Don't call me Protestant," I said,
"All Christians don't belong to sects."

"You're not a Christian, sure, at all;
You're one that mocks God's mother mild."
"Blest above women she,"—says I.
I smiled, and then the women smiled.

This kind of wide-mouthed Irish folk,
Change like a swallow in its flight;
One, two,—they want to shed your blood,
Three, four,— they're friendly and polite.

"Come in, Sir, come," the women said,
And wiping clean their only chair,
They moved it tow'rds me; suddenly
I heard a growl as from a bear,

And off his bed there leaped a man,
A huge, half-drunken, savage beast;
He seized a knife, and ran at me;
I stood, and did not budge the least,

But fixed my eyes upon his eyes,
And cowed him through God's help—as when
An angel stopped the lions' mouths
From eating Daniel in the den.

Then both the women made a rush,
And threw themselves upon the man,
And caught him by his arms and legs:
Oh! what a dreadful scene began.

They reel, they roll, they twist about,
(Like the three Greeks that fought with snakes—
One sees them in the plaster casts—)
The windows dance, the flooring shakes.

As music at a wild-beast show,
With roars and cries combines its strum,
So shouts, yells, howls together rose,
Rap, rap, went oaths like tap of drum.

Crack goes the fellow's rotten shirt,
One half flies this way, one half that;
But ere his trowsers also split,
The broad-backed women laid him flat,

And put him helpless on his bed,
And tossed and turned him as they chose ;
He gave a few indignant snorts,
Then passed into a drunken doze.

Thus fell the mighty—luckily ;
And now came pleasant times indeed,
The women so polite and kind,
So glad to hear me pray and read.

They really scarce would let me go,
They hungered for the food of Life ;
Next week their zeal was just the same ;
The next, they chased me with a knife.

The priest, of course, had come meanwhile,
And heavy threats upon them laid :
I owe no grudge ; as one might say,
He did it in the way of trade.

But still when people take to hunt
A missionary down the street,
Then at their door—in Scripture phrase—
He shakes the dust from off his feet.

Well, after that, I went to see
A far more quiet set than these :
An old Italian and his wife,
Who dealt in stucco images.

Gambetti was their name, I think,
An inoffensive sort of pair;
They scarcely knew one English word,
But treated me with courteous care.

Such funny things upon their shelves,—
Queens, Holy Virgins, Neptune, Mars,
And several naked Goddesses,
Pigs, Angels, and a Prince with stars:

Young Samuel kneeling in his shirt;
Crusoe with parrot, gun, and goat;
St. John in Patmos with a bird;
And baby Moses in his boat:

Dogs, cats, canaries, heroes, saints,
All green and scarlet, gold and blue;
Things much too sacred to be named;
The "Dying Gladiator" too.

(Some lines about that plaster cast
Quite long ago my fancy took—
"Butchered to make a holiday"—
I have them in my extract-book.

And to myself, when people fail
In pious public-speech, I say—
"Butchered is this good gentleman
To make a Christian holiday.")

Leaving Gambetti and his wife,
Another quiet call I made,
Within a rather decent house,
Where a sick, agèd woman stayed.

Midst weakness, loneliness, and pain,
Her every look seemed praise to sing;
In heart she was a holy saint,
Though such a poor old doting thing.

A few small comforts she possessed—
Whose lot is there that nothing mends?—
First place, a store of books, the gift
Of kind Episcopalian friends.

Now, though to favour sect o'er sect
Is not my way, I must attest
That of all pious books I see,
Episcopalian are the best.

So full of manly, simple faith,
So rich in warmth and sweet content,
No harsh malignant threatenings,
No cold hard-hearted argument.

I'm speaking of the genuine thing,
The good old-fashioned stately school;
Asses will bray in lion-skins,
And wolves will howl in coats of wool.

So when I called on Widow Smith,
I chose some volume from her shelf
And read to her, and thus I got
No little profit for myself.

For if a teacher never learns,
His prayers and talk grow weak and cold;
As spiders that go spinning on
Spin webs at last that will not hold.

Another joy the widow had,—
I am not one that strains at gnats,
I did not blame her foolish waste,—
She kept three lazy, greedy cats.

What could the creatures get to eat ?
No rats or mice would enter where
Provisions were so very scarce ;
Cats surely cannot live on air—

Though in such rooms the atmosphere's
Close substance might be almost carved,- -
Quite strange it seemed to see them fat,
While Widow Smith was nearly starved.

This is a contradiction odd,
Which meets you every day you live :
The rich most often like to keep,
The poor most often like to give.

They get so little at a time
That thrift seems scarcely worth their pains ;
At length they lose the power to save,
But spend, give, waste, till naught remains.

Minds are, like bodies, slaves to use,
And wrongful habits mischief breed ;
Crammed stomachs learn to hold too much,
Starved ones can't keep the food they need.

Good Widow Smith !　Some ten days thence,
When last that humble floor I trod,
Her poor old frame was stiff in death,
Her saintly soul had gone to God.

" Had gone to God "—strange phrase, methinks !
As if some special house were His.
Is earth a place where God is not ?
Let's say—" Her soul had gone to bliss."

I saw her just before she died,
Calm, trustful, patient, and resigned ;
She would have been in perfect peace,
But for one thought that vexed her mind.

Grasping my arm she drew me close, —
I scarce could hear her voice at all,—
"Oh ! Jonas, if it were His will,
I'd like a decent funeral."

I kissed her brow, and pledged myself
That what she wished should come to pass ;
Smiles swiftly flitted o'er her face,
As butterflies across the grass.

Once more she smiled, then closed her eye
And never opened them again :
At set of sun she slipped away
Without a struggle or a pain.

———

INFLUENCE OF THE COURSE OF TIME ON NATIONAL LOOKS.

(From the same.)

"OF potent causes that affect
The face or form, to mould or blight—
Disease or violence apart,—
Nerve force exerts the chiefest might.

"And as time rolls, each chance and change
Brings with it change of nervous strain ;
Thus every generation bears
An impress never borne again.

"More quick, more slow, the impress strikes,
As changes quick or slow take place—
Those who would read a nation's past,
May read it in a nation's face."

"Well then," said I, "I'd like to know
What a philosopher would say
About the sort of people, Sir,
One has to do with every day."

Said he, "I should prefer to take
A broader view of things, and try
How far our English portraiture
Illustrates English history."

"How early, Sir, shall we begin ?"
Said I.   "But little can we bring,"
He answered, "of a date more old
Than that of the first Tudor king,

"To help us much.   But yet methinks
On coin, or brass, or burial-stone,
One sees a type of countenance,
Through centuries, quite unlike our own.

"And, speaking in the general mode,
I think one, on the whole, observes
A grave, calm, firm-fleshed, oval face,
Of strong unwavering lines and curves.

" But pass we to those glorious days
When art from her long slumber woke,
When knowledge re-illumed her lamp,
And link by link Rome's fetters broke :

" When England also feels the thrill,
Strong wafted on the breath of time
Full o'er her distant ocean waves,
Of high things revelling in their prime ;—

" Then her whole range of portraiture,
Of statesman, warrior, noble dame,
Bears constant stamp of fleshly waste
Through heat of intellectual flame.

" Till those resplendent years arrive
When Shakespeare trod this honoured earth,
And round him lived the noblest men
That e'er from England drew their birth.

" Ah ! then behold the perfect type,
Where flesh and soul and spirit blend
In measure which the most allows
That glory should in all transcend :

" Long-visaged, strong-chinned, high of nose ;
Large-eyed, with gaze stern, sweet, sublime ;
Well-bearded, grand of chest and arm ;
Browed as if brain to heaven would climb.—

" Ere half a century had flown
A different visage meets the eye,—
Of courtly nobleness in some,
In others of a type less high.

" The Cavalier and Puritan
Two varying types present to view—
The greyhound slim, the mastiff stout ;—
Yet both have in them something new :

" In one a selfish vanity,
In one a dry pedantic pride ;
Their sires and grandsires o'er them tower
As Shakespeare placed at Milton's side.

" Then worse succeeds, both soul and frame
Degenerate ; beauty, strength decay ;
Hard, false, dull logic (called ' good sense '),
And brutal hoggishness, bear sway.

" The Cavalier has now become
A strumous fool with goggled eyes,
And bulbous brow, and fat pink lips,
Small chin, and cheeks of lumpish eyes.

" The Puritan—an atheist now,
Save that he serves a belly-god—
Presents a huge, rough, jowly face,
Topped by a cranium low and broad.

" But ere a deeper depth was plumbed,
(If deeper depth indeed there were),
It pleased the Lord to send a storm
Which cleared the moral atmosphere,—

" The fierce French Revolution.   This
(To change the figure) brought to birth,
By devil-wrought Cæsarean act,
Incarnate health for all the earth.

" Then followed war and furious change,
The nations to their centres shook ;—
Behold the features of mankind
Once more a faithful history-book !

" I know not if that storm set loose
New fiends, but since methinks we trace
A new and potent element
Disturbing, injuring oft, the face,—

" An influence on the nerves, displayed
In the inquiring restless glance
And complex feature-lines, that mark
The nineteenth-century countenance."

Said I, " To judge by pictures, Sir,
Our grandfathers when young appeared
Much like young people nowadays,
Except that then they wore no beard."

" Perhaps," said he ; " it takes some time—
Most oft at least—to fix a brand
So plainly on a race that all
Can see the change.   And yet the hand

" Of change can never bear on minds
And leave the bodies uncontrolled ;
Our sires' or grandsires' minds were young,
Their sons' or grandsons' minds are old.

" The influence of the camp is seen
In their rough, hasty, manly force
Of speech and thought ; our younger race
Is weaker, slower, and less coarse.

"Contrast the mighty torrent-sweep
Of Byron's fierce impassioned lays,
With the meandering placid flow
Of his deep verse who wears the bays

" In these our times ; or gallant Scott,
Whose rhymes rush on like charge of lance ;
Or Campbell, whose heroic strains
Are battle's trumpets of advance.

" It is not that our moderns lack
All fiery essence in their mind ;
But what belongs to flesh and blood
Appears to them so unrefined,

" That to make simple manifold,
And clear obscure, they take much pains—
The grandsires wrote with all their hearts,
The grandsons write with all their brains."

NOVEMBER'S CADENCE.

THE bees about the Linden-tree,
When blithely summer blooms were springing,
Would hum a heartsome melody,
The simple baby-soul of singing :
And thus my spirit sang to me
When youth its wanton way was winging ;
    " Be glad, be sad—thou hast the choice—
    But mingle music with thy voice."

The linnets on the Linden-tree,
Among the leaves in autumn dying,
Are making gentle melody,
A mild, mysterious, mournful sighing :
And thus my spirit sings to me
While years are flying, flying, flying ;
    " Be sad, be sad—thou hast no choice—
But mourn with music in thy voice."

THE ROCKY MOUNTAINS.

YE mountains of rock in the Land of the West,
Ye mountains of glory, for ever be blest !
Blest, blest be your valleys with vast craggy walls,
Your icy blue torrents and white waterfalls.
    But oh ! to be up on the heights, alone,
    Where the pretty grey Siffleur sits still on a stone ;
    Sits on a stone and whistles and sings,
    And trances the heart with his magic spell ;
    Sacredly sad his music rings,
    Clear as the tones of a silver bell,—
    Sounds that weep, that aspire, that pray,
    Like angels calling a soul away.

How grandly, O mountains, your forests are spread
O'er the low sunny slope in the valley's deep bed,
How sweet the pine-fragrance that gladdens the air
In the haunts of the Moose and the grim Grisly Bear !
    But oh ! to be up on the heights, alone,
    Where the curly-horned Mountain Ram dwells with
        his own ;

Dwells with his own on the pleasant steep,
Quenches his thirst at the glacier brook,
Crops the sweet grasses that crisply creep
To cover the sides of a sheltered nook ;
Wanders a while, or rests at his ease
Basking in sunshine and screened from the breeze.

Magnificent mountains ! when dawn has begun
How proudly your pinnacles shine in the sun !
Bright o'er your far summits gold fire-glories glow,
Then descend crag by crag to the valleys below.
　　And oh ! to be up on the heights, alone,
　　Where the snowy Goat climbs on the chaos of stone;
　　Climbs the rock waste with his wide black feet,
　　Scales the ice-cliff whence the waters part,
　　Shades his thick fleece, from the noon-tide heat,
　　In the crater sunk to a mountain's heart—
　　Trees and green grass in the depths of it lie,
　　And a little blue lake that mirrors the sky.

Loved mountains ! blest mountains ! how fair, yet how
　　strange,
When the moon overtops your majestical range !
Shows a thin radiant arc, straight leaps full into sight,
And illumes your vast caves with her silver-sheen light.
　　Then oh ! to be down by the blazing logs,
　　In the midst of good hunters and horses and dogs.
　　Fragrantly smokes the resinous pine,
　　Tall is the spire of its broad red blaze,
　　The eyes of the horses like beryls shine,
　　The torrent glitters with golden rays.
　　Not a sound in the night but is near and small,
　　And vast is the silence that broods on all.

THE GERMAN TOWER KEEPER.

GOD bless our good prince, and establish his crown !
For I am the highest of men in his town.
Of women, however exalted in life,
The highest of all are my daughter and wife.
    Yes, far above folks' heads we dwell,
    And watch the town from hour to hour :
    Their goings-on we see right well
    From off the Margarethen Tower.

Our eight-sided mansion has windows all round—
We fear not foul vapours that cling to the ground,—
Whatever the weather, we get our full share
Of the warmth of the sun and the cool of the air.
    No blinds shut out the light of day,
    But every window has its flower,
    And thus we keep a garden gay
    Up in the Margarethen Tower.

Just under our feet are the tops of the limes,
Great trees of the ancient majestical times ;
They spread their wide billows of blossom abroad,
And smell like a newly-made Eden of God.
    Small birds and pigeons sing and coo
    Within that fragrant yellowy bower,
    And rear their young ones in our view
    Beside the Margarethen Tower.

Hemmed in by the trees are the church's old tiles,
Which gladden our eyes with their ruddy-brown smiles ;

High music the organ and choristers raise, ·
And encompass our home with an ether of praise.
       We trust in God, and fear no shock
       When lightning-clouds around us lour,
       Nor when the furious tempests rock
       The crumbling Margarethen Tower.

How pleasant to stand in the evening's soft light,
And watch the bright backs of the swallows in flight !
These angel-winged swifts heavenly messengers seem,
Though black be their plumage and piercing their scream.
       Give, give me nature's blessêd tones !
       Art's sweets compared with them are sour.
       May swallows ever love the stones
       Of our dear Margarethen Tower !

Three mighty great bells in the belfry are hung—
An earthquake for us when on holidays rung—
The big one a giant beneath it might hold,
The new one is less, but more precious than gold.
       Cast from French cannon is that bell.
       To Him who made the foeman cower
       Its glorious notes thanksgivings tell,
       From the brave Margarethen Tower.

And still, as the minutes creep stealthily on,
We notice the time when each quarter is gone,
And then little Süschen a crank works about,
And a block strikes the bell, and the thunder booms out.
       Strange that a tiny tender maid
       O'er sounds so great should have the power !
       But weight by wit is always swayed,
       As in the Margarethen Tower.

Well pleased are my wife and my daughter and I
To live by ourselves up aloft in the sky.
Our chiefest of wishes is never to part :
We are poor of the pocket, but rich of the heart.
 Six old, four young, canary birds
 Make little Süschen's only dower.
 Oh, sweet is she beyond all words—
 Joy of the Margarethen Tower.

God bless our good prince ! As I sit here installed
And gaze on the spread of the Thüringer Wald,
Its heights all arrayed in the evening's gold glow,
I myself feel a prince o'er the city below.
 God guard our prince and people well,
 And every blessing on them shower—
 On them, and me and mine that dwell
 In the old Margarethen Tower !

THE MOUNTAIN FIR.

THEY sat beneath the mountain fir,
 Beneath the evening sun ;
With all his soul he looked at her—
 And so was love begun.

The titmice blue in fluttering flocks
 Caressed the fir-tree spray ;
And far below, through rifted rocks,
 The river went its way.

As stars in heavenly waters swim
 Her eyes of azure shone ;
With all her soul she looked at him—
 And so was love led on.

The squirrel sported on the bough
 And chuckled in his play ;
Above the distant mountain's brow
 A golden glory lay.

The fir-tree breathed its balsam balm,
 With heather scents united,
The happy skies were hushed in calm—
 And so the troth was plighted.

PIGWORM AND DIXIE.

[Joey Peggram, or "Pigworm," laments over the bygone bachelor days of Ben Dixie, his former boon companion.—ED.]

WELL ! if ever a man is in want of a wife
To poison his pleasure and pester his life,
First place let him go to Ben Dixie's, you know,
And see what that awful example will show.

Oh, such a good fellow was rollicking Ben,
Beloved by the girls and the right sort of men !
You may call me a lie, but—'pon honour 'tis said—
For a twelvemonth he never went sober to bed.

Yes ; rollicking Ben was a fellow of sense,
Who hated all stick-me-up, humbug pretence ;
As to that I can swear, for no hogs in the sty
Were more thick with each other than Dixie and I.

What a jolly old crib was his house in the dale,
A Garden of Eden of 'baccy and ale :
Any hour of the day you could eat at your ease,
There were always some ends of cold bacon or cheese.

Lawk ! now if you enter his prig of a house,
Not a scrap can you find that would serve for a mouse ;
And you wait and you wait till the dinner comes in,
Though perhaps you're as hungry and thirsty as sin.

But at last there's a row,—jingle-jing goes a bell,
And you sit yourself down, and you feed like a swell.
Oh, that shiny new tablecloth !—give me the cheer
Of the old one, all gravy and mustard and beer !

Ah yes, Mrs. Dixie, you're awfully neat,
With your fat little hands and your smart little feet ;
And you trot up and down, and you perk up your head,
And you smell like a rose in a lavender bed.

And you smirk and you smile, and you puff out your
    breast
Like a pigeon a-pouting and walking its best ;
And so mighty polite—why, a fellow can't dare
To chaff when he wants to, and swagger and swear !

Lawk ! I'd like to yell out, like a throttle-choked hen,
When I think of the days of good *bachelor* Ben ;
No wife to torment one, dressed up like a doll,—
But that jolly kind creature, young housekeeper Moll.

She was something to see, as you smoked in your chair,
With her rolling black eyes and the kink in her hair ;
With her shoes down at heel, and her cheeks pink as
        paint,
And holes in her stockings—no beastly constraint !

And her ringlets they smelt like a hairdresser's shop :
And her dress was green stuff, spattered over with slop :
And her hands were good large ones, her ankles were
        thick,
And her nails they were bitten clean down to the quick.

She'd a taste of a temper, but nothing like vice—
It is downright unchristian to be too precise ;
For a shy with a bottle I don't know her match ;
But good lawk ! what is that when a fellow can catch ?

Oh, wasn't it prime ! you could drink, you could smoke,
You could chuck out a curse, you could sing, you could
        joke ;
Things are changed now, alas !—all is bother and bore,—
Why, the Missus looks wild if you spit on the floor !

Faugh ! to hear how they jaw, it quite gives one a turn,—
As if words were hot mealy potatoes that burn ;
" A little more beef, please,"—then faces they pull ;
Can't he say,—" Shove us over some more of the bull " ?

Yes, I hate the whole set with their finikin ways.
It was "live and let live" in the jolly old days,
The hens in the kitchen took all that they chose,
And the pups in the parlour rolled over your toes.

But now (set us up !) they've a precious fine lot
Of young-uns who gobble the pick of the pot ;
And they sit up so pert, each small brat in its place,
And when stuffed nigh to bursting they squeak out a grace !

Well, perhaps I'm not perfect, though fairly so-so ;
But, thank Heav'n, I'm no hypocrite—hang it all, no !
Before I'd go in for that sanctified bosh—
I'd as soon send a red flannel shirt to the wash !

Jolly Ben, bless his soul ! when he used to begin
He would swear till you thought the old Deuce had come
      in :
Now see him with Missus, as prim as a pea,
Trudging slowly to church, with the brats in their lee.

Mrs. Dixie got up in her lavender dress ;
And poor Ben such a swell as no words can express,
With white pants, and a rose, and a tile with a twist,
And a pair of small girls hanging on to his fist.

So they toddle along to the jole of the bell,
And they go to a pew, and get blest with a spell
Of singing and preaching and things in that style—
Ben sleeps, I'll be bound, for the most of the while !

But humbug for ever ! hyprocrisy pays,
Like the bills on the walls about pickles and plays ;
Yes, it's worth heaps of cash to be called "honest Ben,"
And be toadied and praised by all manner of men.

Who but he ! they can't meet to be jolly and dine,
After judging the horses and cattle and swine,
But up starts Squire Blount—"Fill a bumper," says he,
"For a toast in which no one can fail to agree,—

"The health of that pattern to farmers and all,
Mr. Benjamin Dixie of Rosemary Hall !"
Then they clap their fat paws, and they roar, and they
        swill—
Euch ! bring me a basin, I'm going to be ill.

If there's one thing I hate it's that bumptious conceit—
To set up to be tidy and pretty and neat :
It's as much as to say to a fellow, you see,
"What does nicely for you is not fit for big me !"

Instead of the grass and the puddles of muck,
And the sow with her piggies, and goosey and duck,
And a midden, and plenty old kettles and tubs,
They've got gardens and roses, and things they call shrubs.

Just you walk through the garden and tear off a flow'r
For a shy at the hens—don't the Missus look sour !
Or go near those cantankerous buffers of bees—
After you, sir, is manners ; you first, if you please !

Why those brutes won't abide me I really can't say,
For whenever they see me they hunt me away :
They object to bad smells,—but that isn't my case,
Few days but I souse both my hands and my face.

Now Ben Dixie he scrubs in a terrible way,
Till he shines like a sixpence and smells of new hay ;
I liked him far better all mire, muck, and grease,
When the man and his midden were quite of a piece.

What nonsense they talk about scrubbing off dirt—
As if things that come natural ever could hurt !
But Ben, the big booby, has grown like the eels,
The more he is skinned, the more lively he feels.

If you stay for the night at that Rosemary Hall,
You're a mighty queer chap if you like it at all.
" Fresh air," quoth the blockhead ! I say it's a chouse
To hang out in a windmill and call it a house.

And there's lots of oak panels as bright as the stars,
And the place stinks of roses and blue-and-white jars ;
And your bed's got white curtains that can't be drawn
      round,
And you tumble and grunt like a pig in a pound.

And you're nearly sent mad with the peppery smell
Of dead flow'rs dry in bowls, and of live ones as well ;
And the nightingales sing till you wish 'em in Spain,
And at dawn you've the thrushes and blackbirds again.

And your nice morning sleep is disturbed by the noise
Of dear Ben's blessêd darlings, his girls and his boys,
A-feeding the turkeys with stuff from a pail,
And screechy pea-devils with eyes in the tail.

And there's booing of oxen and mooing of cows ;
And the hogs and the horses—confound 'em for rows !
And the sheep, and the cur-dog bow-wowing the flock :
Oh, of course ! Master Dixie keeps excellent stock.

Poor wretch ! I don't fancy that anything pays
For toiling and moiling—I live all *my* days :
A sort of a god, with my 'baccy and bowl,
As jolly and snug as a toad in a hole.

No, it ain't mighty grand, but it suits to a T,
It's a capital den for a fellow like me.
No draughts and dry roses to keep you a-snort,
But a sensible place looking into a court.

On the ground-floor of course,—I object to a stair,
For the higher you go you get more of the air ;
The grate's pretty big, but the window's quite small—
Such a fit, sir ! in fact it won't open at all.

There ain't neither shutter nor bothersome blind,
But there's dust on the glass, and the sun keeps behind ;
And I snooze on my bed for the most of the day,
And the best of the night I am up and away.

Oh, it's jolly to lie on your back half a-doze,
And to kick off the quilt with your lazy old toes;
And you stare at your stockings as long as you please,
And you wriggle your trousers right over your knees.

Then you stretch, and get hold of your pipe for a whiff,
And make matters serene with a drop of the "stiff";
If you're peckish inclined, there is nothing to do
More easy than fry a red herring or two.

As Bill Shakespeare remarks, "There is no place like
    home,"
I'm as proud of my crib as a cock of his comb;
Life's sweet there—though once, I must really confess,
I had nearly dropped in for a bit of a mess.

A young cove he came canting with tracts on the sly,
"Converting" he called it: "Now, Mister," said I,
"Unless your name's 'Walker' this instant, d'ye see,
We'll 'convert' you to sausage, will Towzer and me."

So he turned—did this cove—pretty white in the gill:
"Good-day, sir," says he; "as you like me so ill,
I'll never come in to annoy you no more,—
Though I'm bound to be sometimes a-passing your door."

Well, before it got dark on that very same day,
I was taken all no-how, a queer kind of way;
All my bones and my gizzards were aching like fun,
And my brains were like boots hanging out in the sun.

Oh, I felt monstrous bad, and I soon got so weak
I could scarce raise my head, and I hardly could speak ;
And no creature came near me, I thought I should die,—
When at length sounds the step of a man passing by.

And old Towzer he kicks up a deuce of a din,
And the door opens slow, and a fellow peeps in—
Nick Chousem, my partner ;—says he, "Here's a go !
Bye-bye, Joey Pigworm,—it's small-pox, you know."

And I lay and I blubbered.   The rest I forget.
When I opened my peepers, the first thing they met
Was the mission-cove, watching me anxious and fond,
Like a hen whose small ducks are a-swim in a pond.

Well, of course I recovered—that's middling clear,
For if I'd skedaddled I shouldn't be here :
That good cove pulled me out of Old Gooseberry's gripe,—
And his tracts came quite useful for lighting one's pipe.

Not ungrateful, sir, no ! he declined my advice,
But I showed him neat things with the cards and the
      dice ;
And my dog runs to meet him a-wagging its tail,
And it grins "How d'ye do" like a shark in a gale.

No, it don't pay a bit to be seedy, you see,—
Not, at least, for mere common-sense snobbies like me :
But Ben !—let his thumb ache, they rush to inquire,—
Town, village, and country, lord, parson, and squire.

Lawk, when Ben comes to die ! bless their heads and
    their eyes,
How the crape and the white pocket-wipers will rise !
And the funeral cards will be scattered like peas,
And the folks will come swarming like mites on a cheese.

And they'll drive up a gimcracky hypocrite hearse ;
And they'll shove him inside, like a pig in a purse ;
And they'll carry him off to the burial crib ;
And the parson will come, like a rook in a bib.

Then they'll earth up his corpse in a daisy-bank hole :
And the boom of the organ will sweep off his soul,
As you blow off the froth from a buzzy brown bowl :
And the bloodhound bell will jole—jole—jole.

O lawk ! can't I see it ?   And afterwards too,
The Missus and children all making boohoo ;
And creeping like blackbirds down Sweetbriar Lane,
A-weeping, and wishing him with them again.

And the little pale girls in their bombazine stuff,
With their hair running loose like a parcel of fluff,
And nice flow'rs in their hands for the grave of "Papa"—
Such a comfort to Ben in his coffin, ha ha !

Rum business is life ! but it ends all a-piece
For the easy good chaps and the hard-working geese :
And why should they grudge a poor beast of a man
To be happy and jolly the best way he can ?

Says the mission-cove once,—"You've no sort of excuse
For to cumber the earth, if you're no sort of use."
"How," says I, "could the beggarsome planet be filled,
If the coves that do nothing were taken and killed?"

Some fine day, by and by, I shall likely expire—
They'll not take up Joe Pigworm in char'ots of fire ;—
Well! when Gooseberry wants me I'll meet him quite
      brave :
I wonder what folk will strew over *my* grave !

Nick Chousem, I daresay, will miss me a bit,
And he'll sit on my grave, and he'll smoke there and
      spit ;
And perhaps I'll be missed by my brute of a dog,
For I lick him and kick him, and give him his prog.

Lawk, what do I care ! My blest body will rot,
My blest soul (if I've got one) will toddle to pot,
And I'll treat the poor worms to a famous repast—
Oh yes, I'll be useful to something at last !

THE FLITCH OF DUNMOW.

Come Micky and Molly and dainty Dolly,
    Come Betty and blithesome Bill ;
Ye gossips and neighbours, away with your labours !
    Come to the top of the hill.
For there are Jenny and jovial Joe ;
Jolly and jolly, jolly they go,
    Jogging over the hill.

By apple and berry, 'tis twelve months merry
  Since Jenny and Joe were wed !
And never a bother or quarrelsome pother
  To trouble the board or bed.
So Joe and Jenny are off to Dunmow :
Happy and happy, happy they go,
  Young and rosy and red.

Oh, Jenny's as pretty as doves in a ditty ;
  And Jenny, her eyes are black ;
And Joey's a fellow as merry and mellow
  As ever shouldered a sack.
So quick, good people, and come to the show !
Merry and merry, merry they go,
  Bumping on Dobbin's back.

They've prankt up old Dobbin with ribands and
    bobbin,
  And tethered his tail in a string :
The fat flitch of bacon is not to be taken
  By many that wear the ring !
Good luck, good luck, to Jenny and Joe !
Jolly and jolly, jolly they go.
  Hark ! they merrily sing.

" O merry, merry, merry are we,
Happy as birds that sing in a tree !
All of the neighbours are happy to-day,
Merry are we and merry are they.
O merry are we ! for love, you see,
Fetters a heart and sets it free.

"O happy, happy, happy is life
For Joe (that's me) and Jenny my wife !
All of the neighbours are happy, and say—
' Never were folk so happy as they !'
O happy are we ! for love, you see,
Fetters a heart and sets it free.

"O jolly, jolly, jolly we go,
I and my Jenny, and she and her Joe.
All of the neighbours are jolly, and sing—
' She is a queen, and he is a king !'
O jolly are we ! for love, you see,
Fetters a heart and sets it free."

FEBRUARY IN THE PYRENEES.

THE maidenly snow on the distant peak,
Pure child of the firmament, faultless born,
Gazed fair at the sun, who seemed to seek
To melt into mercy her virgin scorn.

And a stern black rock stood apart, and frowned,
For he envied the snow in her lustrous white ;
And the grim grey shadows closed around,
In dread of the sun and his lordly light.

And the frail young beeches stood shivering near,
With their delicate branches brown and bare ;
But a bird in the thicket sang loud and clear,
For he scented the Spring through the frozen air.

From afar on the wind came the shepherd's cry,
From the grassy slopes and the boxwood bowers,
As his mottled flock to their home drew nigh,
To rest at their ease in the long dark hours.

Then the sun went down, with a last caress
From his golden lips to the fair white snow,
And all Winter came with a deathly stress
On the heights above and the vales below.

Yet a loveliness walked in the quiet dale,
By evening's power from her thrall released ;
For the silence spoke in a tender tale,
When songs and voices had sunk and ceased.

And silence itself more silent grew,
In the murmurous hush of the streamlet's tide
And the lull of the breezes, whispering through
The tall, sad firs on the mountain side.

PROFESSOR VEITCH.

MANORHEAD.

AN urn-round hollow'd glen, clos'd deep within
Its hills, that rise in smoothest symmetry,
To make for it a quiet arch of sky ;
A glen, in far past times deep-fill'd, and scoop'd
By ever-grinding ice, and wind-borne rain,—
The beauteous sculpture of the Unseen Hand
That guides insentient and unthinking powers
To Art's great purpose, through the ages dim,
And 'mid the darkness of the winter nights.

Its arch of sky in summer noon beholds,
From blue, calm height, the quiet depth below,
With heaven's unbroken glory grandly fill'd.
And then, from sparse white fleeting clouds there fall
Tremulous shadows on the pastoral green,—
As passing sadness on a beauteous face,—
That speed a-down the hill-sides, o'er the hollows,
And mingle with the fitful rush of burns,
And the pathetic voice of bleating lambs.

Again, the hollow urn with deep mist fills,
And veils its splendour, yet gives forth a sound
Of hidden waters from its depths remote,

As if the Spirit of the hills had there
Withdrawn within himself, to muse alone,
Deep murmuring o'er the secrets of the glens.

But now, a breath from heaven cleaves through the
    mist,
And bares before the ardent eye blue rifts
Of sky, and sunny slopes of mottled hills ;
And then, the west'ring sun strikes slantingly,
And with a golden tide the glen o'erflows,
Of shimm'ring splendour, short-liv'd, fast pursued
Across the hollow, up the radiant slope
By hast'ning evening shadow, until at length
Day's one last passionate glow burns on the brow
Of the sun-fronting height, and passes thence
For ever into gloamin' of the moor.

THE CLOUD-BERRY FLOWER.

From "ON THE SCRAPE: LOOKING SOUTHWARDS."

AROUND me cluster quaint cloud-berry flowers,
That love the moist slopes of the highest tops,
Pale white, and delicate, and beautiful,
Yet lowly growing 'mid the black peat moss,—
No life with darker root and fairer bloom :
As if the hand of God had secret wrought
Amid the peaty chaos and decay
Of long deep buried years, and from the grave
Set free a form of beauty rare and bright,
To typify the glory and the grace
Which from the dust of death He will awake,
In course of time, on Resurrection morn !

From "OLD BORDER LIFE AND POETRY."

THINK, once in these old towers what feelings wrought,—
There bridal joy, and children's sunny smiles,
A mother's hopes and fears, a father's cares,
And all strong thrillings of this life have been,—
Home-welcome flashed to victor from old wars,
Dead burden borne from fatal feud o' night;
Ay such that 'tis a marvel this dull earth
Should lie so callous 'neath the memories,
Unless it be that surely in its breast
It keeps them latent for the final morn.

There, where the mounds rise green o'er ancient home,
And all is silence save the ceaseless dash
Of passing waters o'er the whitened stones,—
There, was a sweet wife's clinging parting sad,
When husband 'bodin' in the feir of war,'
Boune for dire Flodden's reckless chivalry,
Rode forth a gleaming wonder to young eyes
That eager peered from height of bartizan.
Long dread suspense there was, long hoped return,
And then dim sough of that disastrous day,
That passed, ill-omen'd, through the shuddering land !
But him his vassals' love bore, faithful, back
From hated southern field, from strangers' earth,
That he might lie beside his kindred dead ;
O'er moss and moor, and o'er brown mountain ways,
They wended with their burden, shoulder-borne.

At sundown, resting in a valley low,
They saw, between them and the western sky,
A solitary tower, grey, roofless, rise,
Where once a powerful lord had ruled the land ;

A darkening mass, but through a narrow bole
High near the top, there gleamed a ray serene,
As cast from heaven beyond ; and, lingering there,
The day slow dwined to shade, thus passed and died,
A strange, weird way of death on that tower-top,
That moved and thrilled in hearts of all these men
The waiting spirits of old memories !
Then sadly looked they on their own mailed dead,
And thought of all the prowess of his house,
And of the fair slight maidens orphaned there.

And on they wended through the moonlit night,
'Neath shadows of the crags, as passing palls
That softly touched the rigid, armoured form
They bore aloft ; by mountain burns they went,
That poured sad requiem, now paused, now moaned ;
Till, as the robins waked the Autumn morn,
They reached his own grey tower, and passed within
The iron gate ; and, 'neath the vaulted roof
Of däis hall, they laid him down,—where oft
He princely sat,—his piercëd hauberk on,
His visor down ; on moveless shoulder spread
The silver shield that bore the sable heads :
Now, utmost feat of loyal duty done,
When o'er him widow sobbed and children wailed,
Sprung the first tears of those stern loving men.

Slow passing forth there was from that grey house,
And in the grave beside the dead was laid
Joy of one living heart, and that fresh mound
Seemed in a widow's eye earth's dearest thing.
Yet now, nor mound, nor stone is found to mark
His resting-place, and tower slow follows tomb,
Till house of life and house of death alike,

Beyond all memory gone, are smoothly dressed
In folds of summer grass, where dull sheep browse,
And shepherds, heedless, tread upon the fame,
The nameless fame, that lived in other days.

———

THE HART OF MOSSFENNAN.

" They hunted it up, they hunted it doun,
They hunted it in by Mossfennan toun,
And aye they gie'd it another turn,
Round by the links of the Logan Burn."
—OLD BALLAD.

'NEATH Powmood Craig the hart was born,
And thence in the dawn of a summer morn,
By startled mother's side as it lay,
'Twas brought by a youth for his sweetheart's play.

She was a blue-eyed maiden fair,
Of stately mien and flaxen hair,
The daughter meet of an olden race,
Remote as a flower in a moorland place,
That blooms to all the great world lost,
And yet once seen is prized the most,—
Pure wood nymph she of Caledon,
Who loved all creatures wild and lone.

The gift to her was priceless, dear,
Since the giver, laid on a plaited bier,
Was borne away from a far-off field,
With a spotless name, with a blood-stained shield.

To her of an eve the creature bent,
While to him a simple grace she lent,
As she comely wreathed his noble head,
And decked his brow with the heather red.
Fond she gazed on those lustrous eyes
That met her look with a sweet surprise
At a face so tender, sad, and fair ;
She thought they read her soul's despair ;
And through her frame strange thrill would go,
As she caught the chequer'd pass and flow
Of trembling motions in their great deeps,
As light and shade o'er the mountain-steeps.

Far o'er the moors on a summer day
He'd pass and roam and freely stray ;
But ever, as shade of evening fell,
He turned to the home he loved so well.
His heart yearned aye to the lonely wild,
While his love was that of a human child,—
That set a bound to his nature free,—
For the maiden's face on Mossfennan Lee.

The hunters are out this summer morn,
They sweep the moors by hag and burn,
By rock and crag, each high resort,
For dear they love their noble sport.
They started a fee at Stanhope Head,
And down the glen the raches sped,
Fire-flauchts lanced up from each horse's side,
For the galling spur was prompt to chide.

Round he ran by Hopcarton Stell,
The spotted hounds pressed on him fell ;
I' the haugh he took the Tweed at the wide,
Then tossed his horns on Mossfennan side.

Still the cruel hounds are on his track,
In his ear the yell of the hurrying pack,
Fain to Mossfennan Tower he would turn,
But the chace is hot,—to the hill by the burn.

They hunted him high, they hunted him low,
They hunted him up by the mossy flow ;
The lee-long day, from early morn,
The Hopes rung loud with bouts of the horn.
No bloom of heather brae them stayed,
No birk-tree quiver or sheen of glade,
No touch of nature bent their will,
In hot blood onward, onward still.

Powmood, that ever in clear or mist,
In fray or hunt the foremost pressed,
Now speeding keen as north-west wind,
Late i' the day left all behind ;
Save Dreva's Laird, ne'er boding good,
Wide was he famed for a reiver rude,—
And hand that took kindly aye to blood,—
Left blacken'd walls where the homestead stood.

They hunted the hart these two alone,
Till the shadows lay in the afternoon ;
Where brae was stey and bank was steep,
The noble fee fell in a gallant leap.
They blew the mort on the Wormhill Head,
Where sore he sighed and then lay dead!

Oh ! why not let the creature be,
Bear his noble head o'er hill and lee,—
That ate but the wild roots, drank o' the spring
And roamed the moor a seemly thing,—

Joyed in the sun, flashed fleet in the storm,
Free in the grace of his God-given form !

The merry sport of the day is o'er;
I' the gloamin' at the old tower door,
No gentle creature is there to greet
Her eyes that seek him, sad and sweet,—
Oh ! with love's last link 'tis sore to part,
And feel but the void of the aching heart

The merry sport of the day is o'er;
Rose the creature's sigh its God before?
Hearts harder growing through breach of ruth,
I ween this is eternal truth :
That gloamin', after words of strife,
Saw Powmood's blood on Dreva's knife !

MERLIN APOSTROPHISES THE SUN.

From "MERLIN."

THIS morn I bow before thee, lord of light
And life !—my hope, my fear, my reverence !
Of thee unworthy, and my early vows.
Far-gleaming arrows, piercing feeble mists,
Herald thine uprise ; low down in the vales,
That pour their loving tribute to the Tweed,
The waters shimmer 'mid the morning's joy ;
Around me burn-heads croon, and moorland birds
Awake, a-wing, pipe brief glad notes to thee,
The brightening lord of happy melody.

Now part in twain the curtains of the dawn,
Each hill-top is aflame, and thou hast set

Thyself, full-orbed, in empire o'er the day :—
Aglow as in that dawn when first enthroned,
The wasting ages taking nought from thee,
Nor tainted by the evil of this earth,
Thou layest now, as new birth of the morn,
Thy strength of glory on the circling hills.
I worship thee, O sovereign of the sky,
The symbol of the God who is unseen.

———

GWENDYDD'S SONG.

(*From the same.*)

Gwendydd *takes Merlin's harp and sings.*

Fresh as of old the breeze of the morn,
   Plaintive the notes that float
O'er the moor with the sunny thyme,
   And the blue forget-me-not.

The rock-rose lifts its face to the sun,
   It droops when its lord is set ;
The tormentil peers, the heather-bell glows ;
   Sweet-eyed is the violet.

The lowly gale looks forth from the grass,
   Silver-starring the brae ;
Th' Idæan vine holds its cup for the dew,
   High where the burn-heads play,

As they flash in ripples of light,
   Ere down they break to the glen
By green bank, red scaur, and grey rock,
   Where the rowan shades the linn :

And the sun o'er all is moving in joy,
    The strong lord of the sky ;
He stoops to bless the earth with his love,
    Benign in his majesty.

And nought but raises its face to him,
    Both herb and flower of earth ;
He, lord of all, that rules in heaven,
    Hath care for the lowliest birth.

And thou art far from the face of God—
    Whate'er thy craft or power—
Who knowest not first to bless with thy might,
    As the sun in the morning hour.

———

THE VOICE OF THE DANISH BOY.

A TRADITION OF THE BORDER HILLS.

THE sun is passing behind the hill,
The eventide falls soft and still,
And down the glen from the western steep
The shadow moves in a dream-like sleep.
Peace there is for each farm and tower,
And the bliss and the rest of the gloamin' hour.

Around the vale on each wavy height
There streams the glow of a mellow light,
The farewell boon of the parting sun
To the hills that watch till his race is run.

But list !   A strange deep-passioned tone
Is borne from the height that light shines on,
As of harp-strings touched with a gentle hand,
And the voice as of song of a foreign land.

Not loud or strained is the mingled note,
Only loving ear can hear it float ;
It breaks not the calm of eve profound,
How gentle, yet deep, is that mountain sound
Now it thrills in hope, then it falls in pain,
Rises and thrills and falls again,
As if passion had sunk to soft regret
O'er its fruitless day of strife with fate,
And empire held and the pride of power
Were a mournful dream of the evening hour.

From the hill there came a shepherd fair,—
" Had he heard the voice in the silent air?"
" Yes !" was his answer,—" I know it well ;
Oft in the evening I hear it swell,
When the stillness comes in the summer night,
And the far hill-tops are aglow with light.
'Tis suddenly born, 'tis speedily dead ;
As the gleam that glows on the mountain's head,
So suddenly comes and speedily goes
This strange weird song at the evening's close.
It dies with the light in a softening strain,
Till in the quiet eve it wakes again—
The plaint that follows the note of joy—
And I know 'tis the voice of ' the Danish Boy,'
Who sits a brief space on that green grave-mound,
Where say they his forebears' bones are found."

Sweet burst of regret for the olden time,
When hope was high and life in its prime,—

The theme is old, the strain ever young,
Nor heard alone in a foreign tongue.
From many a heart in this life of ours
There comes a like strain in the evening hours,—
A thrill from hope perished, and effort unblessed,
When our day is o'er, and our sun's in the west !

IN MANOR.

AN AFTERNOON PICTURE, SEPTEMBER 11, 1887.

ITS deepest song the Manor sings,
　　This day of mist and grey-cloud rain,
And in its rising swell and fall
　　I hear again the sad refrain,

That meets me on an autumn day,
　　Has touched my ear in youthful morn,
When first by thee, loved stream, I strayed,—
　　A sorrowing voice, yet not forlorn.

Corn-fields are bare, and on the hills
　　The heather fades, the bent is white,
The bracken yellow 'mid the green ;
　　Yet through the rain a golden light

'Mid clouds and towers in heaven is tossed,
　　Strays on the hills, strikes mists beneath,
That rise and pass against the sky,
　　Blown by the mountain-spirit's breath.

'Tis a strange land 'mid those weird hills,
    Where cloud and gleam are trailing high ;
What glances there ? one daring bird,
    Hath pierced the tumult of the sky !

OCTOBER IN THE SCOTTISH LOWLANDS.

THE russet's o'er the heather,
    The grace of the bracken gone ;
Sere and dun each moorland space,
    Where the gleam of summer shone

The mist creeps o'er the height,
    The burn comes hoarser down,
The wandering wind is wailing
    Among the bent " sae brown."

The blaeberry leaf, blood-red,
    Flushes the face of the brae,
As a crimson drop distilled
    From a deed in an olden fray.

The last golden sheaves of the haugh
    Are borne on the creaking wain ;
Another year is upgathered,
    Ne'er to be mine again !

The varied days may pass,
    The varied times go by !
Let the spirit in me grow,
    Seasons may ceaseless fly !

On the sun-bright hues of summer
  May come a sober grey,
And the wreath on autumn's mellow crown
  Have the pathos of decay.

For the sunny hours I've known
  No vain regrets I find,
If, passing, they but leave me
  Fresh heart and a wider mind !

In Memoriam.

JOCKIE :

COMPANION AND FRIEND, WHO DIED OF OLD AGE,
DEC. 18, 1876, IN HIS EIGHTEENTH YEAR.

COLD, stiff, and dead, thou liest to-day,
My friend on many a pathless way,
Up glen, o'er hill, and moorland lone :
No fear hadst thou, aye bounding on,
    For I was there !

On many a misty top we've been,
For long where nought was heard or seen,
Thou by my side,—thy lint-white hair,
To me a gladsome vision there,
    Lighting the gloom !

By weird grey cairn on windy height,
Where, far away from human sight,
We sat an hour in storm or shine,
Thy wondering eyes would peer in mine,
        In wistful gaze.

If but a crust I gave to thee,
How grateful was thy look to me !
Thou ne'er didst want, yet well I knew
Thou wert as faithful and as true,
        Whate'er thy lot.

One common joy, one common life,
We had apart from human strife ;
I was thy trust, and thou didst lend
To me the charm of single friend,
        A blessing rare.

Wilful sometimes, as mountain hare,
The source to me of heartfelt care,
Would tempt thee to a vagrant chase ;
Threatened, till back thou cam'st apace,
        To be forgiven.

Since first we went among the heather,
'Tis fourteen years, and, there together,
Thou hast pursued thy silent thought,
And in my brain have fancies wrought,
        Some marked, some lost.

But, gentle soul, I cannot say
That any gleam of fancy's ray
E'er touched me with the softening power
Thy love and faith, from hour to hour,
        Aye had for me.

And now this eve thy grave is low,
And white beneath the Christmas snow ;
The silent moon gleams calm o'er thee,
As it shall steal one night o'er me,
      When laid as thou.

Thy simple faith, thy loving trust,
Thy kindling eye,—are these but dust ?
Cast forth as weeds to rot in earth,
With nothing of immortal worth ?
      No ! God is just !

PROFESSOR NICHOL.

DONNA VERA.

Take my homage, Dea certe ! crowned among the stars
   above,
Goddess, passionless, disdaining ebbs and flows of human
   love ;
Seated in thy palace, queenly, where thy radiance glows
   serenely,
O'er the mists and wandering meteors that amid our
   vapours move :
>   Donna Vera, Donna Vera !

Hard thy service : Thou demandest all the treasures of
   our store ;
Jealous of a rival worship, and constraining to adore ;
Ancient altars overturning, tearful pleading for them
   spurning,
Flinging into air the phantoms, pressed Ixion-like of
   yore :
>   Donna Vera, Donna Vera !

Aphrodite wooed and won me, rising roseate from the
   sea,
When the spring of life was flushing, and the fresh blood
   throbbing free ;

Swift-heeled Hermes, bright thoughts bringing, Phœbus,
    wars and wisdoms singing,
Twining Nymphs and Graces lured me, ere my longing
    set on thee :
          Donna Vera, Donna Vera !

Then the solemn glooms and glories of the dim transition
    days,
Vestals chanting Roman anthems, Covenanters Hebrew
    lays—
Broken fragments of thy meaning, simple Faith's
    impatient gleaning—
Held me in religious rapture, till thy Presence broke
    the maze :
          Donna Vera, Donna Vera !

Cold and rocky, uncompanioned pathways lead us to the
    height
Where thou reignest, Maiden Mistress, in thy majesty
    and might.
Who would find thee must surrender oft more gentle
    hearts and tender ;
But thy smile is our life's splendour, and thy eyes are
    wells of light :
          Donna Vera, Donna Vera !

Stern the call to quit our homesteads, put away all
    childish things ;
Hence the weak world fears thee, clinging to long-
    cherished leading strings.
Let me sing thy praises only,—whatsoever summit lonely
Bears thee skyward—saved and sheltered in the shadow
    of thy wings :
          Donna Vera, Donna Vera !

From "Pictures by the Way."

I.

THE CHAPEL.

Just after the sunset, yesterday,
When the last of the crowd had passed away,
I went to the little church to pray.

They had jostled me so, the rabble rout,
That my radical zeal was half worn out :
I wished them cleaner and less devout.

My spirit was clouded with discontent,
And the faith I had was nearly spent,
When I came, like a thief impenitent,

Weary and foiled in the weary race,
To hide myself from my own disgrace,
And steal some comfort from the place.

Nothing for naught, in the world, they say,
And little they get who have little to pay:
But the chapel was open all the day.

The choir was as free as the aisles of a wood,
And I found, when under its shade I stood,
That the air of the church was doing me good.

In the silence, after the city's smoke,
My spirit grew calmer, and thoughts awoke
From sleep, that I fancied dead.—I spoke:—

" Perchance they were not unwisely bold
Who called this God's house—the men of old—
Does the Shepherd wait within the fold?"

So, up the choir, with footsteps faint,
In the fading light of each shining saint,
I wondered if He would hear my plaint.

There was something surely in kneeling where
A thousand hearts had left their care,
That helped to contradict despair.

"No hope remains in the world," I cried,
"So far I have wandered, so much denied;
Is there any way left as yet untried?

I love; but it only makes death more drear
And truth more distant; I love in fear,
'Tis not with the love that seeth clear.

I toil; but the range of my restless glance
Still stretches afar; an aimless dance
I see, and name it the whirl of chance.

They are blown together, like dust in the wind—
The feeble frame and the lordly mind—
And only their ashes are left behind.

My words are bitter, what proof remains
To mark them false? Are a prisoner's chains
Lighter because he forgets his pains?

Athwart the vista of vanished time,
Is a mocking gleam of a ruined prime
And discord that drowns the morning chime.

Idly we long for the innocent days,
When life was worship and prayer was praise,
Now all is wrapt in a blinding maze.

Idly we beat at the iron gates,
If the sole response that our cry awaits
Is the heartless law of the heedless fates.

The fires of our passion are spent in vain,
The stars went out long since in the rain ;
Can Faith once lost be found again ?

'Tis dark without it ; but how can we,
When the cloud murk thickens, pretend to see,
Across the darkness, an image of Thee.

Hear me ; for mine is a soul in need.
On the cold damp ground, I sink and bleed.
Hear me, and show Thou art God indeed ! ''

At the word, a torrent of music rolled
From arch to arch, like a flood of gold,
Fraught with the burden of thoughts untold.

The chords, as struck by a seraph band,
Seemed an answering thrill from the spirit land—
'' Let there be light ! '' while, near at hand,

The crucifix shone o'er the altar stair,
Till its beacon made me at last aware
Of the lamp that was burning faintly there.

I fixed my gaze on the steadfast ray,
Till it seemed as if earth and its troubles lay
In the valley of restlessness far away.

A dream-like procession of early years
Swept through my spirit ; the frost that sears
Our life fell from me in soothing tears.

Then throbbed out slowly the organ blast,
But still the unfading lustre cast
A glimmer on labyrinths of my Past.

God makes each heart a cathedral dim,
With its vaults where gloomy vapours swim,
And its altar burning still for Him.

I woke from my trance, in the church alone,
And the church-bell marked that an hour had flown,
As it pealed in a sombre monotone.

Like a deep voice singing a noble song,
It bade me arise, and amid the throng
Keep bright my lamp, my courage strong.

II.

MARE MEDITERRANEUM.

A LINE of light ! it is the inland Sea,
  The least in compass and the first in fame ;
The gleaming of its waves recalls to me
    Full many an ancient name.

As through my dreamland float the days of old,
  The forms and features of their heroes shine :
I see Phœnician sailors bearing gold
    From the Tartessian mine.

Seeking new worlds, storm-tossed Ulysses ploughs
  Remoter surges of the winding main ;
And Grecian captains come to pay their vows,
    Or gather up the slain.

I see the temples of the "Violet Crown"
  Burn upward in the hour of glorious flight ;
And mariners of uneclipsed renown,
    Who won the great sea fight.

I hear the dashing of a thousand oars,
  The angry waters take a deeper dye ;
A thousand echoes vibrate from the shores
    With Athens' battle-cry.

Again the Carthaginian rovers sweep,
  With sword and commerce, on from shore to shore :
In visionary storms the breakers leap
    Round Syrtes, as of yore.

Victory, sitting on the Seven Hills,
  Had gained the world when she had mastered thee:
Thy bosom with the Roman war-note thrills,
    Wave of the inland sea.

Then, singing as they sail in shining ships,
  I see the monarch minstrels of Romance,
And hear their praises murmured through the lips
    Of the fair dames of France.

Across the deep another music swells,
  On Adrian bays a later splendour smiles;
Power hails the marble city where she dwells
    Queen of a hundred isles.

Westward the galleys of the Crescent roam,
  And meet the Pisan challenge in the breeze,
Till the long Dorian palace lords the foam
    With stalwart Genovese.

But the light fades; the vision wears away;
  I see the mist above the dreary wave.
Blow winds of Freedom, give another day
    Of glory to the brave!

III.

LUCERNE.

THE lake beneath, and the city,
  And the quiet glorious hills,
Bending beneath the sunset,
  With strong submissive wills;

The mound above, and the ramparts,
　And the river that swiftly flows,
Between the walls, to the meadows :
　In the evening's deep repose.

Three towers above, in the sunlight,
　Are gleaming in burnished gold,
Over one the twilight is creeping,
　It stands in the shadow, cold :—

Four stages of life recalling—
　Our birth, our love, our toil,
And the last that lies in the shadow,
　And waits to receive the spoil.

IV.

ST. POL DE LÉON.

In Finisterre, between two winding bays
　Where northern billows beat the craggy shore,
Steeped in a dream of dim religious days,
　The sombre village nestles as of yore :
　　Careless of changes come and gone,
　　St. Pol de Léon slumbers on.

Safe in the hush of convent hall, and spire
　Star-lit by foils that pierce the tapering stone,
While anthems echo through the listening choir,
　Or monk or sister haunts the aisles alone,
　　Remote from ways of modern strife
　　Lingers the mediæval life.

Pinnacle, turret, belfry, shaft and tower,
  Cloister and transept keep the same repose ;
As, in secluded haunt, the lily flower.
  In white tranquillity, regardless grows ;
    While, o'er the sheltered garden wall,
    The tides of passion rise and fall.

Ere saintly Louis led the last crusade,
  This Breton Minster was a beacon light ;
Serene in distance and secure in shade
  From sound of Creçy's charge or Poitiers' fight ;
    Nor storm of Jacquerie awoke,
    Nor Agincourt the silence broke.

The Maid whose lustre shames the envious years,
  Rekindles Freedom in a thankless land ;
The Sceptre oversways the banded peers ;
  Rash Francis yields to Charles' o'er-mastering hand :
    New worlds are found, new creeds have birth,
    Here all is of the earlier earth.

On Roscoff's ledge alights the Fay, whose spell
  Lures love to death, first Queen of Ronsard's lays :
Now it is " Henri Quatre et Gabrielle,"
  And now the shifting tune is " Louis Treize " :
    Let mistress rule, or courtiers lie,
    Here vespers chime where surges die.

Richelieu may write and reign, or Mazarin
  Crush in his coils of craft the wrestling Fronde,
Turenne or Condé rival laurels win
  To crown the "grand Monarque" : far leagues
        beyond
      The cannon music on the Rhine,
      They worship here in peace divine.

The clash and clamour of the ceaseless fray,
　Round Blenheim, ·Ramillies, Malplaquet, beats:
Orgies of Orleans stain the graceless day,
　And Rosbach seals a kingdom.　In these streets,
　　Nought but the lapse of time is told,
　　And shepherds' tales to simple fold.

The Earthquake of uplifted misery shakes
　Peoples and princes, ancient Faith and Throne:
On wastes of snow the Gallic fury breaks:
　Caged in his isle the Eagle dies alone:
　　On this, far drawn, sequestered strand
　　They roll the chaunts of Hildebrand.

Again the Drapeau of the Fleur-de-Lys
　Flaunts forth and falls; but Blanche or Oriflamme
Or Rouge or Tricolor, by this strange sea,
　Seem as the interchange of breeze and calm:
　　Through all life's tempests come and gone,
　　St. Pol de Léon slumbers on.

v.

H. W. L.

The roar of Niagara dies away,
　The fever heats of war and traffic fade,
While the soft twilight melts the glare of day
　In this new Helicon, the Muses' glade.

The roof that sheltered Washington's retreat,
　Thy home of homes, America, I find
In this memorial mansion, where we greet
　The full-toned lyrist, with the gentle mind.

Here have thy chosen spirits met and flowered,
  Season on season, 'neath magnetic spells
Of him who, in his refuge, rose-embowered,
  Remote from touch of envious passion dwells.

Here Concord's sage and Harvard's wit contend
  The wise, the true, the learnéd of the land,
Grave thoughts, gay fantasies together blend
  In subtle converse, 'neath his fostering hand.

With other forms than those of mortal guest
  The house is haunted ; visions of the morn,
Voices of night that soothe the soul to rest,
  Attend the shapes, by aery wand reborn.

Serene companions of a vanished age,
  Noiseless they tread the once familiar floors ;
Or, later offspring of the poet's page,
  Throng the threshold, crowd the corridors.

"Sweet Preciosa" beside the listening stair
  Flutters expectant while Victorian sings ;
Evangeline, with cloistral eyes of prayer,
  Folds her white hands, in shade of angels' wings.

Conquistadors of Castile pace the hall ;
  Or red-skinned warriors pass the challenge round ;
Or Minnehaha's laughter, as the fall
  Of woodland waters, makes a silver sound.

Thor rolls the thunders of his fiery vaunt,
  The answering battle burns in Olaf's eyes ;
Or love crowned Elsie, lures us with the chaunt
  That lulled the waves, 'neath star-hung Genoan skies.

Here grim-faced captains of colonial days
  Salute the builders of old German rhyme ;
And choral troops of children hymn the praise
  Of their own master minstrel of all time.

Fair shrine of pure creations ! linger long
  His bright example, may his fame increase :
Discord nor distance ever dim his song,
  Whose ways are pleasantness, whose paths are
    peace.

Nor Hawthorne's manse, with ancient moss bespread,
  Nor Irving's hollow is with rest so rife,
As this calm haven, where the leaves are shed
  Round Indian summers of a golden life.

CONTRASTS.

I.

Yes ! it was simply greatness,
  There was nothing else I could say ;
I had fenced my path more straightly,
  But his was the kinglier way.

He had all the march of a monarch,
  And the eye that claims command,
And he looked around on his kingdom,
  As he led us by the hand.

In the reckoning of little virtues
  'Twas I who bore the palm ;
But he faced the world more nobly
  With that imperial calm.

Wrestling where he was conquered,
  I waged, till eve, the fight ;
But he fell like the stars, as grandly,
  ·And he rose as the dawning light.

Whatever new fields await us,
  However new lands employ,
'Twill be mine the ceaseless struggle
  And his the serener joy.

And if ever we meet in the future,
  When an æon has rolled away,
On the heights of the great Hereafter
  He will rule as he rules to-day.

For wherever we stand together,
  In the light of that larger morn,
'Mid all those wondrous changes
  He will still be the elder born.

II.

PRIZES at school, and places
  Of honour in life he won ;
Now he claims to have finished
  The task that we both begun.

Keen to perceive, and steadfast
  In working out his plan,
Success is his, and the homage
  That marks a successful man.

I am a broken pillar,
  Left on the sands alone:
He is a gilded column,
  Under a royal throne.

Finding his fortune fairly,
  Prudently true and kind;
There is something he can't get over,
  He has but a little mind.

He rose, by honest efforts,
  To the promise of wealth and fame;
And yet, for thrice his station,
  I would not wear his name.

He strove—but never boldly;
  Attained—but was never great;
More like a childish marvel
  Than a brave man breasting fate.

The smallness of his boyhood,
  The weakness of his prime,
He will bear with him, like nature,
  However high he climb.

He dare not write a sentence
  Of good old English ring;
But hovers, both ways smiling,
  And winds about a thing.

Safe o'er the summer waters,
   When sunshine floods them through ;
Far from the reach of rapids,
   He paddles his canoe.

He fronts his fawning world,
   And triumphs in his way,
But what he'll think to-morrow
   Was my thought yesterday.

Since first he sought my counsel,
   I have been half his creed ;
His fashion is to follow,
   My humour is to lead.

———

From "THE DEATH OF THEMISTOCLES."

Themistocles.   I lived
Two lives apart ; for, while the noonday sun
Burnt on the passions of the fiery strife,
In hours of rest withdrawn from restless day,
I bent o'er mounds of half-forgotten dead,
And roamed by citadels of Argive kings,
Compeers of Cecrops, ere or Minos ruled
Or Jason clove the deep.   Here Inachus,
The first earth-born of Tethys, left his name ;
And Io suffered woe, till, Hermes' dart
Smiting the watcher with the hundred eyes,
From Hera's wrath she wandered on, like me
O'er floods and hills and by the desert track
Of winding continents to utmost Nile.
Hither Egyptian Danaos brought his maids

Fatal to marriage, but for one true wife.
Here Danae blossomed 'neath the golden shower
And bore the Gorgon-slayer to the world.
Here, of the race so oft by Zeus renewed,
Sprang Heracles, whom Tiryns' square-stone walls
Attest the mightiest, and Lernean font—
Poseidon's gift for Amymone's love,
Whence Nauplius—with the Nemean vale crag-set
And cataract smitten ; all which haunts I saw ;
And musing by Mycenæ's lion gate
Recalled Atrides' doom, Orestes' curse,
Electra's solace, and Athene's aid.
So sped my years in Argolis, the crown
Of Hellas, and the front ere Spartan coils
Closed round her stifling, while the air was full
Of tidings from my city, how she grew
Greater in war and art to celebrate
The splendour of her nuptials with the sea.

———

Themistocles.   Peace, boy !
Hast thou not known me better, all those years
Of so long silence, as thou floutest them,
As dream my watchful spirit, never bent
Before their worst revilings, would accept
Mercy misnamed for Justice still denied,
Alms from the men who never gave my due,
But for a moment's flash ?   Insulting boon
Designed, if hinted, for disgrace !   Am I,
Hunted from land to land, from sea to sea,
Panting and breathless o'er Epirus' wastes,
Reft of my own by rage of enemies,
The sport of waves that seemed to serve their hate,
Till I found refuge where I stand so sure
Though profitless,—am I to beg the stale

And wretched charities of men who snatched
Their profits, grudged my glories, slurred my name ?—
The crowd who ever asking never gave,
Laid all their burdens on me, cast aside
When I had borne them, wearied of my gifts,
Scowled at my presence, then assailed my life—
Once wingless kites, who, nurtured in my nest,
As soon as fledged found beaks to peck at me,
Their master, who had forged them arms to strike,
And given them tongues to mutter or to shriek
Their rancorous venoms.

———

Themistocles.   Aristides talked
Of his old comrade in the fight, and sought
To keep our public free from private jars ;
Yet stood apart in grim integrity
And wisdom held infallible, his course
Being set as firm to thwart me in debate
As Cimon's own.   I grant his patriot zeal
But fail to clear him of a jealous shade.
So with another whom I once advanced,
Slighter Lysimachus, whose lusty limbs,
Unmatched in the Pentathlon, left his mind
To veer, as if aspiring to some place
The rabble have for auction.   When acclaim
Followed my lightest breath, no more applause
Came from a score of clappers than from him ;
But when they hooted, with apologies,
And courteous manner cloaking matter's lack,
He joined, by nature, the majority.
Others of subtler sort, my downward steps
Pursued with smiles and, offering service, slipt
Into the hearts that I was ousted from.

Some shifts I laugh to think on of good men ;
'Mong these, the archon, leader of the year,
A genial comrade when the winds were mild,
But weak in storms, and with his soul so fed
On plaudits, that the murmur of a mob
Seared it like iron, till his nature grew
Barren of battle, and his humour changed
Smothered in caution, to mere mimicry.
So with the rest, in fear or hope they turned,
Or hid themselves from compromise with me,
When Fortune shook her wings.

Extracts from " HANNIBAL."

CAUTION'S a virtue that o'ercharged is vice,
And dull content is poverty of soul.
Who shuns offence and holds with neither side,
Who dreads the deep and never dares to swim,
Who fears to trip and never tries to run,
May yet in walking stumble.

                Who works for dues
Of honour, and a following of friends,
Is but a prouder kind of mercenary,
Drawing upon a bank that often breaks.

The Gods who rule the earth are far removed,
Their dwelling-place is all the round of Heaven.
The stars, the moon, the hill-tops, and the sea,
The sun himself, are but their sentinels.
Their temples are the oracles that stand

Nigh to the gates of their serene abodes ;
They come there, when we meet them, with a heart
That has a single aim, and with a voice
That speaks their language.

ON THE SOUTH SHORE OF AVERNUS.

Hannibal.   The Gods are not of Rome or Italy:
They dwell in earth's abyss or with the stars,
Their shrines are where we bring heroic hearts :
Yet there are spots which to the minds of men
Seem set apart for converse with the Gods.
On temples by the sea our fancy roams
To Hercules the Roamer : on high hills
Astarte pours her radiance : Tanais bends
Her bow in tempests, and the thunder hails
Chrysaor's sword-flash.   On this sultry marge
Of nether night and Hades, let us bow
Before the Powers of Silence, Death and Dreams ;
Of that chaotic Air that, o'er the deep
Long brooding, brought forth lightnings in the sky ;
And of the Fires pent up, ere Æon rose,
Parent of all our world, nor first nor last.

Myra.   Ah, none can know how soon the world
        forgets,
But they whose heroes have a second death
When their name vanishes.   To-morrow's sun
Puts out the light of all her yesterdays.
We pass, and make a space for those who pass
In the same careless Lethe, that rolls on,
Whether we live, or die, or stand, or fall,
Without a tremble on its even way.

Who spurns at "images"

Proclaims his fathers nameless, taints himself
With envy that decries the thing it longs for
And vanity that ridicules the pride
It vainly apes.

THE PASSAGE OF THE ALPS.

Sosilus.   What sights, what sounds, what wonders
      marked our way !
Terrors of ice, and glories of the snow,
Wide treacherous calms, and peaks that rose in storm
To hold the stars, or catch the morn, or keep
The evening with a splendour of regret ;
Or, jutting through the mists of moonlight, gleamed
Like pearly islands from a seething sea ;—
On dawn-swept heights, the war-cry of the winds ;
The wet wrath round the steaming battlements,
From which the sun leapt upward, like a sword
Drawn from its scabbard ;—the green chasms that cleft
Frost to its centre ; echoes drifting far,
Down the long gorges of the answering hills ;
The thunders of the avalanche ;—the cry
Of the strange birds that hooted in amaze
To see men leaving all the tracks of men ;—
Snow-purpling flowers, first promise of the earth ;
Then welcome odours of the woods less wild ;
Grey lustres looming on the endless moor ;
The voice of fountains, in eternal fall
From night and solitude to life and day !

Of men who rise above the common herd
Of goats and sheep, that butt and breed and die,
The most are clipped in pieces by themselves ;

Frittered in flickering fancies; half inclined
To fleet delights and then, with brief resolves,
Taking up languid duties; mingling arts
Irreconcilable, or balancing
Prudence and valour, and their like's esteem,
Which is a weakness added to their own :
And so they dance like puppets jerked awry.
Who sets himself one way and pulls one string,
His Will, become a Fate, compels the world,
And while the rest stand gazing, he commands.

Now all is still.   The Night, that waves aside,
And shames the discords of the clamorous Day,
Sheds a false peace upon the weary land.
Her stars, from soundless deeps, despise our storms.
They glance, through avenues of time to come,
On all the races of the world at rest.
But, while the fevers of our passion burn,
In this the childish age of vexed mankind,
Our march is made, our music set, in strife.
The red right hand beats back usurping wrong :
And Justice lies o'er heights of angry war.

ROBERT BUCHANAN.

THE DEAD MOTHER.

I.

As I lay asleep, as I lay asleep,
Under the grass as I lay so deep,
As I lay asleep in my white death-serk
Under the shade of Our Lady's Kirk,
I waken'd up in the dead of night,
I waken'd up in my shroud o' white,
And I heard a cry from far away,
And I knew the voice of my daughter May:
" Mother, mother, come hither to me !
Mother, mother, come hither and see !
Mother, mother, mother dear,
Another mother is sitting here :
My body is bruised, in pain I cry,
All night long on the straw I lie,
I thirst and hunger for drink and meat,
And mother, mother, to sleep were sweet !"
I heard the cry, though my grave was deep,
And awoke from sleep, and awoke from sleep.

II.

I awoke from sleep, I awoke from sleep,
Up I rose from my grave so deep !
The earth was black, but overhead

The stars were yellow, the moon was red ;
And I walk'd along all white and thin,
And lifted the latch and enter'd in.
I reach'd the chamber as dark as night,
And though it was dark my face was white :
" Mother, mother, I look on thee !
Mother, mother, you frighten me !
For your cheeks are thin and your hair is grey ! "
But I smiled, and kiss'd her fears away ;
I smooth'd her hair and I sang a song,
And on my knee I rock'd her long.
"O mother, mother, sing low to me—
I am sleepy now, and I cannot see ! "
I kiss'd her, but I could not weep,
And she went to sleep, she went to sleep.

III.

As we lay asleep, as we lay asleep,
My May and I, in our grave so deep,
As we lay asleep in the midnight mirk,
Under the shade of Our Lady's Kirk,
I waken'd up in the dead of night,
Though May my daughter lay warm and white,
And I heard the cry of a little one,
And I knew 'twas the voice of Hugh my son :
" Mother, mother, come hither to me
Mother, mother, come hither and see !
Mother, mother, mother dear,
Another mother is sitting here :
My body is bruised and my heart is sad,
But I speak my mind and call them bad ;
I thirst and hunger night and day,
And were I strong I would fly away ! "
I heard the cry, though my grave was deep,
And awoke from sleep, and awoke from sleep !

IV.

I awoke from sleep, I awoke from sleep,
Up I rose from my grave so deep,
The earth was black, but overhead
The stars were yellow, the moon was red;
And I walk'd along all white and thin,
And lifted the latch and enter'd in.
" Mother, mother, and art thou here?
I know your face, and I feel no fear;
Raise me, mother, and kiss my cheek,
For oh, I am weary and sore and weak."
I smooth'd his hair with a mother's joy,
And he laugh'd aloud, my own brave boy;
I raised and held him on my breast,
Sang him a song, and bade him rest.
" Mother, mother, sing low to me—
I am sleepy now and I cannot see !"
I kiss'd him, and I could not weep,
As he went to sleep, as he went to sleep.

V.

As I lay asleep, as I lay asleep,
With my girl and boy in my grave so deep,
As I lay asleep, I awoke in fear,
Awoke, but awoke not my children dear,
And heard a cry so low and weak
From a tiny voice that could not speak :
I heard the cry of a little one,
My bairn that could neither talk nor run,
My little, little one, uncaress'd,
Starving for lack of the milk of the breast;
And I rose from sleep and enter'd in,
And found my little one pinch'd and thin,

And croon'd a song and hush'd its moan,
And put its lips to my white breast-bone;
And the red, red moon that lit the place
Went white to look at the little face,
And I kiss'd, and kiss'd, and I could not weep,
As it went to sleep, as it went to sleep.

VI.

As it lay asleep, as it lay asleep,
I set it down in the darkness deep,
Smooth'd its limbs and laid it out,
And drew the curtains round about;
Then into the dark, dark room I hied,
Where awake *he* lay, at the woman's side;
And though the chamber was black as night,
He saw my face, for it was so white!
I gazed in his eyes, and he shriek'd in pain,
And I knew he would never sleep again,
And back to my grave crept silently,
And soon my baby was brought to me;
My son and daughter beside me rest,
My little baby is on my breast;
Our bed is warm and our grave is deep,
But **he** cannot sleep, he cannot sleep!

THE BALLAD OF JUDAS ISCARIOT.

'Twas the body of Judas Iscariot
 Lay in the Field of Blood;
'Twas the soul of Judas Iscariot
 Beside the body stood.

Black was the earth by night,
    And black was the sky;
Black, black were the broken clouds,
    Tho' the red Moon went by.

'Twas the body of Judas Iscariot
    Strangled and dead lay there;
'Twas the soul of Judas Iscariot
    Look'd on it in despair.

The breath of the World came and went
    Like a sick man's in rest;
Drop by drop on the World's eyes
    The dews fell cool and blest.

Then the soul of Judas Iscariot
    Did make a gentle moan—
" I will bury underneath the ground
    My flesh and blood and bone.

" I will bury deep beneath the soil,
    Lest mortals look thereon,
And when the wolf and raven come
    The body will be gone!

" The stones of the field are sharp as steel,
    And hard and cold, God wot;
And I must bear my body hence
    Until I find a spot!"

'Twas the soul of Judas Iscariot
    So grim, and gaunt, and grey,
Raised the body of Judas Iscariot,
    And carried it away.

And as he bare it from the field
  Its touch was cold as ice,
And the ivory teeth within the jaw
  Rattled aloud, like dice.

As the soul of Judas Iscariot
  Carried its load with pain,
The Eye of Heaven, like a lanthorn's eye,
  Open'd and shut again.

Half he walk'd, and half he seem'd
  Lifted on the cold wind;
He did not turn, for chilly hands
  Were pushing from behind.

The first place that he came unto
  It was the open wold,
And underneath were prickly whins,
  And a wind that blew so cold.

The next place that he came unto
  It was a stagnant pool,
And when he threw the body in
  It floated light as wool.

He drew the body on his back,
  And it was dripping chill,
And the next place he came unto
  Was a Cross upon a hill.

A Cross upon the windy hill,
  And a Cross on either side,
Three skeletons that swing thereon,
  Who had been crucified.

And on the middle cross-bar sat
  A white Dove slumbering;
Dim it sat in the dim light,
  With its head beneath its wing.

And underneath the middle Cross
  A grave yawn'd wide and vast,
But the soul of Judas Iscariot
  Shiver'd, and glided past.

The fourth place that he came unto
  It was the Brig of Dread,
And the great torrents rushing down
  Were deep, and swift, and red.

He dared not fling the body in
  For fear of faces dim,
And arms were waved in the wild water
  To thrust it back to him.

'Twas the soul of Judas Iscariot
  Turn'd from the Brig of Dread,
And the dreadful foam of the wild water
  Had splash'd the body red.

For days and nights he wander'd on
  Upon an open plain,
And the days went by like blinding mist,
  And the nights like rushing rain.

For days and nights he wander'd on,
  All thro' the Wood of Woe;
And the nights went by like moaning wind,
  And the days like drifting snow.

'Twas the soul of Judas Iscariot
  Came with a weary face—
Alone, alone, and all alone,
  Alone in a lonely place !

He wander'd east, he wander'd west,
  And heard no human sound ;
For months and years, in grief and tears,
  He wander'd round and round.

For months and years, in grief and tears,
  He walk'd the silent night ;
Then the soul of Judas Iscariot
  Perceived a far-off light.

A far-off light across the waste,
  As dim as dim might be,
That came and went like the lighthouse gleam
  On a black night at sea.

'Twas the soul of Judas Iscariot
  Crawl'd to the distant gleam ;
And the rain came down, and the rain was blown
  Against him with a scream.

For days and nights he wander'd on,
  Push'd on by hands behind ;
And the days went by like black, black rain,
  And the nights like rushing wind.

'Twas the soul of Judas Iscariot,
  Strange, and sad, and tall,
Stood all alone at dead of night
  Before a lighted hall.

And the wold was white with snow,
  And his foot-marks black and damp,
And the ghost of the silver Moon arose,
  Holding her yellow lamp.

And the icicles were on the eaves,
  And the walls were deep with white,
And the shadows of the guests within
  Pass'd on the window light.

The shadows of the wedding guests
  Did strangely come and go,
And the body of Judas Iscariot
  Lay stretch'd along the snow.

The body of Judas Iscariot
  Lay stretch'd along the snow ;
'Twas the soul of Judas Iscariot
  Ran swiftly to and fro.

To and fro, and up and down,
  He ran so swiftly there,
As round and round the frozen Pole
  Glideth the lean white bear.

'Twas the Bridegroom sat at the table-head,
  And the lights burnt bright and clear—
" Oh, who is that," the Bridegroom said,
  " Whose weary feet I hear ? "

'Twas one look'd from the lighted hall,
  And answer'd soft and slow,
" It is a wolf runs up and down
  With a black track in the snow."

The Bridegroom in His robe of white
  Sat at the table-head—
" Oh, who is that who moans without ?"
  The blessëd Bridegroom said.

'Twas one look'd from the lighted hall,
  And answer'd fierce and low,
" 'Tis the soul of Judas Iscariot
  Gliding to and fro."

'Twas the soul of Judas Iscariot
  Did hush itself and stand,
And saw the Bridegroom at the door
  With a light in His hand.

The Bridegroom stood in the open door,
  And He was clad in white,
And far within the Lord's Supper
  Was spread so broad and bright.

The Bridegroom shaded His eyes and look'd,
  And His face was bright to see—
" What dost thou here at the Lord's Supper
  With thy body's sins ?" said He.

'Twas the soul of Judas Iscariot
  Stood black, and sad, and bare—
" I have wander'd many nights and days ;
  There is no light elsewhere."

'Twas the wedding guests cried out within
  And their eyes were fierce and bright—
" Scourge the soul of Judas Iscariot
  Away into the night !"

The Bridegroom stood in the open door,
  And He waved hands still and slow,
And the third time that He waved His hands
  The air was thick with snow.

And of every flake of falling snow,
  Before it touch'd the ground,
There came a dove, and a thousand doves
  Made sweet sound.

'Twas the body of Judas Iscariot
  Floated away full fleet,
And the wings of the doves that bare it off
  Were like its winding-sheet.

'Twas the Bridegroom stood at the open door,
  And beckon'd, smiling sweet ;
'Twas the soul of Judas Iscariot
  Stole in, and fell at His feet.

" The Holy Supper is spread within,
  And the many candles shine,
And I have waited long for thee
  Before I pour'd the wine ! "

The supper wine is pour'd at last,
  The lights burn bright and fair,
Iscariot washes the Bridegroom's feet,
  And dries them with his hair.

THE STARLING.

THE little lame Tailor
    Sat stitching and snarling—
Who in the world
    Was the Tailor's darling ?
To none of mankind
Was he well inclined,
    But he doted on Jack the Starling.

For the bird had a tongue,
    And of words good store,
And his cage was hung
    Just over the door ;
And he saw the people,
    And heard the roar,—
Folk coming and going
    Evermore,—
And he looked at the Tailor—
    And swore !

From a country lad
    The Tailor bought him,—
His training was bad,
    For tramps had taught him ;
On alehouse benches
    His cage had been,
While louts and wenches
    Made jests obscene,—
But he learn'd, no doubt,
    His oaths from fellows

Who travel about
        With kettle and bellows;
And three or four
        [The roundest by far
That ever he swore!]
        Were taught by a Tar.
And the Tailor heard—
        "We'll be friends," thought he;
" You're a clever bird,
        And our tastes agree.
We both are old,
        And esteem life base,
The whole world cold,
        Things out of place;
And we're lonely too,
        And full of care—
So what can we do
        But swear?

The devil take you,
        How you mutter!
Yet there's much to make you
        Fluster and flutter.
You want the fresh air
        And the sunlight, lad,
And your prison there
        Feels dreary and sad;
And here *I* frown
        In a prison as dreary,
Hating the town,
        And feeling weary:
We're too confined, Jack,
        And we want to fly,
And you blame mankind, Jack,
        And so do I!"

A haggard and ruffled
    Old fellow was Jack,
With a grim face muffled
    In ragged black,
And his coat was rusty
    And never neat,
And his wings were dusty
    With grime of the street,
And he sidelong peer'd,
    With eyes of soot,
And scowl'd and sneer'd,—
    And was lame of a foot !
And he longed to go
    From whence he came ;—
And the Tailor, you know,
    Was just the same.

All kinds of weather
    They felt confined,
And swore together
    At all mankind ;
For their mirth was done,
    And they felt like brothers,
And the railing of one
    Meant no more than the other's.
'Twas just a way
    They had learn'd, you see,—
Each wanted to say
    Only *this*—" Woe's me ;
I'm a poor old fellow,
    And I'm prison'd so,
While the sun shines mellow,
And the corn waves yellow,
    And the fresh winds blow,—

And the folk don't care
　　If I live or die,
But I long for air,
　　And I wish to fly !"
Yet unable to utter it,
　　And too wild to bear,
They could only mutter it,
　　And swear.

Many a year
　　They dwelt in the City,
In their prisons drear,
　　And none felt pity,—
Nay, few were sparing
　　Of censure and coldness,
To hear them swearing
　　With such plain boldness.
But at last, by the Lord,
　　Their noise was stopt,—
For down on his board
　　The Tailor dropt,
And they found him, dead,
　　And done with snarling,
Yet over his head
　　Still grumbled the Starling.
But when an old Jew
　　Claim'd the goods of the Tailor,
And with eye askew
　　Eyed the feathery railer,
And with a frown
　　At the dirt and rust,
Took the old cage down,
　　In a shower of dust,—

Jack, with heart aching,
  Felt life past bearing,
And shivering, quaking,
All hope forsaking,
  Died, swearing.

—— ——

THE WAKE OF O'HARA.

(SEVEN DIALS.)

To the Wake of O'Hara
  Came company ;
All St. Patrick's Alley
  Was there to see,
With the friends and kinsmen
  Of the family.
On the long deal table lay Tim in white,
And at his pillow the burning light.
Pale as himself, with the tears on her cheek,
The mother received us, too full to speak ;
But she heaped the fire, and on the board
Set the black bottle with never a word,
While the company gather'd, one and all,
Men and women, big and small—
Not one in the Alley but felt a call
  To the Wake of Tim O'Hara.

At the face of O'Hara,
  All white with sleep,
Not one of the women
  But took a peep,
And the wives new-wedded
  Began to weep.

The mothers gather'd round about,
And praised the linen and laying out,—
For white as snow was his winding-sheet,
And all was peaceful, and clean, and sweet ;
And the old wives, praising the blessèd dead,
Were thronging around the old press-bed,
Where O'Hara's widow, tatter'd and torn,
Held to her bosom the babe new-born,
And stared all around her, with eyes forlorn,
    At the Wake of Tim O'Hara.

    For the heart of O'Hara
      Was good as gold,
    And the life of O'Hara
      Was bright and bold,
    And his smile was precious
      To young and old !
Gay as a guinea, wet or dry,
With a smiling mouth, and a twinkling eye !
Had ever an answer for chaff and fun ;
Would fight like a lion, with any one !
Not a neighbour of any trade
But knew some joke that the boy had made ;
Not a neighbour, dull or bright,
But minded *something*—frolic or fight,
And whisper'd it round the fire that night,
    At the Wake of Tim O'Hara !

    " To God be glory
      In death and life,
    He's taken O'Hara
      From trouble and strife ! "
    Said one-eyed Biddy,
      The apple-wife.

" God bless old Ireland !" said Mistress Hart,
Mother to Mike of the donkey-cart ;
" God bless old Ireland till all be done,
She never made wake for a better son !"
And all join'd chorus, and each one said
Something kind of the boy that was dead ;
And the bottle went round from lip to lip,
And the weeping widow, for fellowship,
Took the glass of old Biddy and had a sip,
    At the Wake of Tim O'Hara.

      Then we drank to O'Hara,
        With drams to the brim,
      While the face of O'Hara
        Look'd on so grim,
      In the corpse-light shining
        Yellow and dim.
The cup of liquor went round again,
And the talk grew louder at every drain ;
Louder the tongues of the women grew !—
The lips of the boys were loosening too !
The widow her weary eyelids closed,
And, soothed by the drop o' drink, she dozed ;
The mother brighten'd and laugh'd to hear
Of O'Hara's fight with the grenadier,
And the hearts of all took better cheer,
    At the Wake of Tim O'Hara.

      Tho' the face of O'Hara
        Lookt on so wan,
      In the chimney-corner
        The row began—
      Lame Tony was in it,
        The oyster-man ;

For a dirty low thief from the North came near,
And whistled " Boyne Water " in his ear,
And Tony, with never a word of grace,
Flung out his fist in the blackguard's face ;
And the girls and women scream'd out for fright,
And the men that were drunkest began to fight,—
Over the tables and chairs they threw,—
The corpse-light tumbled,—the trouble grew,—
The new-born join'd in the hullabaloo,—
        At the Wake of Tim O'Hara.

            " Be still ! be silent !
                Ye do a sin !
            Shame be his portion
                Who dares begin ! "
            'Twas Father O'Connor
                Just enter'd in !—
All look'd down, and the row was done—
And shamed and sorry was every one ;
But the Priest just smiled quite easy and free—
" Would ye wake the poor boy from his sleep ? "
        said he :
And he said a prayer, with a shining face,
Till a kind of brightness fill'd the place :
The women lit up the dim corpse-light,
The men were quieter at the sight,
And the peace of the Lord fell on all that night
        At the Wake of Tim O'Hara !

From "CORUISKEN SONNETS."

(Written at or near Loch Coruisk, Island of Skye.)

I.

THE HILLS ON THEIR THRONES.

GHOSTLY and livid, robed with shadow, see !
  Each mighty mountain silent on its throne,
  From foot to scalp one stretch of livid stone,
Without one gleam of grass or greenery.
Silent they take the immutable decree—
  Darkness or sunlight come,—they do not stir ;
Each bare brow lifted desolately free,
  Keepeth the silence of a death-chamber.
Silent they watch each other until doom ;
  They see each other's phantoms come and go,
Yet stir not.   Now the stormy hour brings gloom,
  Now all things grow confused and black below,
Specific through the cloudy drift they loom,
  And each accepts his individual woe.

II.

KING BLAABHEIN.

MONARCH of these is Blaabhein.   On his height
  The lightning and the snow sleep side by side,
Like snake and lamb ; he waiteth in a white
  And wintry consecration.   All his pride
Is husht this dimly-gleaming autumn day—
  He broodeth o'er the things he hath beheld—
Beneath his feet the rains crawl still and grey,
  Like phantoms of the mighty men of eld.
A quiet awe the dreadful heights doth fill,
  The high clouds pause and brood above their King ;

The torrent murmurs gently as a rill ;
  Softly and low the winds are murmuring ;
A small black speck above the snow, how still
Hovers the eagle, with no stir of wing !

III.

THE FIERY BIRTH OF THE HILLS.

O HOARY Hills, though ye look aged, ye
  Are but the children of a latter time !—
  Methinks I see ye in that hour sublime
When from the hissing cauldron of the Sea
Ye were upheaven, while so terribly
    The clouds boil'd, and the lightning scorch'd you
        bare.
Wild, new-born, blind, Titans in agony,
  Ye glared at heaven through folds of fiery hair ! . . . .
Then, in an instant, while ye trembled thus
A Hand from heaven, white and luminous,
    Pass'd o'er your brows, and husht your fiery breath.
Lo ! one by one the still stars gather'd round,
The great Deep glass'd itself, and with no sound
    A cold snow fell, till all was still as death.

THE VISION OF THE MAN ACCURST.

From "THE BOOK OF ORM."

JUDGMENT was over ; all the world redeem'd
Save one Man,—who had sinn'd all sins, whose soul
Was blackness and foul odour. Last of all,
When all was lamb-white, thro' the summer Sea

Of ministering Spirits he was drifted
On to the white sands; there he lay and writhed,
Worm-like, black, venomous, with eyes accurst
Looking defiance, dazzled by the light
That gleam'd upon his clench'd and blood-stain'd hands;
While, with a voice low as a funeral bell,
The Seraph, sickening, read the sable scroll,
And as he read, the Spirits ministrant
Darken'd and murmur'd, " Cast him forth, O Lord ! "
And, from the shrine where unbeheld He broods,
The Lord said, " 'Tis the basest mortal born—
Cast him beyond the Gate ! "

                          The wild thing laugh'd
Defiant, as from wave to wave of light
He drifted, till he swept beyond the Gate,
Past the pale Seraph with the silvern eyes;
And there the wild Wind, that for ever beats
About the edge of brightness, caught him up,
And, like a straw, whirl'd round and wafted him,
And on a dark shore in the Underworld
Cast him, alone and shivering; for the Clime
Was sunless, and the ice was like a sheet
Of glistening tin, and the faint glimmering peaks
Were twisted to fantastic forms of frost,
And everywhere the frozen moonlight steam'd
Foggy and blue, save where the abysses loom'd
Sepulchral shadow.   But the Man arose,
With teeth gnash'd beast-like, waved wild feeble hands
At the white Gate (that glimmer'd far away,
Like to the round ball of the Sun beheld
Through interspaces in a wood of pine),
Cast a shrill curse at the pale Judge within,
Then groaning, beast-like crouch'd.

                                   Like golden waves
That break on a green island of the south,
Amid the flash of many plumaged wings,
Pass'd the fair days in Heaven.   By the side
Of quiet waters perfect Spirits walk'd,
Low singing, in the star-dew, full of joy
In their own thoughts and pictures of those thoughts
Flash'd into eyes that loved them ; while beside them,
After exceeding storm, the Waters of Life
With soft sea-sound subsided.   Then God said,
" 'Tis finish'd—all is well !"   But as He spake
A voice, from out the lonely Deep beneath,
Mock'd !
                    Then to the pale Seraph at the Gate,
Who looketh on the Deep with steadfast eyes
For ever, God cried, " What is he that mocks ? "
The Seraph answer'd, " 'Tis the Man accurst ! "
And, with a voice of most exceeding peace,
God ask'd, " What doth the Man ? "

                                   The Seraph said :
" Upon a desolate peak, with hoar-frost hung,
Amid the steaming vapours of the Moon,
He sitteth on a throne, and hideously
Playeth at judgment ; at his feet, with eyes
Slimy and luminous, squats a monstrous Toad ;
Above his head pale phantoms of the Stars
Fulfil cold ministrations of the Void,
And in their dim and melancholy lustre
His shadow, and the shadow of the Toad
Beneath him, linger.   Sceptred, throned, and crown'd,
The foul judgeth the foul, and sitting grim,
Laughs ! "
                    With a voice of most exceeding peace
The Lord said, " Look no more ! "

                              The Waters of Life
Broke with a gentle sea-sound gladdening—
God turn'd and blest them ; as He blest the same,
A voice, from out the lonely Void beneath,
Shriek'd !

              Then to the Seraph at the Gate,
Who looketh on the Deep with steadfast eyes
For ever, God cried, " What is he that shrieks?"
The Seraph answer'd, "'Tis the Man accurst !"
And, with a voice of most exceeding peace,
God ask'd, " What doth the Man ?"

                              The Seraph said :
" Around him the wild phantasms of the fog
Moan in the rheumy hoar-frost and cold steam.
Long time, crown'd, sceptred, on his throne he sits
Playing at judgment ; then with shrill voice cries—
'' 'Tis finish'd, thou art judged !' and, fiercely laughing,
He thrusteth down an iron heel to crush
The foul Toad, that with dim and luminous eyes
So stareth at his soul.   Thrice doth he lift
His foot up fiercely—lo ! he shrinks and cowers—
Then, with a wild glare at the far-off gate,
Rushes away, and rushing thro' the dark,
Shrieks ! "
              With a voice of most exceeding peace
The Lord said, " Look no more !"

                              The Waters of Life,
The living, spiritual Waters, broke,
Fountain-like, up against the Master's Breast,
Giving and taking blessing.   Overhead
Gather'd the shining legions of the Stars,

Led by the ethereal Moon, with dewy eyes
Of lustre : these have been baptised in fire,
Their raiment is of molten diamond,
And 'tis their office, as they circling move
In their blue orbits, evermore to turn
Their faces heavenward, drinking peace and strength
From that great Flame which, in the core of Heaven,
Like to the white heart of a violet burns,
Diffusing rays and odour.   Blessing all,
God sought their beauteous orbits, and behold !
The Eyes innumerably glistening
Were turn'd away from Heaven, and with sick stare,
Like the blue gleam of salt dissolved in fire,
They search'd the Void, as human faces look
On horror.

            To the Seraph at the Gate,
Who looketh on the Deep with steadfast eyes,
God cried, " What is this thing whereon they gaze ?"
The Seraph answer'd, " 'Tis the Man accurst."
And, with a voice of most exceeding peace,
God ask'd, " What doth the Man ?"
                              The Seraph said :
" O Master ! send Thou forth a tongue of fire
To wither up this worm !   Serene and cold,
Flooded with moon-dew, lies the World, and there
The Man roams ; and the image of the Man
In the wan waters of the frosty sphere
Falleth gigantic.   Up and down he drifts,
Worm-like, black, venomous, with eyes of hate,
Waving his bloody hands in fierce appeal,
So that the gracious faces of Thy Stars
Are troubled, and the stainless tides of light
Shadow pollution.   With wild, ape-like eyes,

The wild thing whining peers thro' horrent hair,
And rusheth up and down, seeking to find
A face to look upon, a hand to touch,
A heart that beats ; but all the World is void
And awful.   All alone in the Cold Clime,
Alone within the lonely universe,
Crawleth the Man accurst ! ''
                              Then said the Lord,
" Doth he repent ? "   And the fair Seraph said,
" Nay, he blasphemeth !   Send Thou forth Thy fire ! "
But with a voice of most exceeding peace,
Out of the Shrine where unbeheld He broods,
God said, " What I have made, a living Soul,
Cannot be unmade, but endures for ever."
Then added, "Call the Man ! "

                              The Seraph heard,
And in a low voice named the lost one's name ;
The wild Wind that for ever beats the Gate
Caught up the word, and fled thro' the cold Void.
'Twas murmur'd on, as a lorn echo fading,
From peak to peak.   Swift as a wolf the Man
Was rushing o'er a waste, with shadow streaming
Backward 'gainst a frosty gleaming wind,
When like a fearful whisper in his ear
'Twas wafted ; then his blanch'd lips shook like leaves
In that chill wind, his hair was lifted up,
He paused, his shadow paused, like stone and shadow,
And shivering, glaring round him, the Man moan'd,
" Who calls ? " and in a moment he was 'ware
Of the white light streaming from the far Gate,
And looming, blotted black against the light,
The Seraph with uplifted forefinger,
Naming his name !

　　　　　　　　And ere the Man could fly,
The wild Wind in its circuit swept upon him,
And lifted him, and whirl'd him like a straw,
And cast him at the Gate,—a bloody thing—
Mad, moaning, horrible, obscene, unclean ;
A body swollen and stainëd like the wool
Of sheep that in the rainy season crawl
About the hills, and sleep on foul damp beds
Of bracken rusting red.　There, breathing hard,
Glaring with fiery eyes, panted the Man,
With scorch'd lips drooping, thirsting as he heard
The flowing of the Fountains far within.

　　Then said the Lord, " Is the Man there?" and "Yea,"
Answered the Seraph pale.　Then said the Lord,
" What doth the Man ?"　The Seraph, frowning, said :
" O Master, in the belly of him is fire,
He thirsteth, fiercely thrusting out his hands,
And threateneth, seeking water !"　Then the Lord
Said, " Give him water—let him drink !"

　　　　　　　　　　　　　　The Seraph,
Stooping above him, with forefinger bright
Touched the gold kerbstone of the Gate, and lo !
Water gush'd forth and gleamed ; and lying prone
The Man crawl'd thither, dipt his fever'd face,
Drank long and deeply ; then, his thirst appeased,
Thrust in his bloody hands unto the wrist,
And let the gleaming Fountain play upon them,
And looking up out of his dripping hair,
Grinn'd mockery at the Giver.

　　　　　　　　　　　　　Then the Lord
Said low, " How doth the Man ?"　The Seraph said :
" It is a Snake !　He mocketh all Thy gifts,

And, in a snake's voice, half articulate,
Blasphemeth!"   Then the Lord: "Doth the Man crave
To enter in?"   "Not so," the Seraph said,
"He saith——"   "What saith he?"   "That his Soul
    is fill'd
With hate of Thee and of Thy ways; he loathes
Pure pathways where the fruitage of the Stars
Hangeth resplendent, and he spitteth hate
On all Thy Children.   Send Thou forth Thy fire!
In no wise is he better than the beasts,
The gentle beasts, that come like morning dew
And vanish.   Let him die!"   Then said the Lord:
"What I have made endures; but 'tis not meet
This thing should cross my perfect work for ever.
Let him begone!"   Then cried the Seraph pale:
"O Master! at the frozen Clime he glares
In awe, shrieking at Thee!"   "What doth he crave?"
"Neither Thy Heaven nor Thy holy ways.
He murmureth out he is content to dwell
In the Cold Clime for ever, so Thou sendest
A face to look upon, a heart that beats,
A hand to touch—albeit like himself,
Black, venomous, unblest, exiled, and base:
Give him this thing, he will be very still,
Nor trouble Thee again."

                        The Lord mused.

                                        Still,
Scarce audible, trembled the Waters of Life—
Over all Heaven the Snow of the same Thought
Which rose within the Spirit of the Lord
Fell hushedly; the innumerable Eyes
Swam in a lustrous dream.

                              Then said the Lord :
" In all the waste of worlds there dwelleth not
Another like himself—behold he is
The basest Mortal born.   Yet 'tis not meet
His cruel cry, for ever piteous,
Should trouble my eternal Sabbath-day.
Is there a Spirit here, a human thing,
Will pass this day from the Gate Beautiful
To share the exile of this Man accurst,—
That he may cease the shrill pain of his cry,
And I have peace ? "

                              Hushedly, hushedly,
Snow'd down the Thought Divine—the living Waters
Murmur'd and darken'd.   But like mournful mist
That hovers o'er an autumn pool, two Shapes,
Beautiful, human, glided to the Gate
And waited.
                      " What art thou ? " in a stern voice
The Seraph said, with dreadful forefinger
Pointing to one.   A gentle voice replied,
" I will go forth with him whom ye call curst !
He grew within my womb—my milk was white
Upon his lips.   I will go forth with him ! "
" And *thou ?* " the Seraph said.   The second Shape
Answer'd, " I also will go forth with him ;
I have kist his lips, I have lain upon his breast,
I bare him children, and I closed his eyes ;
I will go forth with him ! "

                              Then said the Lord,
" What Shapes are these which speak ? "   The Seraph
          answer'd :
" The woman who bore him and the wife he wed—
The one he slew in anger—the other he stript,

With ravenous claws, of raiment and of food."
Then said the Lord, " Doth the Man hear ?"   " He
    hears,"
Answer'd the Seraph ; " like a wolf he lies,
Venomous, bloody, dark, a thing accurst,
And hearkeneth with no sign !"   Then said the Lord :
" Show them the Man," and the pale Seraph cried.
" Behold ! "
            Hushedly, hushedly, hushedly,
In heaven fell the Snow of Thought Divine,
Gleaming upon the Waters of Life beneath,
And melting,—as with slow and lingering pace,
The Shapes stole forth into the windy cold,
And saw the thing that lay and throbb'd and lived,
And stoop'd above him.   Then one reach'd a hand
And touch'd him, and the fierce thing shrank and spat,
Hiding his face.
            " Have they beheld the Man ? "
The Lord said ; and the Seraph answer'd " Yea ; "
And the Lord said again, " What doth the Man ? "

" He lieth like a log in the wild blast,
And as he lieth, lo ! one sitting takes
His head into her lap, and moans his name,
And smoothes his matted hair from off his brow,
And croons in a low voice a cradle song ;
And lo ! the other kneeleth at his side,
Half-shrinking in the old habit of her fear,
Yet hungering with her eyes, and passionately
Kissing his bloody hands."

            Then said the Lord,
" Will they go forth with him ? "   A voice replied,
" He grew within my womb—my milk was white
Upon his lips.   I will go forth with him ! "

And a voice cried, "I will go forth with him ;
I have kist his lips, I have lain upon his breast,
I bare him children, and I closed his eyes ;
I will go forth with him !"

                Still hushedly
Snow'd down the Thought Divine, the Waters of Life
Flow'd softly, sadly ; for an alien sound,
A piteous human cry, a sob forlorn
Thrill'd to the heart of Heaven.

                The Man wept.

And in a voice of most exceeding peace
The Lord said (while against the Breast Divine
The Waters of Life leapt, gleaming, gladdening) :
"The Man is saved ; let the Man enter in !"

FIDES AMANTIS.

(L'ENVOI TO "THE OUTCAST.")

DEAREST and Best !   Light of my way !
  Soul of my Soul, whom God hath sent
To be my guardian night and day,
To make me humbly kneel and pray,
  When proudest and most turbulent !
Calm of my Life ! dear Angèl mine !
  Come to me, now I faint and fail,
And guide me softly to the Shrine,
  Where thro' the deep'ning gloom doth shine
  Life's bleeding Heart, Love's Holy Grail,

Where Soul feels Soul, and Instinct, stirred
  To Insight, looks Creation thro',
And hear me murmur, word by word,
  The Creed I owe to Heaven and *you !*

" I do believe in GOD ; that He
Made Heaven and Earth, and you and me !
Nay, I believe in all the host
  Of Gods, from Jesus down to Joss,
But honour best and reverence most
  That guileless God who bore the Cross.
I do believe that this dark scheme,
  This riddle of our life below,
Is solved by Insight and by Dream,
  And not by aught mere Sense can know ;
That the one sacrifice whereby
We attest a faith which cannot die,
Is the burnt-offering we place
  On Truth's pure Altar day by day,
Whereby the sensual and the base
  Within us is consumed away ;
That just as far as we forego
  Our selfish claim to stand *alone*,
Proving our gladness or our woe
  Is Humankind's and not our own,
So far as for another's sake
  Our cup of sorrow we accept,
And crave, although our hearts should break,
  The pain supreme of God's Adept,
So far shall we attain the height
Of Freedom, in the Master's sight.
I do believe that our salvation
  Lies in the little things of life,
Not in the pomp and acclamation

Of triumph, or in battle-strife,
Not on the thrones where men are crown'd,
  Not in the race where chariots roll,
But in the arms that clasp us round
  And hold us *backward* from the goal !
In Love, not Pride ; in stooping low,
  Not soaring blindly at the sun ;
In power to feel, not zeal to know ;
  Not in rewards, but duties done.

" *Corollary :* all gain is base,
  The Victor's wreath, the Poet's crown,
If conquest in the giddy race
  Means one poor struggler trampled down,
If he who gains the sunless throne
Of Fame, sits silent and alone,
Without Humanity to share
His happiness, or his despair !

" This Gospel I uphold, the one
  The latter Adam comes to prove :
To every Soul beneath the sun
  Wide open lies a Heaven of Love ;
But none, however free from sin,
  However cloth'd in pomp and pride,
However fair, may enter in,
  Without some Witness at his side,
To attest before the Judge and King
Vicarious love and suffering.
Who stands alone, shall surely fall !
  Who folds the falling to his breast
Stands sure and firm in spite of all,
  While angel-choirs proclaim him blest."

Dearest and Best ! Soul of my Soul !
   Life of my Life, kneel here with me !
Pray while the Storms around us roll,
   That God may keep us frail, yet free !
Be Love our strength ! be God our goal !
   Amen, et Benedicite !

ANDREW LANG.

TWILIGHT ON TWEED.

THREE crests against the saffron sky,
  Beyond the purple plain,
The kind remembered melody
  Of Tweed once more again.

Wan water from the border hills,
  Dear voice from the old years,
Thy distant music lulls and stills,
  And moves to quiet tears.

Like a loved ghost thy fabled flood
  Fleets through the dusky land;
Where Scott, come home to die, has stood,
  My feet returning stand.

A mist of memory broods and floats,
  The Border waters flow;
The air is full of ballad notes,
  Borne out of long ago.

Old songs that sung themselves to me,
  Sweet through a boy's day-dream,
While trout below the blossom'd tree
  Plashed in the golden stream.

   .   .   .   .   .

Twilight, and Tweed, and Eildon Hill,
  Fair and too fair you be ;
You tell me that the voice is still
  That should have welcomed me.

MARTIAL IN TOWN.

LAST night, within the stifling train,
  Lit by the foggy lamp o'erhead,
  Sick of the sad Last News, I read
Verse of that joyous child of Spain,

Who dwelt when Rome was waxing cold,
  Within the Roman din and smoke.
  And like my heart to me they spoke,
These accents of his heart of old :—

Brother, had we but time to live,
  And fleet the careless hours together,
With all that leisure has to give
  Of perfect life and peaceful weather,

The Rich Man's halls, the anxious faces,
The weary Forum, courts, and cases
  Should know us not; but quiet nooks,
But summer shade by field and well,
  But country rides, and talk of books,
At home, with these, we fain would dwell !

Now neither lives, but day by day
  Sees the suns wasting in the west,
And feels their flight, and doth delay
  To lead the life he loveth best.

So from thy city prison broke,
  Martial, thy wail for life misspent,
And so, through London's noise and smoke
  My heart replies to the lament.

For dear as Tagus with his gold,
  And swifter Salo, were to thee,
So dear to me the woods that fold
  The streams that circle Fernielea !

ENGLAND.

"We are rather disposed to laugh when poets or orators try
to conjure with the name of England."—Professor Seeley.

When Nelson's sudden signal came
  Men's hearts leaped up the word to hail :
Not vainly with his England's name
  He "conjured," but to some avail !
When o'er the *Birkenhead* her fate
  Closed, and our men arose to die,
The name of England yet was great,
  And yet upheld their hearts on high.

For England's honour Gordon chose,
  When England would not guard her own,
Serene amidst a world of foes,
  Alone to live, to die alone.
But that great name, to Milton dear,
  Of England's ocean-circled isle,
The voters greet it with a jeer,
  The witling sniffs it with a smile.

Well, if indeed that name no more
　　Must, like a trumpet, stir the blood ;
Of all our fathers wrought and bore
　　For England, on the field and flood,
If naught endures, if all must pass,
　　Then speed the hour when we shall be,
Unmoved, unshamed beneath the grass,
　　Deaf to the mountains and the sea !

Deaf to the Voices Wordsworth heard
　　Reverberant from height and deep ;
Dull to the sights and sounds that stirred
　　Our fathers ; heedless and asleep.
For so, at least, we shall not hear
　　The noises from the Meetings borne,
Where England's children, with a sneer
　　Hail " England " as a word of scorn.

———

Translations.

From " THE LITTLE GARLAND."

Leonidas of Tarentum.

THE FISHERMAN'S TOMB.

THERIS the Old, the waves that harvested
　　More keen than birds that labour in the sea,
With spear and net, by shore and rocky bed,
　　Not with the well-manned galley laboured he ;
Him not the star of storms, nor sudden sweep
　　Of wind with all his years hath smitten and bent,

But in his hut of reeds he fell asleep,
  As fades a lamp when all the oil is spent :
This tomb nor wife nor children raised, but we
His fellow-toilers, fishers of the sea.

THE WAYSIDE WELL.

Not where the sultry pool is fouled by sheep,
  Drink, wayfarer; but climb a little way,
By yonder pastoral pine above the steep,
  The grassy hillock where the heifers stray :
There shalt thou find the snow-cold springs that leap
  Forth from the rock, and babble through the day.

Asclepiades.

DEWY GARLANDS.

There hang, my garlands, by her gate,
  My love's gate wreathing o'er :
Nor cast your blossoms now, but wait
  Until she opes the door ;
Then, dank with dew love's eyes have shed,
  Fall, petals drenched in brine,
That so, at least, her golden head
  May drink these tears of mine.

ALEXANDER ANDERSON.

("SURFACEMAN.")

CUDDLE DOON.

THE bairnies cuddle doon at nicht
 Wi' muckle faught an' din;
"Oh try and sleep, ye waukrife rogues,
 Your faither's comin' in."
They never heed a word I speak;
 I try to gie a froon,
But aye I hap them up an' cry,
 "Oh, bairnies, cuddle doon."

Wee Jamie wi' the curly heid—
 He aye sleeps next the wa',
Bangs up an' cries, "I want a piece"—
 The rascal starts them a'.
I rin an' fetch them pieces, drinks,
 They stop awee the soun',
Then draw the blankets up an' cry,
 "Noo, weanies, cuddle doon."

But ere five minutes gang, wee Rab
 Cries out, frae 'neath the claes,
"Mither, mak' Tam gie ower at ance,
 He's kittlin' wi' his taes."

The mischief's in that Tam for tricks,
  He'd bother half the toon ;
But aye I hap them up and cry,
  " Oh, bairnies, cuddle doon."

At length they hear their faither's fit,
  An', as he steeks the door,
They turn their faces to the wa',
  While Tam pretends to snore.
" Hae a' the weans been gude ?" he asks,
  As he pits aff his shoon ;
" The bairnies, John, are in their beds,
  An' lang since cuddled doon."

An' just afore we bed oorsel's,
  We look at our wee lambs,
Tam has his airm roun' wee Rab's neck,
  And Rab his airm round Tam's.
I lift wee Jamie up the bed,
  An' as I straik each croon,
I whisper, till my heart fills up,
  " Oh, bairnies, cuddle doon."

The bairnies cuddle doon at nicht
  Wi' mirth that's dear to me ;
But soon the big warl's cark an' care
  Will quaten doon their glee
Yet, come what will to ilka ane,
  May He who rules aboon
Aye whisper, though their pows be bald,
  " Oh, bairnies, cuddle doon."

JENNY WI' THE AIRN TEETH.

WHAT a plague is this o' mine,
  Winna steek an e'e ;
Tho' I hap him o'er the heid,
  As cosy as can be.
Sleep an' let me to my wark—
  A' thae claes to airn—
Jenny wi' the airn teeth,
  Come an' tak' the bairn !

Tak' him to your ain den,
  Whaur the bogie bides,
But first put baith your big teeth
  In his wee plump sides ;
Gie your auld grey pow a shake,
  Rive him frae my grup,
Tak' him whaur nae kiss is gaun
  When he waukens up.

Whatna noise is that I hear
  Comin' doon the street ?
Weel I ken the dump, dump,
  O' her beetle feet ;
Mercy me ! she's at the door !
  Hear her lift the sneck ;
Wheesht, an' cuddle mammy noo,
  Closer roun' the neck.

Jenny wi' the airn teeth,
  The bairn has aff his claes ;
Sleepin' safe an' soun', I think—
  Dinna touch his taes.

Sleepin' bairns are no for you,
    Ye may turn aboot,
An' tak' awa' wee Tam next door—
    I hear him screichin' oot.

Dump, dump, awa' she gangs
    Back the road she cam',
I hear her at the ither door,
    Speirin' after Tam ;
He's a crabbit, greetin' thing –
    The warst in a' the toon,
Little like my ain wee wean—
    Losh, he's sleepin' soun' !

Mithers hae an awfu' wark
    Wi' their bairns at nicht,
Chappin' on the chair wi' tangs,
    To gie the rogues a fricht ;
Aulder bairns are fleyed wi' less,
    Weel eneuch we ken,
Bigger bogies, bigger Jennies,
    Frichten muckle men.

———

BIG FITTIE JOCK.

THE wee'st bit wean, when the schule scaled at nicht,
If it steekit its nieve, could hae gi'en him a fricht ;
An', if it but touched him, he grat lood an' lang,
Till the neebors ran oot, thinkin' something was wrang.
He slaver'd an' rubbit his een for an oor,
Till his face was as black as if row'd amang stour ;
But they took little heed, for they a' made a mock—
Little pity ava could be got for Big Jock.

It was months ere the letters would stick in his brains,
Though the maister himsel' spared nae trouble or pains;
But he often turned roun', sair in heart an' perplex'd—
What he learned him ae day he forgot it the next;
But Jock plodded on wi' the same solemn face,
Stood up for his task in the auld usual place,
Till the hale o' the schule an' the half o' the folk
Made a nickname, an' ca'd him at ance " Fittie Jock."

He was left by the rest in the class far ahin';
They were writin' sma' text when he tried to begin !
But, losh, what a sicht was he whiles to our view,
Wi' the ink on his face frae the chin to the broo,
His tongue half shot oot, as if ready to lick,
While his " strokes " micht hae ser'd for a guid walkin'-
    stick.
His " kloopies " were no unlike han's for a crock :
Nae clerk, ane could see, wad be made oot o' Jock.

He next tried the countin', and got to the length
O' simple addition, but that tried his strength.
He swat till the draps fell in blabs on his sklate
As he countit his fingers, for that was his gate.
In short, it was seen by ilk ane in the toon
That Jock in the lang run wad hae to gang doon.
A barrow wi' mills or a rag-gatherin' pock
Were trades that were laid oot for Big Fittie Jock.

Weel, years cam' an' gaed, an' the schule time gaed by,
While the boys, noo half-men, were all eager to try
Their fortune in life.   Some, fu' quick wi' the pen,
Gaed into the city to fecht among men ;

Ithers took to the sea, or in far stranger lan's
Made their hame, an' laid frae them wi' wealth-seekin'
    han's.
But, strange to relate, the big barrow an' pock
Was the trade that fell into the han's o' Big Jock.

His mither, puir body, focht lang, lang and sair
To mak' him gie't up, but he stack till't the mair ;
The first time he took wi' his pock to the street,
She screen'd her bit window, no likin' to see't ;
But Jock hoy'd awa' whistlin' oot o' the toon,
Wi' his barrow to cadge a' the parish aroon' ;
The weans, unco glad o' the fun, in a flock,
Ran ahint him a mile, then took fareweel o' Jock.

Three weeks after that, on a bright afternoon,
When the weans wi' their lessons for ae day were dune,
A loud cry got up as they took to their feet,
For Jock wi' his barrow cam' into the street.
Ye could scarce see his face, it was hidden by mills
Made up o' braw paper, and fine fancy frills,
A lang sack o' rags, just as fu' as could chock,
Lay across the stoot trams, an' between them was Jock.

" Hey, rags for braw mills," an' Jock blew on his horn,
While the neebors cam' roun' scarcely hidin' their scorn ;
He ne'er fash'd his thoom, but gied toots ane an' twa,
While a neebor cried, " Jock, man, wha learn'd ye to
    blaw ? "
They a' lauch'd at this, but he gied them a smile
As he took in the rags an' gied oot mills the while.
He sune got his barrow cleared oot o' its stock,
For the weans were a' daft to hae mills frae Big Jock.

His mither at first took his trade sair to heart,
But she brichten'd when Jock got a cuddy an' cart ;
Then hareskins an' sheepskins, brass, lead, an' auld airn,
Rags frae a gudewife, or sma' cloots frae a bairn,
Ocht, in fact, that could draw a bawbee was ta'en in,
Till the auld wives said—"Certes, Big Jock's makin' tin—
The purse that he keeps is as lang as a sock."
But hoo muckle was in't nane could ken but Big Jock.

When he got his cairt fu', he set aff to the toon,
Selt his cargo, an' then made a lang circuit roun',
Wi' dishes o' a' kin' o' shapes, frae the mug
To the muckle saut crock wi' a hole for a lug.
But when he cam' back, in his cairt could be seen
A gude stieve bit horse where the cuddy had been ;
Then the neebors began less to jeer an' to mock—
Na, some o' them struck up a freendship wi' Jock.

Weel, as time row'd alang, it was easy to see
That the warl' to Jock was as kin' as could be.
He biggit a hoose wi' a front to the street,
Whase windows to see fell na short o' a treat,
An' a' were stuck fu' o' the choicest o' things,
Frae the sappy big cheese to the ham row'd wi' strings,
Forbye sma'er things, sic as candy an' rock,
Were in plenty within the braw hoose built by Jock.

His mither had noo got abune thae ill days,
When he took to the rags wi' the same on his claes,
An' the greatest delicht that the puir body kent,
Was to look at the sign bricht wi' varnish and pent,

Whereon in big letters was seen her son's name,
Wi' " General Grocer " put in 'neath the same.
My certes, nae sma' drink was she 'mang the folk,
An' next to the sign in her worship was Jock.

But O, what a nicht did she spen' in her hoose,
When her son wi' some frien's entered briskly an' croose.
" Look here," cried the first, an' he gied a hurraih,
" There's your son, an' we've made him a Bailie this day!"
She sprang to the fire an' made ready the tea,
While a bottle or twa plainly hinted a spree.
A braw spleet new mutch an' a gown were put on,
No to please, but to honour, her son, Bailie John.

When the toddy had gotten a haud o' Jock's heid,
He rose to reply to the toast o' gude speed.
He stammer'd an' said, wi' a claw at his croon—
" When I gaed wi' a barrow," an' then he sat doon—
But no till he pointed to where on the wa'
Hung the big horn that noo he had nae need to blaw.
The pride o' his mither at this got a shock,
But the rest a' declared it was honest o' Jock.

An' what cam' o' a' thae bricht han's at the schule
Wha lauch'd an' consider'd Big Jock as a fule?
Tam Tamson, the coonter, sae gleg an' sae fell,
Made a figure owre mony an' did for himsel';
Rab Dobs, wha was thocht to be steady an' rich,
Cam' hame, took a shool, an' gaed into a ditch;
Dick Dips, wi' his pride, that was aye on the cock,
Gaed a' to the dirt, and turned ostler to Jock.

An' Geordie, the poet, wha thocht it a splore
To mak' rhymes for the rest to put in at Jock's door,
Instead o' becomin' a star as he ocht,
Noo works on a line wi' nae rhymes in his thocht.
"'Od," quo' the auld joiner, to some o' the lave,
Lookin' ow'r his braid specks as he morticed a nave,
"O' a' that we thocht wad gie this warl' a knock,
Deil ane o' them a' has dune weel but Big Jock."

BOWL ABOOT.

LANG Jock Maclean, the toozie loon,
Was ken'd an' noted roun' an' roun'
As ane wha couldna let abee
The drink when signboards took his e'e ;
But in wad bang wi' richt gudewill,
Cryin', "Landlady, bring in a gill."
Then, if some drouthie frien's cam' in,
The glasses roun' an' roun' wad spin,
Till ilka ane began to feel
His noddle spinnin' like a wheel.

But Jock is noo fu' snod an' douce,
An' never heeds a public-hoose ;
An' hoo this cam' to be wrocht oot,
Was simply dune by "bowl aboot."

Ae nicht as Jock cam' frae the toun,
As usual wi' a dizzy croon,
He staucher'd on fu' gruff an' grim,
For a' things had gane wrang wi' him.

So he resolved to lay the blame
O' a', if he got safely hame,
On Jean, wha sat her lane, puir body,
Cursin' late 'oors an' steamin' toddy.
At length she heard him at the sneck,
But never jee'd or turned her neck ;
Then in he cam' wi' ae lang stagger,
An', lookin' roun' him wi' a swagger,
Roar'd oot, as he tried to be steady,
" Jean, whaur's my supper ?—get it ready."
But aye she sat upon the stule,
Nor spak' a sentence guid or ill.

Then wi' an oath that wasna made
For print, Jock to the dresser gaed,
Took up a bowl, an' turnin' roun',
He heaved it up abune his croon,
An' crash ! it gaed upon the fluir
In fifty different bits an' mair.

Then Jean, as mad as mad could be,
Sprang up sic spitefu' wark to see,
Ran to the dresser, took anither,
An' clashed it doon withoot a swither,
Then turned to Jock, half skreighin' oot,
" Come on, ye deevil, bowl aboot."

Then, mercy me ! what wark began—
Bowl after bowl in flinners span,
An' aye as Jock himsel' took ane,
Jean seized its mate, an' made it spin.
Baith wrocht as if for life an' death,
Nor stoppit to recruit their breath,

But crash on crash gaed bowl an' plate,
Till Jock, half-ruein' at their fate,
Began to parley for cessation
O' siccan dreid extermination.
"Haud, Jean," he cried, wi' savage broo,
"Own that this ploy began wi' you,
An' no anither bowl by token
This nicht between us will be broken."
"Na, faith I, Jock," Jean cried, "ower lang
I've listened to the same auld sang ;
Hae borne your bickerin', snash, an' talk,
Nor gied ye an ill answer back ;
Hae sat up mony a weary nicht,
My heart up in my throat wi' fricht,
Thinkin' ye micht fa' ower the brig,
When rains had made the water big.
But come what may, be't guid or ill,
This nicht I'll let you hae your fill.
So bowl aboot, an' see wha's winner,
Ye guid-for-naething drucken sinner !
There's mine "--an' ere he was aware,
Jean smash'd her bowl upon the fluir.
An' Jock (his peacefu' thochts in vain),
Swore, an' fell to his wark again,
Till ashets, bowls, broth plates, an' a',
That looked sae nicely in a raw,
Lay on the fluir—a broken harl—
The ruins o' a crockery warl'.

Next mornin', when Jock rase an' saw
The awfu' smash he scarce could draw
His trousers on, but glower'd to see't,
Until he nearly cut his feet
Among the broken skelps that lay
Like snawflakes on a winter's day ;

Then, wi' a scart at his braid croon,
He gied a grum'le an' sat doon
To sup his parritch oot the pot,
For nae hale plate was in the lot.
But just afore he daun'ered oot
He gied a hoast an' turned aboot,
Flung doon his purse upon a chair,
Then pointed to the dresser bare:
Sic action said to Jean fu' plain,
"There, get the dresser fill'd again."

That nicht, when Jock frae wark cam' hame,
The fire shot oot a cheerfu' flame
As far's the dresser, where new delf
Was nicely ranged upon each shelf.
The table sat afore the fire,
An' on't was a' ane could desire;
An' by it Jean sat, a' the while
Upon her face a cheerfu' smile.
Jock glower'd an' wonner'd when he saw
His hoose sae snod, an' trig, an' braw.
At length, when he had ate his fill,
He sat, but keepit thinkin' still,
Until at last he turned to Jean,
An' said, the big tears in his een,
" Wife, I hae thocht, an' still I think,
I've been ower lang the fule o' drink;
But here this very nicht I voo
To be a better man to you,
An' leave gill stoups, an' a' their mirth,
For purer joys beside the hearth.
See, there's my han' t'ye as a proof."
Jean rase an' took his honest loof,
Kiss'd him, an' ca'd him John, an' grat
Wi' joy that it had come to that,

Blessin', sic was her happy state,
The breakin' o' each bowl an' plate,
For plainly it was that brocht on
The wish'd-for happy change in John.

Frae that to this, as far's I've heard,
Jock aye has stickit to his word ;
Comes hame fu' sober, ticht, and square
At nicht frae big Drumshauchle Fair.
An' Jean, since he has left the drappie,
Is noo fu' cheerfu', bien, an' happy ;
But aye when Jock prepares to gang
To fairs an' roups an' sic-like thrang,
She snods him up wi' great respeck ;
Twines a big gravit roun' his neck,
Convoys him half-way doon the green,
Then wi' a smile aboot her een,
Stops, pu's his beard, an' whispers oot—
" Noo, Jock, keep min', or bowl aboot ! "

TOSHIE NORRIE.

O, BONNIE Toshie Norrie
    To Inverard is gane,
An' wi' her a' the sunshine
    That made us unco fain.
The win' is cauld an' gurly,
    An' winter's in the air,
But where dwells Toshie Norrie,
    O, it's aye simmer there.

O, bonnie Toshie Norrie,
  What made you leave us a'?
Your hame is no the Heelands,
  Though there the hills are braw.
Come back wi' a' your daffin',
  An walth o' gowden hair,
For where dwells Toshie Norrie,
  O, it's aye simmer there.

O, bonnie Toshie Norrie,
  The winter nichts are lang,
An' aft we sit an' weary
  To hear an auld Scotch sang ;
Come back, an' let your music,
  Like sunshine, fill the air,
For where dwells Toshie Norrie,
  O, it's aye simmer there.

LANGSYNE, WHEN LIFE WAS BONNIE.

LANGSYNE, when life was bonnie,
  An' a' the skies were blue,
When ilka thocht took blossom,
  An' hung its heid wi' dew,
When winter wasna winter,
  Though snaws cam' happin' doon
Langsyne, when life was bonnie,
  Spring gaed a twalmonth roun'.

Langsyne, when life was bonnie,
  An' a' the days were lang ;
When through them ran the music
  That comes to us in sang,
We never wearied liltin'
  The auld love-laden tune ;
Langsyne, when life was bonnie,
  Love gaed a twalmonth roun'.

Langsyne, when life was bonnie,
  An' a' the warld was fair,
The leaves were green wi' simmer,
  For autumn wasna there.
But listen hoo they rustle,
  Wi' an eerie, weary soun',
For noo, alas, 'tis winter
  That gangs a twalmonth roun'.

NOTTMAN.

THAT was Nottman waving at me,
But the steam fell down, so you could not see ;
He is out to-day with the fast express,
And running a mile in the minute, I guess.

Danger? none in the least, for the way
Is good, though the curves are sharp as you say,
But bless you, when trains are a little behind,
They thunder around them—a match for the wind.

Nottman himself is a devil to drive,
But cool and steady, and ever alive
To whatever danger is looming in front,
When a train has run hard to gain time for a shunt.

But he once got a fear, though, that shook him with pain,
Like sleepers beneath the weight of a train.
I remember the story well, for, you see,
His stoker, Jack Martin, told it to me.

Nottman had sent down the wife for a change
To the old folks living at Riverly Grange,
A quiet sleepy sort of a town,
Save when the engines went up and down.

For close behind it the railway ran
In a mile of a straight if a single span ;
Three bridges were over the straight, and between
Two the distant signal was seen.

She had with her her boy—a nice little chit
Full of romp and mischief, and childish wit,
And every time that we thunder'd by,
Both were out on the watch for Nottman and I.

"Well, one day," said Jack, "on our journey down,
Coming round on the straight at the back of the town,
I saw right ahead, in front of our track,
In the haze, on the rail, something dim-like and black.

"I look'd over at Nottman, but ere I could speak,
He shut off the steam, and, with one wild shriek,
A whistle took to the air with a bound ;
But the object ahead never stirr'd at the sound.

" In a moment he flung himself down on his knee,
Leant over the side of the engine to see,
Took one look, then sprung up, crying, breathless and pale,
' Brake, Jack, it is some one asleep on the rail ! '

" The rear brakes were whistled on in a trice,
While I screw'd on the tender brake firm as a vice,
But still we tore on with this terrible thought
Sending fear to our hearts—' Can we stop her or not ? '

" I took one look again, then sung out to my mate,
' We can never draw up, we have seen it too late.'
When, sudden and swift, like the change in a dream,
Nottman drew back the lever and flung on the steam.

" The great wheels stagger'd and span with the strain,
While the spray from the steam fell around us like rain,
But we slacken'd our speed, till we saw with a wild
Throb at the heart, right before us—a child !

" It was lying asleep on the rail, with no fear
Of the terrible death that was looming so near ;
The sweat on us both broke as cold as the dew
Of death as we question'd—' What can we do ? '

" It was done—swift as acts that take place in a dream—
Nottman rushed to the front and knelt down on the beam,
Put one foot in the couplings ; the other he kept
Right in front of the wheel for the child that still slept.

I stood close behind him, and, standing could feel
Underneath the wild roar of the merciless wheel,
And I knew—and this thought made me catch at my breath,
That the very next moment would be life or death.

"'Saved!' I burst forth, my heart leaping with pride,
For one touch of the foot sent the child to the side,
But Nottman look'd up, his lips white as with foam,
'My God, Jack,' he cried, 'it's my own little Tom!'

"He shrunk, would have slipp'd, but one grasp of my
        hand
Held him firm till the engine was brought to a stand,
Then I heard from behind a shriek take to the air,
And I knew that the voice of a mother was there.

"The boy was all right, had got off with a scratch :
He had crept through the fence in his frolic to watch
For his father ; but, wearied with mischief and play,
Had fallen asleep on the rail where he lay.

"For days after that on our journey down,
Ere we came to the straight at the back of the town,
As if the signal were up with its gleam
Of red, Nottman always shut off the steam."

THE APOLLO BELVIDERE.

From "IN ROME."

BACK to the grand Apollo !   Tell me not
    A mortal had to do with this.   I know
    That if a god content him here below,
A mightier one must bind him to the spot.

Can this be genius that can so enthral,
    And lift us like a whirlwind till we feel
    The very heaven around us, and we reel
In the delight of worship?   Who can call
This splendid triumph stone?   Say rather we
    Behold a god who came to men, and met
His punishment in marble.   Yet he lives;
    While we, with all our throbbing being set,
Worship with the bold thought that it may be
    Idolatry that Heaven itself forgives.

J. LOGIE ROBERTSON.

("HUGH HALIBURTON.")

From "NORWEGIAN SONNETS."

I.

THE CLIMB FROM VALLË.

STEEP was the climb from Vallë : far below
  The sæter[1] we had left lay lost in mist,
  And still the height rose higher than we wist
Beyond the ravings of the Otteraa.[2]
And now a thin bleak air began to blow,
  And now the bispevei[3] to turn and twist,
  Here round a tjern[4] no summer ever kissed,
And there behind a hide of hoarded snow.
The stars dissolved anon ; and airy trills
  Of wavering music showed the day begun :
We toiled to meet the morn—o'er rocks, o'er rills ;
  And, breathless, but at last our wish we won—
The top ! and lo, a countless herd of hills
  Tossing their shining muzzles in the sun !

[1] Farm.
[2] Pronounced Ottero.
[3] Bridle-path.
[4] Mountain lake, tarn.

II.

"PAA HEJA:" LIFE ON THE HEIGHTS.

Is there a pleasure can with this compare ?—
    To leap at sunrise from your mountain-bed,
    Roused by a skylark revelling overhead,
And drink great draughts of golden morning air ;
A plunge, and breakfast—simple rural fare ;
    Then forth with vigorous brain, elastic tread,
    Hope singing at your heart o'er sorrow dead,
And strength for fifty miles, and still to spare !
That joy was ours !—O memory ! oft restore us
    Those autumn runs, here in the smoky town,
When through the woods our mad nomadic chorus
    Rang freedom up and civilisation down !
Io ! my hearts ! the world was all before us,
    And we nor owned nor envied king nor crown !

III.

THE MOUNTAIN LAUREATE.

MORNING is flashing from a glorious sun
    On the broad shoulders of the giant fells
    That outreach arms across the narrow dells
And form a silent brotherhood of one
Listening their skylark laureate !   New begun
    He up the heavens in ever-rising swells
    Carries their thanksgiving in song that wells
From his small breast as if 'twould ne'er be done.
What life his music gives them !   They are free
    In the wild freedom of his daring wing ;
And in the cataract of his song, the sea
    Of poetry that fills all heaven, they sing ;
—He is their poet-prophet in his glee,
    And in his work and worth their priest and king !

IV.

MORNING—THE MOUNTAIN FAMILY AT THEIR DEVOTIONS.

I SEE across the lofty table-lands
    A hundred regal mountains at the least
    Inclining mutely towards the opening East,—
As many little tjerns and queenly vands[1]
Kneeling at different levels : Phœbus stands
    Beaming benevolence like a great High Priest
    Blessing a nation for some holy feast
At his wide temple-door with lifted hands.—
Rejoice, ye hills ! ye happy mountains, fling
    Your arms aloft in worship wildly free !
Ye vands, and rivers in the valleys, sing !
    Shout ! till the heavens ring with your choral glee ;
And God Himself with mild face wondering
    Looks out at last, and smiles well-pleased to see !

———

From " HORACE IN HOMESPUN."

I.

HUGHIE'S ADVICE TO HIS BROTHER JOHN.

" *Omnes eodem cogimur.*"—CAR. II. 3.

DEAR Jock, ye're higher up the brae
    Than me, your aulder brither—
Keep mind the higher up ye gae
    The mair ye're in the weather.

[1] Lakes.

I'm no' misdootin' that ye're wice,
  An', for your ploo-share, speed it !
But I may better gi'e advice,
  An' ye may better need it.

The higher up the brae ye speel
  The farrer it's below ye,—
Tak' tent ye dinna gi'e the deil
  Occasion to dounthrow ye.
Be douce an' ceevil wi' success,
  For Fortune's no' to trust aye ;
Then if your head should tak' the gress
  Ye're whaur ye were at first aye.

An honest fa', wi' conscience clear,
  It never brak' a bane yet ;
There's aye the honest course to steer
  For a' that's come an' gane yet.
But letna lucre be your aim,
  Pursued thro' thick an' thin aye ;
The honour o' an honest name,
  That's what you first should win aye.

For happiness (to God be thanks !)
  Is no' the gift o' Fortun' ;
Wi' place the limmer plays her pranks,
  Wi' men like puppets sportin'—
Rich folk lookin' idly on
  At puir folk busy dargin'—
But happiness, my brither John,
  It wasna in the bargain.

The ups an' douns o' human life
  Are like a fairy revel;
But a' the warld, an' his wife,
  Maun lie at ae great level.
An' that's a thocht for me an' you
  When Fate's awards perplex us;
In calm eternity's wide view
  There's little that should vex us.

Fate's like the waves aneth the mune,
  An' we are vessels ridin';
It's doon an' up, an' up an' doon,
  An' here there's nae abidin';
But on the far horizon's edge,
  To which we're ever driftin',
The changes on oor pilgrimage
  Are but a paltry shiftin'.

II.

HUGHIE'S INDIGNATION AT THE CONDUCT OF THE ABSCONDING ELDER.

" *Mala soluta navis exit alite.*"—CAR. V. 10.

HE's aff the kintra at a spang!
  He's on the sea—they've tint him!
The warst o' weather wi' him gang!
  Gude weather bide ahint him!
O for a rattlin' bauld Scots blast
  To follow an' owretak' him—
To screed his sails, an' brak' his mast,
  An' grup his ship, an' shak' him.

Yet wha was less possessed wi' guile,
  Or prayed wi' readier unction?
He brocht the sweetness o' a smile
  To every public function.
There wasna ane had half the grace
  Or graciousness o' Peter ;
There wasna ane in a' the place
  For the millennium meeter.

He's fairly aff, he's stown awa',
  A wolf that wore a fleece, man !
He's cheated justice, jinkit law,
  An' lauch'd at the policeman.
The mission fund, the parish rate.
  He had the haill control o't ;
The very pennies i' the plate—
  He's skirtit wi' the whole o't !

It's juist a year—it's no' a year,
  I'm no' a hair the belder,
Since in the Session Chaumer here
  We made him rulin' elder.
An' juist a month as Feursday fell
  He gat the gold repeater,
That in a speech I made mysel
  We handit owre to Peter.

A bonnie lever, capp'd an' jew'ld,
  Perth never saw the mak' o't,
An' wi' his character in goold
  Engraven on the back o't.

He's aff !   IIe's aff wi' a' the spoil,
    Baith law and justice jinkit !
O for a wind o' winds the wale
    To chase his ship an' sink it !

To lift the watter like a fleece
    An' gie him sic a drookin',
Whaur on his growf he groans for grace
    But canna pray for pukin'.
Then wash'd owre seas upon a spar,
    Wi' seaweeds roun' the head o'm,
Let neither licht o' sun nor star
    Shine down upon the greed o'm !

But let a shark fra oonderneath,
    Its jaws wi' hunger tichtenin',
Soom round him, shawin' izzet teeth
    At every flash o' lichtnin' !
Till in the end the angry waves
    Transport him to a distance
To herd wi' wolves an' sterve in caves
    An' fecht for an existence !

III.

IIUGHIE REFUSES TO EMIGRATE.

> "*Ibi tu calentem
> Debita sparges lacrima favillam
>   Vatis amici.*"—CAR. II. 6.

MATTHIE, nae mair ! ye'se gang your lane !
    Tak' my best wishes wi' ye,
An' may guid fortun' owre the main
    An' snugly settled see ye !

I wuss ye weel ! the kintra's lairge,
  An' ye're but twa wi' Mary ;
Ye'll shortly hae the owner's chairge
  Nae doot o' half a prairie.
There's ample room in sic a park
  To foond a score o' nations,
An' flourish like a patriarch
  Amon' your generations.

But me may Scotland's bonnie hills
  Maintain to utmost auld age,
Leadin' my flocks by quiet rills,
  An' lingerin' thro' the gold age ;
Untemptit wi' a foreign gain
  That mak's ye merely laird o't,
An' thinkin' Scotland a' min' ain
  Tho' ownin' ne'er a yaird o't !

What hills are like the Ochil hills ?
  There's nane sae green, tho' grander ;
What rills are like the Ochil rills ?
  Nane, nane on earth that wander !
There Spring returns amon' the sleet,
  Ere Winter's tack be near thro' ;
There Spring an' Simmer fain wad meet
  To tarry a' the year thro' !

An' there in green Glendevon's shade
  A grave at last be found me,
Wi' daisies growin' at my head
  An' Devon lingerin' round me !
Nae stane disfigurement o' grief
  Wi' lang narration rise there ;

A line wad brawly serve, if brief,
    To tell the lave wha lies there.
But ony sculptur'd wecht o' stane
    Wad only overpow'r me ;
A shepherd, musin' there his lane,
    Were meeter bendin' owre me.

IV.

HUGHIE TAKES HIS EASE IN HIS INN.

*" Vates quid orat de patera novum
    Fundens liquorem."*—CAR. I. 31.

Noo, by my croon, the sun sends doun
    Uncommon drouthy weather,
But here's an inn—if it were sin
    We'll spill a dram thegither !
An' while we sit an' rest oor fit,
    Surveyin' man's dominion,
We'll tak' a glance at things that chance,
    An' freely pass opinion.

Yon stookit grain that dots the plain—
    We canna ca' a lead o't ;
The herd that strays on yonder braes—
    We canna claim a head o't.
It's no' in beeves an' baundit sheaves
    That we can coont oor wealth, Tam ;
Yet, nane the less, there's happiness
    To puir folk wi' their health, Tam.

There needs but sma' estate to ca'
    Awa' the wants that fear folk,
While mony wares bring mony cares
    That never trouble puir folk.

An' for the yield o' hill or field—
   It's little that we're spar'd o't,
But to the ee it's juist as free
   To hiz as him that's laird o't.

Gie knaves their wine—this drink be mine,
   Auld Scotland's native brewin'!
O' this bereft, there's watter left,
   Wi' that we'll e'en be doin'!
Gie fules their braws—they've aiblins cause
   To be sae finely wrappit;
The man that's in a healthy skin
   He's brawly if he's happit.

Gie him a horse wha wants the force
   To drive his ain shanks' naigie;
What can he ken o' wud or glen,
   Or mountain wild an' craigie?
Wad Fortun' grant me what I want
   I'd pray for health o' body,
A healthy mind to sang inclin'd,
   An' nae distaste for toddy!

v.

HUGHIE'S MONUMENT.

"*Non omnis moriar.*"—CAR. III. 30.

IN vain the future snaps his fangs,
The tyke may rage—he canna wrang's,
I put my haund upon my sangs
      Withoot a swither;
To me this monument belangs,
      I need nae ither.

It's no' in granite to endoor,
Sandstane comes ripplin' doon like stoor,
Marble—it canna stand the shoo'r,
    It lasts nae time;
There's naething yet has hauf the poo'r
    O' silly rhyme.

The pyramids hae tint their tale,
It's lang sin' they begoud to fail,
They're either murlin' doun to meal
    Or fog-enwrappit,
While Homer at this hoor's as hale
    As e'er he stappit.

Sae I may say't withoot a lee,
I dinna a'thegither dee;
Therefore forbear to greet for me
    When I'm awa',
An' keep a dry, a drouthie ee,
    I chairge ye a'.

When at my door the hearse draws up
An' Kate haunds roun' the dirgy-cup,
Nae friend o' mine will tak' a sup
    For that the less,
But calmly wi' a steady grup
    Cowp owre his gless.

The better pairt o' me remains!
Whaur Allan Watter weets the plains,
An' Devon, crystal but for rains,
    Gangs wanderin' wide,
Lang after me ye'll hear my strains
    On Ochilside.

VI.

HUGHIE'S WINTER EXCUSE FOR A DRAM.

·· Vides ut alta stet nive candidum
Soracte."—CAR. I. 9.

FRA whaur ye hing, my cauldrife frien',
  Your blue neb owre the lowe,
A snawy nichtcap may be seen
  Upon Benarty's pow;
An' snaw upon the auld gean stump,
  Whas' frostit branches hang
Oot-owre the dyke abune the pump
  That's gane clean aff the fang.
The pump that half the toun's folk ser'd,
  It winna gie a jaw,
An' rouch, I ken, sall be your beard
  Until there comes a thaw!

Come, reenge the ribs, an' let the heat
  Doun to oor tinglin' taes;
Clap on a gude Kinaskit peat
  An' let us see a blaze.
An' since o' watter we are scant
  Fess ben the barley-bree—
A nebfu' baith we sanna want
  To wet oor whistles wi'!
Noo let the winds o' Winter blaw
  Owre Scotland's hills an' plains,
It maitters nocht to us ava—
  We've simmer in oor veins!

The pooers o' Nature, wind an' snaw,
  Are far abune oor fit,
But while we scoog them, let them blaw ;
  We'll aye hae simmer yet.
An' sae wi' Fortune's blasts, my frien',—
  They'll come an' bide at will,
But we can scoog ahint a screen
  An' jook their fury still.
Then happy ilka day that comes,
  An' glorious ilka nicht ;
The present doesna fash oor thooms,
  The future needna fricht !

The future !—man, there's joys in store,
  An' joys ye little ken,
The warld has prov'd them sweet afore,
  The warld will again !
The lasses, min ! the dearest gift
  An' treasure time can gie—
Here's to the love that lichts the lift
  O' woman's witchin' ee !
An' vainly till that licht expire
  Should storm or winter low'r—
It's sune aneuch to seek the fire
  When simmer days are owre !

From "OCHIL IDYLLS."

AULD FERMER'S ADDRESS TO THE "PRODIGAL" SUN,

WHA CAM' HAME IN SEPTEMBER AFTER WEEL NEAR SAX MONTHS' ABSENCE.

SCENE—*The middle of a half-cut field—Auld Fermer in a sleeved waistcoat, liftin' the fa'en sheaves, an' biggin' the blawn stooks.*

Hoo daur ye blink upon the stooks
　That wadna shine upon the grain,
But left us to oorsel's for ooks,
　Or the waur company o' the rain?

We did oor pairt; we teel'd the laund,
　An' cuist oor corn into the yird;
We micht wi' profit held oor haund
　Wi' you, an' wi' your broken wird.

Noo that the sizzen's owre ye haste,
　Wi' fogs an' cranreuch i' your train,
Thinkin' to share the shearer's feast—
　Gae to the launds ye ca' your ain!

Swith to the launds that had your lauch,
　An' sorn on them for horn an' spune;
It's no' for you the fatted calf,
　It's a' for you the pair o' shoon!

Nae robe—as you may weel suppose ;
　Nor ring—’faith, that wad be a sham !
Unless I had it i’ your nose
　To lead ye back the gate ye cam’ !

We’ve managed in a kind o’ wey
　Withoot the favour o’ your face ;
We’ve raw’d oor neeps, an’ made oor hey,
　An’ towl’d amang the weet like beass !

Look whaur your wark negleckit lay,
　An’ meditate what micht hae been ;
But dinna think to mend the day
　By blinkin’ for an hoor at een !

Look on the weary-waitin’ craps
　That ne’er will come to hervest-hame—
On stookit strae wi’ scowther’d taps,
　An’ skeps that canna turn the beam.

We’ve dune withoot ye in a kind,
　We’ll dae withoot ye better yet ;
Whaur promises are no’ to mind,
　There disappointment’s no’ to get !

We’ll gang for girse an’ craps o’ green,
　An’ get oor laids o’ corn abroad ;
We’ll dae withoot ye, morn an’ e’en,
　Sae—ye may turn an’ tak’ the road !

THE TINKLERS.

THE mist lies like a plaid on plain,
The dyke-taps a’ are black wi’ rain,
A soakit head the clover hings,
On ilka puddle rise the rings.

Sair dings the rain upon the road,
It dings—an’ nae devallin’ o’t ;
Adoun the gutter rins a rill
Micht halflins ca’ a country mill.

The very roadman’s left the road :
The only kind o’ beas’ abroad
Are dyucks rejoicin’ i’ the flud,
An’ pyots clatterin’ i’ the wud.

On sic a day wha tak’s the gate ?
The cadger ? maybe ! but he’s late ;
The carrier ? na, he doesna flit
Unless D. P.—the deil permit !

On sic a day wha tak’s the gate ?
The tinkler an’ his towsie mate ;
He, foremost wi’ a nose o’ flint,
She, sour an’ sulky, yairds ahint.

A blanket frae her shouthers doun
Wraps her an’ a’ her bundles roun’ ;
A second rain rins aff the skirt ;
She skelps alang thro’ dub an’ dirt.

Her cheeks are red, her een are sma',
Her head wi' rain-draps beadit a';
The yellow hair, like wires o' bress,
Springs, thrivin' in the rain, like gress.

Her man an' maister stalks in front,
Silent mair than a tinkler's wont ;
His wife an' warkshop there ahint him—
This day he caresna if he tint them.

His haunds are in his pooches deep,
He snooves alang like ane in sleep,
His only movement's o' his legs,
He carries a' aboon like eggs.

Sma' wecht ! his skeleton an' skin,
An' a dour, heavy thocht within !
His claes, sae weel wi' weet they suit him,
They're like a second skin aboot him.

They're doun the road, they're oot o' sicht ;
They'll reach the howff by fa' o' nicht,
In Poussie Nancy's cowp the horn,
An' tak' the wanderin' gate the morn.

They'll gie their weasans there a weet,
Wi' kindred bodies there they'll meet,
Wi' drookit gangerels o' the clan,
The surgeons o' the pat an' pan.

Already on the rain-wash'd wa'
A darker gloom begins to fa' ;
Sooms frae the sicht the soakin' plain,—
It's closin' for a nicht o' rain.

HOBNOBBING ON THE OCHILS.

(A NOTE OF EXCUSE.)

Vide HOR., Car. III. 17.

GEORGE, son of lairds that awn'd the laund,
    Sin' Scotland was a nation—
And yet ye tak' a higher staund
    Than that o' generation:
What tho' your pedigree ye trace
    Frae maister an' frae madam?
The meanest figure wi' a face,
    He bude to come fra Adam.

George, worthy son o' honest folk!
    I canna rank ye high'r—
I spend this nicht at aucht o'clock
    Beside my ain peat fire.
The mune, sair burden'd wi' a broch,
    Shaws nouther face nor form;
And there's a moanin' aff the loch
    That bodes the comin' storm.

Gie Borlan' Jock, the cadger loon,
    An' poacher tho' he is,
As he gangs drookit by your toon,
    A dram for bringin' this:
An' for oorsel's—we'll play the joke
    We've play'd sae aften noo:
Drink up to me at aucht o'clock,
    And I'll drink doun to you!

QUEM TU, MELPOMENE.

HOR., Car. IV. 3.

WHAM at his birth wi' mournfu' smile
  The Muse has ance regairdet,
Shall ne'er in field o' battle toil
  To be with bays rewairdet.

Yet shall he haunt, a lanely ghost,
  The placid battle plain—
To mourn the lives that there were lost,
  The loves that there were slain.

Hoo caulder for thae stricken lives
  Maun mony a hearth hae been;
Hoo blank to mony bairns an' wives
  The social hoor at e'en!

Nae hunter on the heather hills
  Bird-slaughterin' shall he be,
Nor fisher rivin' fra the gills
  O' some puir troot his flee.

Yet shall he love the dusky pools
  And speel the mountain stairs,
Unburdened wi' the murderin' tools
  O' guns an' gauds an' snares,—

O'erjoy'd to find attractions rife
  In Nature's ilka feature,
And share the brotherhood of life
  With every happy creature.

Oh, what avails a victor's name
   At close of battle clangour ?
This warld is far owre sma' for fame,
   And life owre short for anger.

TO THE LAIRD.

"*Mea nec Falernæ
Temperant vites neque Formiani
Pocula colles.*"—HOR., Car. I. 20.

DEAR Laird, ye're comin' up the brae
   As lang's gude weather haulds ?
Ye're surely welcome to a day
   Amang your ain sheep-faulds.

If caller air, an' caperin' lamb,
   An' knowes o' noddin' green,
Wi' noo an' then a social dram
   Or twa-haund crack atween ;

The food whar'on your fathers fared
   A girdle scone an' cheese—
Ye're freely welcome to them, laird,
   If thae hae power to please ;

But if your craig maun hae its waucht
   O' wines I canna name,—
They're no' within a shepherd's aucht :
   Ye'd better bide at hame.

SPRING ON THE OCHILS.

> "*Audire et videor pios*
> *Errare per lucos, amœnæ*
> *Quos et aquæ subeunt et auræ.*"
>
> — HOR., Car. III. 4.

I.

FRA whaur in fragrant wuds ye bide
   Secure fra winter care,
Come, gentle Spring, to Ochilside
   And Ochil valleys fair.
For sweet as ony pagan spring
   Are Devon's watters clear;
And life wad be a lovely thing
   Gif ye were only here.

II.

She comes! the waffin' o' her wings
   Wi' music fills the air;
An' wintry thochts o' men an' things
   Vex human hearts nae mair.
On Devon banks wi' me she strays,
   Her poet for the while,
And Ochil brooks and Ochil braes
   Grow classic in her smile!

—————

THE HIND'S DANCE.

*" Gaudet invisam pepulisse fossor
    Ter pede terram."*—HOR., Car. III. 18.

Now Jocky's freed !   The bands are broke
That tied him to the hated yoke ;
Rejoicing in his freedom found,
With heavy heel he hits the ground.   .

In thraldom to the red earth bound,
Sweet Jocky's griefs were of the ground ;
Now, bondsman with a broken chain,
He leaps upon his tyrant slain.

Leeze me on simmer !—but she brings
A heavy load of hempen strings ;
She ties sweet Jocky to the wark
Fra morning dim till gloaming dark.

His haunds are hard, his banes are sair ;
Wi' but the gift o' caller air,
He plants his feet in many a soil,
He leaves in many a clod his toil.

But noo nae mair he'll drag his feet ;
The labour o' the year's complete :
Now beat the stibble-laund wi' glee,
And fling aloft with fetlock free !

On loft with rural joy he jumps,
He beats the ground with triple thumps !
The lingering vigour of his legs
He leaves upon the hated rigs !

Now heap the hearth with peats an' whins ;
And, Jocky, rest and roast your shins,—
Till Candlemas with blustering shout
Cry Jocky and his oxen out !

———

A WINTER VIEW.

I.

THE rime lies cauld on ferm an' fauld,
   The lift's a drumlie grey ;
The hill-taps a' are white wi' snaw,
   An' dull an' dour's the day.
The canny sheep thegither creep,
   The govin' cattle glower ;
The plooman staunds to chap his haunds
   An' wuss the storm were ower.

II.

But ance the snaw's begoud to fa'
   The cauld's no' near sae sair :
'Neth stingin' drift oor herts we lift
   The winter's warst to dare.
Wi' frost an' cauld we battle bauld,
   Nor fear a passin' fa',
But warstle up wi' warmer grup
   O' life, an' hope, an' a'.

III.

An' sae, my frien', when to oor een
　Oor warldly ills appear
In prospect mair than we can bear,
　An outlook cauld and drear ;
Let's bear in mind—an' this, ye'll find,
　Has heartened not a few—
When ance we're in the battle's din
　We'll find we're half gate thro'.

AN OCHIL FARMER.

ABUNE the braes I see him stand,
The tapmost corner o' his land,
An' scan wi' care, owre hill an' plain,
A prospect he may ca' his ain.

His yowes ayont the hillocks feed,
Weel herdit in by wakefu' Tweed ;
An' canny thro' the bent his kye
Gang creepin' to the byre doun-by.

His hayfields lie fu' smoothly shorn,
An' ripenin' rise his rigs o' corn ;
A simmer's evenin' glory fa's
Upon his hamestead's sober wa's.

A stately figure there he stands
An' rests upon his staff his hands :
Maist like some patriarch of eld,
In sic an evenin's calm beheld.

A farmer he of Ochilside,
For worth respectit far an' wide;
A friend of justice and of truth,
A favourite wi' age an' youth.

There's no' a bairn but kens him weel,
And ilka collie's at his heel;
Nor beast nor body e'er had ocht
To wyte him wi', in deed or thocht.

Fu' mony a gloamin' may he stand
Abune the brae to bless the land!
Fu' mony a simmer rise an' fa'
In beauty owre his couthie ha'!

For peacefu' aye, as simmer's air,
The kindly hearts that kindle there;
Whase friendship, sure an' aye the same,
For me mak's Ochilside a hame.

DAVE (*sc. Daphnis*).

" *Ton Mosais philon andra, ton ou Numphaisin
apechthe.*"

WITH the smell of the meads in his plaiden dress,
He comes from the broomy wilderness.

The dewdrop burns in his bushy hair,
His forehead shines, and is free from care.

He looks round-orb'd thro' the blue of his eyes,
With the fearless fulness of summer skies.

The red that breaks on the brown of his cheek,
Is the russet apple's ripen'd streak.

White as the milk of nuts are his teeth,
And crisp and black is his beard beneath.

What can he show to the strife of towns ?
A vision of peace on the distant downs.

Green hollows and hillocks, and skies of blue,
And white sheep feeding the long day thro'.

The apples are ruddy, the nuts are ripe,
By every pool there grows a pipe.

How can he touch the world's dull'd ear ?
What can he play that the world will hear ?

His pipe is slender, and softly blown,
The music sinks ever in undertone.

Yet sweet to hear of an autumn night,
When the sheaves on the shorn rigs glimmer white,

It sounds in the dusk like the joy of a star,
When the lattice of heaven is left ajar,

To clasping lovers that thread the threaves
Like a shadow moving among the sheaves.

ROBERT LOUIS STEVENSON.

THE HOUSE BEAUTIFUL.

A naked house, a naked moor,
A shivering pool before the door,
A garden bare of flowers and fruit
And poplars at the garden foot:
Such is the place that I live in,
Bleak without and bare within.

Yet shall your ragged moor receive
The incomparable pomp of eve,
And the cold glories of the dawn
Behind your shivering trees be drawn ;
And when the wind from place to place
Doth the unmoored cloud-galleons chase,
Your garden gloom and gleam again,
With leaping sun, with glancing rain.
Here shall the wizard moon ascend
The heavens, in the crimson end
Of day's declining splendour ; here
The army of the stars appear.
The neighbour hollows dry or wet,
Spring shall with tender flowers beset ;
And oft the morning muser see
Larks rising from the broomy lea,
And every fairy wheel and thread
Of cobweb dew-bediamonded.

When daisies go, shall winter time
Silver the simple grass with rime;
Autumnal frosts enchant the pool
And make the cart-ruts beautiful;
And when snow-bright the moor expands,
How shall your children clap their hands!
To make this earth, our hermitage,
A cheerful and a changeful page,
God's bright and intricate device
Of days and seasons doth suffice.

REQUIEM.

UNDER the wide and starry sky,
Dig the grave and let me lie.
Glad did I live and gladly die,
   And I laid me down with a will.
This be the verse you grave for me:
Here he lies where he longed to be;
Home is the sailor, home from sea,
   And the hunter home from the hill.

OUR LADY OF THE SNOWS.

OUT of the sun, out of the blast,
Out of the world, alone I passed
Across the moor and through the wood
To where the monastery stood.
There neither lute nor breathing fife,
Nor rumour of the world of life,

Nor confidences low and dear,
Shall strike the meditative ear.
Aloof, unhelpful, and unkind,
The prisoners of the iron mind,
Where nothing speaks except the bell
The unfraternal brothers dwell.

Poor passionate men, still clothed afresh
With agonising folds of flesh ;
Whom the clear eyes solicit still
To some bold output of the will,
While fairy Fancy far before
And musing Memory-Hold-the-door
Now to heroic death invite
And now uncurtain fresh delight :
O, little boots it thus to dwell
On the remote unneighboured hill !

O to be up and doing, O
Unfearing and unshamed to go
In all the uproar and the press
About my human business !
My undissuaded heart I hear
Whisper courage in my ear.
With voiceless calls, the ancient earth
Summons me to a daily birth.
Thou, O my love, ye, O my friends—
The gist of life, the end of ends—
To laugh, to love, to live, to die,
Ye call me by the ear and eye !

Forth from the casemate, on the plain
Where honour has the world to gain,

Pour forth and bravely do your part,
O knights of the unshielded heart !
Forth and forever forward !—out
From prudent turret and redoubt,
And in the mellay charge amain,
To fall but yet to rise again !
Captive ? ah, still, to honour bright,
A captive soldier of the right !
Or free and fighting, good with ill ?
Unconquering but unconquered still !

And ye, O brethren, what if God,
When from Heav'n's top he spies abroad,
And sees on this tormented stage
The noble war of mankind rage :
What if his vivifying eye,
O monks, should pass your corner by ?
For still the Lord is Lord of might ;
In deeds, in deeds, he takes delight ;
The plough, the spear, the laden barks,
The field, the founded city, marks ;
He marks the smiler of the streets,
The singer upon garden seats ;
He sees the climber in the rocks :
To him, the shepherd folds his flocks.
For those he loves that underprop
With daily virtues Heaven's top,
And bear the falling sky with ease,
Unfrowning caryatides.
Those he approves that ply the trade,
That rock the child, that wed the maid,
That with weak virtues, weaker hands,
Sow gladness on the peopled lands,
And still with laughter, song and shout,
Spin the great wheel of earth about.

But ye ?—O ye who linger still
Here in your fortress on the hill,
With placid face, with tranquil breath,
The unsought volunteers of death,
Our cheerful General on high
With careless looks may pass you by.

A LOWDEN SABBATH MORN.

THE clinkum-clank o' Sabbath bells
Noo to the hoastin' rookery swells,
Noo faintin' laigh in shady dells,
        Sounds far an' near,
An' through the simmer kintry tells
        Its tale o' cheer.

An' noo, to that melodious play,
A' deidly awn the quiet sway—
A' ken their solemn holiday,
        Bestial an' human,
The singin' lintie on the brae,
        The restin' plou'man.

He, mair than a' the lave o' men,
His week completit joys to ken;
Half-dressed, he daunders out an' in,
        Perplext wi' leisure;
An' his raxt limbs he'll rax again
        Wi' painfu' pleesure.

The steerin' mither strang afit
Noo shoos the bairnies but a bit ;
Noo cries them ben, their Sinday shüit
    To scart upon them,
Or sweeties in their pouch to pit,
    Wi' blessin's on them.

The lasses, clean frae tap to taes,
Are busked in crunklin' underclaes ;
The gartened hose, the weel-filled stays,
    The nakit shift,
A' bleached on bonny greens for days,
    An' white's the drift.

An' noo to face the kirkward mile :
The guidman's hat o' dacent style,
The blackit shoon, we noo maun fyle
    As white's the miller :
A waefü' peety tae, to spile
    The warth o' siller.

Our Marg'et, aye sae keen to crack,
Douce-stappin' in the stoury track,
Her emeralt goun a' kiltit back
    Frae snawy coats,
White-ankled, leads the kirkward pack
    Wi' Dauvit Groats.

A' thocht ahint, in runkled breeks,
A' spiled wi' lyin' by for weeks,
The guidman follows closs, an' cleiks
    The sonsie missis ;
His sarious face at aince bespeaks
    The day that this is.

And aye an' while we nearer draw
To whaur the kirkton lies alaw,
Mair neebours, comin' saft an' slaw
    Frae here an' there,
The thicker thrang the gate an' caw
    The stour in air.

But hark ! the bells frae nearer clang ;
To rowst the slaw, their sides they bang ;
An' see ! black coats a'ready thrang
    The green kirkyaird ;
And at the yett, the chestnuts spang
    That brocht the laird.

The solemn elders at the plate
Stand drinkin' deep the pride o' state :
The practised hands as gash an' great
    As Lords o' Session ;
The later named, a wee thing blate
    In their expression.

The prentit stanes that mark the deid,
Wi' lengthened lip, the sarious read ;
Syne wag a moraleesin' heid,
    An' then an' there
Their hirplin' practice an' their creed
    Try hard to square.

It's here our Merren lang has lain,
A wee bewast the table-stane ;
An' yon's the grave o' Sandy Blane ;
    An' further ower,
The mither's brithers, dacent men !
    Lie a' the fower.

Here the guidman sall bide awee
To dwall amang the deid; to see
Auld faces clear in fancy's e'e;
    Belike to hear
Auld voices fa'in saft an' slee
    On fancy's ear.

Thus, on the day o' solemn things,
The bell that in the steeple swings
To fauld a scaittered faim'ly rings
    Its walcome screed;
An' just a wee thing nearer brings
    The quick an' deid.

But noo the bell is ringin' in;
To tak' their places, folk begin;
The minister himsel' will shiine
    Be up the gate,
Filled fu' wi' clavers about sin
    An' man's estate.

The tiines are up—*French*, to be shiire,
The faithfii' *French*, an' twa-three mair;
The auld prezentor, hoastin' sair,
    Wales out the portions,
An' yirks the tiine into the air
    Wi' queer contortions.

Follows the prayer, the readin' next,
An' than the fisslin' for the text—
The twa-three last to find it, vext
    But kind o' proud;
An' than the peppermints are raxed,
    An' southernwood.

For noo's the time whan pows are seen
Nid-noddin' like a mandareen;
When tenty mithers stap a preen
          In sleepin' weans;
An' nearly half the parochine
          Forget their pains.

There's just a waukrif' twa or three:
Thrawn commentautors sweer to 'gree,
Weans glowrin' at the bumlin' bee
          On windie-glasses,
Or lads that tak a keek a-glee
          At sonsie lasses.

Himsel', meanwhile, frae whaur he cocks
An' bobs belaw the soundin'-box,
The treesures of his words unlocks
          Wi' prodigality,
An' deals some unco dingin' knocks
          To infidality.

Wi' sappy unction, hoo he burkes
The hopes o' men that trust in works,
Expounds the fau'ts o' ither kirks,
          An' shaws the best o' them
No muckle better than mere Turks,
          When a's confessed o' them.

Bethankit! what a bonny creed!
What mair would ony Christian need?—
The braw words rumm'le ower his heid,
          Nor steer the sleeper;
And in their restin' graves, the deid
          Sleep aye the deeper.

"IT'S AN OWERCOME SOOTH."

IT'S an owercome sooth for age an' youth
   And it brooks wi' nae denial,
That the dearest friends are the auldest friends
   And the young are just on trial.

There's a rival bauld wi' young an' auld
   And it's him that has bereft me;
For the sürest friends are the auldest friends
   And the maist o' mines hae left me.

There are kind hearts still, for friends to fill
   And fools to take and break them;
But the nearest friends are the auldest friends
   And the grave's the place to seek them.

———

From "A CHILD'S GARDEN OF VERSES."

I.

PIRATE STORY.

THREE of us afloat in the meadow by the swing,
   Three of us aboard in the basket on the lea.
Winds are in the air, they are blowing in the spring,
   And waves are on the meadow like the waves there are
      at sea.

Where shall we adventure, to-day that we're afloat,
　Wary of the weather and steering by a star?
Shall it be to Africa, a-steering of the boat,
　To Providence, or Babylon, or off to Malabar?

Hi! but here's a squadron a-rowing on the sea—
　Cattle on the meadow a-charging with a roar!
Quick, and we'll escape them, they're as mad as they
　　　can be,
　The wicket is the harbour and the garden is the shore.

II.

MY BED IS A BOAT.

My bed is like a little boat;
　Nurse helps me in when I embark;
She girds me in my sailor's coat
　And starts me in the dark.

At night, I go on board and say
　Good-night to all my friends on shore;
I shut my eyes and sail away
　And see and hear no more.

And sometimes things to bed I take,
　As prudent sailors have to do:
Perhaps a slice of wedding-cake,
　Perhaps a toy or two.

All night across the dark we steer:
　But when the day returns at last,
Safe in my room, beside the pier,
　I find my vessel fast.

III.

NORTH-WEST PASSAGE.

1. Good Night.

WHEN the bright lamp is carried in,
The sunless hours again begin ;
O'er all without, in field and lane,
The haunted night returns again.

Now we behold the embers flee
About the firelit hearth ; and see
Our faces painted as we pass,
Like pictures, on the window-glass.

Must we to bed indeed ? Well then,
Let us arise and go like men,
And face with an undaunted tread
The long black passage up to bed.

Farewell, O brother, sister, sire !
O pleasant party round the fire !
The songs you sing, the tales you tell,
Till far to-morrow, fare ye well !

2. Shadow March.

ALL round the house is the jet-black night ;
  It stares through the window-pane ;
It crawls in the corners, hiding from the light,
  And it moves with the moving flame.

Now my little heart goes a-beating like a drum,
    With the breath of the Bogie in my hair;
And all round the candle the crooked shadows come
    And go marching along up the stair.

The shadow of the balusters, the shadow of the lamp,
    The shadow of the child that goes to bed—
All the wicked shadows coming, tramp, tramp, tramp,
    With the black night overhead.

3. IN PORT.

LAST, to the chamber where I lie
My fearful footsteps patter nigh,
And come from out the cold and gloom
Into my warm and cheerful room.

There, safe arrived, we turn about
To keep the coming shadows out,
And close the happy door at last
On all the perils that we past.

Then, when mamma goes by to bed,
She shall come in with tip-toe tread,
And see me lying warm and fast
And in the Land of Nod at last.

IV.

THE UNSEEN PLAYMATE.

WHEN children are playing alone on the green,
In comes the playmate that never was seen.
When children are happy and lonely and good,
The Friend of the Children comes out of the wood.

Nobody heard him and nobody saw,
His is a picture you never could draw,
But he's sure to be present, abroad or at home,
When children are happy and playing alone.

He lies in the laurels, he runs on the grass,
He sings when you tinkle the musical glass;
Whene'er you are happy and cannot tell why,
The Friend of the Children is sure to be by!

He loves to be little, he hates to be big,
'Tis he that inhabits the caves that you dig;
'Tis he when you play with your soldiers of tin
That sides with the Frenchmen and never can win.

'Tis he, when at night you go off to your bed,
Bids you go to your sleep and not trouble your head;
For wherever they're lying, in cupboard or shelf,
'Tis he will take care of your playthings himself!

V.

MY KINGDOM.

Down by a shining water well
I found a very little dell,
　　No higher than my head.
The heather and the gorse about
In summer bloom were coming out,
　　Some yellow and some red.

I called the little pool a sea;
The little hills were big to me;
　　For I am very small.
I made a boat, I made a town,
I searched the caverns up and down,
　　And named them one and all.

And all about was mine, I said,
The little sparrows overhead,
    The little minnows too.
This was the world and I was king ;
For me the bees came by to sing,
    For me the swallows flew.

I played there were no deeper seas,
Nor any wider plains than these,
    Nor other kings than me.
At last I heard my mother call
Out from the house at evenfall,
    To call me home to tea.

And I must rise and leave my dell,
And leave my dimpled water well,
    And leave my heather blooms.
Alas ! and as my home I neared,
How very big my nurse appeared,
    How great and cool the rooms !

CHRISTMAS AT SEA.

The sheets were frozen hard, and they cut the naked
    hand ;
The decks were like a slide, where a seaman scarce could
    stand ;
The wind was a nor'wester, blowing squally off the sea ;
And cliffs and spouting breakers were the only things
    a-lee.

They heard the surf a-roaring before the break of day;
But 'twas only with the peep of light we saw how ill we
    lay.
We tumbled every hand on deck instanter, with a shout,
And we gave her the maintops'l, and stood by to go
    about.

All day we tacked and tacked between the South Head
    and the North;
All day we hauled the frozen sheets, and got no further
    forth;
All day as cold as charity, in bitter pain and dread,
For very life and nature we tacked from head to head.

We gave the South a wider berth, for there the tide-race
    roared;
But every tack we made we brought the North Head
    close aboard:
So's we saw the cliffs and houses, and the breakers
    running high,
And the coastguard in his garden, with his glass against
    his eye.

The frost was on the village roofs as white as ocean foam;
The good red fires were burning bright in every 'long-
    shore home;
The windows sparkled clear, and the chimneys volleyed
    out;
And I vow we sniffed the victuals as the vessel went
    about.

The bells upon the church were rung with a mighty jovial
    cheer;
For it's just that I should tell you how (of all days in the
    year)

This day of our adversity was blessèd Christmas morn,
And the house above the coastguard's was the house
    where I was born.

O well I saw the pleasant room, the pleasant faces there,
My mother's silver spectacles, my father's silver hair ;
And well I saw the firelight, like a flight of homely elves,
Go dancing round the china-plates that stand upon the
    shelves.

And well I knew the talk they had, the talk that was of
    me,
Of the shadow on the household and the son that went
    to sea ;
And O the wicked fool I seemed, in every kind of way,
To be here and hauling frozen ropes on blessèd Christmas
    Day.

They lit the high sea-light, and the dark began to fall.
" All hands to loose topgallant sails," I heard the captain
    call.
" By the Lord, she'll never stand it," our first mate,
    Jackson, cried.
. . . " It's the one way or the other, Mr. Jackson," he
    replied.

She staggered to her bearings, but the sails were new
    and good,
And the ship smelt up to windward just as though she
    understood.
As the winter's day was ending, in the entry of the night,
We cleared the weary headland, and passed below the
    light.

And they heaved a mighty breath, every soul on board
but me,
As they saw her nose again pointing handsome out to
sea ;
But all that I could think of, in the darkness and the
cold,
Was just that I was leaving home and my folks were
growing old.

WILLIAM SHARP.

From "ROMANTIC BALLADS."

THE WEIRD OF MICHAEL SCOTT.

PART III.

ALL day the curlew wailed and screamed,
All day the cushat crooned and dreamed,
All day the sweet muir-wind blew free :
Beyond the grassy knowes far gleamed
The splendour of the singing sea.

Above the myriad gorse and broom
And miles of golden kingcup-bloom
The larks and yellowhammers sang :
Where the scaur cast an hour-long gloom
The lintie's falling notes out-rang.

Oft as he wandered to and fro—
As idly as the foam-bells flow
Hither and thither on the deep—
Michael the Wizard's face would grow
From death to life, and he would weep—

Weep, weep hot tears of bitter pain
For what might never be again :
Yet even as he wept his face
Would gleam with mockery insane.
With laughter fierce on would he race,

Screaming a wild and savage cry,
Till awed to silence by the sky
Unfathomable, vast, serene :
Then would he wayfare silently
With hush'd and furtive mien.

At times he watch'd the white clouds sail
Across the wastes of azure pale ;
Or oft would haunt some moorland pool
Fringed round with thyme and fragrant gale
And canna-tufts of snow-white wool.

Long in its depths would Michael stare,
As though some secret thing lay there :
Mayhap the moving water made
A gloom where crouched a Kelpie fair
With death-eyes gleaming through the shade.

Then on with weary listless feet
He fared afar, until the sweet
Cool sound of mountain brooks drew nigh,
And loud he heard the strayed lambs bleat
And the white ewes responsive cry.

High up among the hills full clear
He heard the belling[1] of the deer
Amid the corries where they browsed,
And, where the peaks rose gaunt and sheer,
Fierce swirling echoes eagle-roused.

He watched the kestrel wheel and sweep,
He watched the dun fox glide and creep,
He heard the whaup's long-echoing call,
Watched in the stream the brown trout leap
And the grilse spring the waterfall.

[1] Noise of a roe in rutting time.

Along the slopes the grouse-cock whirred ;
The grey-blue heron scarcely stirred
Amid the mossed grey tarn-side stones :
The burns gurg-gurgled through the yird
Their sweet clear bubbling undertones.

Above the tarn the dragon-fly
Shot like a flashing arrow by ;
Vague in a moving shifting haze
The gnat-clouds sank or soared on high
And danced their wild aërial maze.

As the day waned he heard afar
The hawking fern-owl's dissonant jar
Disturb the silence of the hill :
The gloaming came : star after star
He watched the skiey spaces fill.

But as the darkness grew and made
Forest and mountain one vast shade,
Michael the Wizard moaned in dread—
A long white moonbeam like a blade
Swept after him where'er he fled.

Swiftly he leapt o'er rock and root,
Swift o'er the fern his flying foot,
But swifter still the white moonbeam :
Wild was the grey-owl's dismal hoot,
But wilder still his maniac scream.

Once in his flight he paused to hear
A hollow shriek that echoed near :—
The louder were his dreadful cries,
The louder rang adown the sheer
Gaunt cliffs the echoing replies.

As though a hunted wolf, he raced
To the lone woods across the waste
Steep granite slopes of Crammond-Low—
The haunted forest where none faced
The terror that no man might know.

Betwixt the mountains and the sea
Dark leagues of pine stood solemnly,
Voiceful with grim and hollow song,
Save when each tempest-stricken tree
A savage tumult would prolong.

Beneath the dark funereal plumes,
Slow waving to and fro—death-blooms
Within the void dim wood of death—
Oft shuddering at the fearful glooms
Sped Michael Scott with failing breath.

Once, as he passed a dreary place,
Between two trees he saw a face—
A white face staring at his own :
A weird strange cry he gave for grace,
And heard an echoing moan.

" Whate'er you be, O thing that hides
Among the trees—O thing that bides
In yonder moving mass o' shade
Come forth tae me ! "—wan Michael glides
Swift, as he speaks, athwart the glade :

" Whate'er you be, I fear ye nought !
Michael the Wizard has na fought
Wi' men and demons year by year
To shirk ae thing he has na sought
Or blanch wi' any mortal fear ! "

But not a sound thrilled thro' the air—
Not even a she-fox in her lair
Or brooding bird made any stir—
All was as still and blank and bare
As is a vaulted sepulchre.

Then awe, and fear, and wild dismay
O'ercame mad Michael, ashy grey,
With eyes as of one newly dead :
" If wi' my sword I canna slay,
Thou'lt dree thy weird when it is said !

" Whate'er you be, man, beast, or sprite,
I wind ye round wi' a sheet o' light—
Aye, round and round your burning frame
I cast by spell o' wizard might
A fierce undying sheet of flame ! "

Swift as he spoke a thing sprang out,
A man-like thing, all hemmed about
With blazing blasting burning fire !
The wind swoop'd wi' a demon-shout
And whirled the red flame higher and higher !

And as, appalled, wan Michael stood
The flying flaughts swift fired the wood ;
And even as he shook and stared
The gaunt pines turned the hue of blood
And all the waving branches flared.

Then with wild leaps the accursëd thing
Drew ever nigher : with a spring
Michael escaped its fiery clasp,
Although he felt the fierce flame sting
And all the horror of its grasp.

Swift as an arrow far he fled,
But swifter still the flames o'erhead
Rushed o'er the waving sea of pines,
And hollow noises crashed and sped
Like splitting blasts in ruin'd mines.

A burning league—leagues, leagues of fire
Arose behind, and ever higher
The flying semi-circle came :
And aye beyond this dreadful pyre
There leapt a man-like thing in flame.

With awful scream doom'd Michael saw
The flying furnace reach Black-Law :
" ' *Blood, bride, and bier,' the auld rune saith,*
Hell's wind tae me ae nicht sall blaw,
The nicht I ride unto my death !

" *The blood of Stair is round me now :*
My bride can laugh to scorn my vow :
My bier, my bier, ah sall it be
Wi' a crown o' fire around my brow
Or deep within the cauld saut sea !"

Like lightning, over Black-Law's slope
Michael fled swift with sudden hope :
What though the forest roared behind—
He yet might gain the cliff and grope
For where the sheep-paths twist and wind.

The air was like a furnace-blast
And all the dome of heaven one vast
Expanse of flame and fiery wings :
To the cliff's edge, ere all be past,
With shriek on shriek lost Michael springs.

But none can hear his bitter call,
None, none can see him sway and fall—
Yea, one there is that shrills his name !
" O God, it is my ain lost saul
That I hae girt wi' deathless flame !"

With waving arms and dreadful cries
He cowers beneath those glaring eyes—
But all in vain—in vain—in vain !
His own soul clasps him as its prize
And scorches death upon his brain.

Body and soul together swing
Adown the night until they fling
The hissing sea-spray far and wide :
At morn the fresh sea-wind will bring
A black corpse tossing on the tide.

THE DEATH-CHILD.

SHE sits beneath the elder-tree
And sings her song so sweet,
And dreams o'er the burn that darksomely
Runs by her moonwhite feet.

Her hair is dark as starless night,
Her flower-crown'd face is pale,
But O her eyes are lit with light
Of dread ancestral bale.

She sings an eerie song, so wild
With immemorial dule—
Though young and fair Death's mortal child
That sits by that dark pool.

And oft she cries an eldritch scream
When red with human blood
The burn becómes a crimson stream,
A wild, red, surging flood :

Or shrinks, when some swift tide of tears—
The weeping of the world—
Dark eddying 'neath man's phantom-fears
Is o'er the red stream hurl'd.

For hours beneath the elder-tree
She broods beside the stream ;
Her dark eyes filled with mystery,
Her dark soul rapt in dream.

The lapsing flow she heedeth not
Through deepest depths she scans :
Life is the shade that clouds her thought,
As Death's the eclipse of man's.

Time seems but as a bitter thing
Remember'd from of yore :
Yet ah (she thinks) her song she'll sing
When Time's long reign is o'er.

Erstwhiles she bends alow to hear
What the swift water sings,
The torrent running darkly clear
With secrets of all things.

And then she smiles a strange sad smile
And lets her harp lie long ;
The death-waves oft may rise the while,
She greets them with no song.

Few ever cross that dreary moor,
Few see that flower-crown'd head ;
But whoso knows that wild song's lure
Knoweth that he is dead.

From "Sospiri di Roma."

I.

HIGH NOON AT MIDSUMMER ON THE CAMPAGNA.

High noon,
And from the purple-veilèd hills
To where Rome lies in azure mist,
Scarce any breath of wind
Upon this vast and solitary waste,
These leagues of sunscorch'd grass
Where i' the dawn the scrambling goats maintain
A hardy feast,
And where, when the warm yellow moonlight floods the
　　flats,
Gaunt laggard sheep browse spectrally for hours,
While not less gaunt and spectral shepherds stand
Brooding, or with hollow vacant eyes
Stare down the long perspectives of the dusk.
Now not a breath :
No sound ;
No living thing,

Save where the beetle jars his bristling shards,
Or where the hoarse cicala fills
The heavy heated hour with palpitant whirr.
Yet hark !
Comes not a low deep whisper from the ground,
A sigh as though the immemorial past
Breathed here a long, slow, breath?
Lost nations sleep below ; an empire here
Is dust ; and deeper, deeper still,
Dim shadowy peoples are the mould that warms
The roots of every flower that blooms and blows :
Even as we, too, bloom and fade,
Frail human flowers, who are so bitter fain
To be as the wind that bloweth evermore,
To be as this dread waste that shroudeth all
In garments green of grass and wilding sprays,
To be as the Night that dies not, but forever
Weaves her immortal web of starry fires ;
To be as Time itself,
Time, whose vast holocausts
Lie here, deep buried from the ken of men,
Here, where no breath of wind
Ruffles the brooding heat,
The breathless blazing heat
Of Noon.

II.

RED POPPIES.

(In the Sabine valleys near Rome.)

THROUGH the seeding grass,
And the tall corn,
The wind goes :
With nimble feet,
And blithe voice,

Calling, calling,
The wind goes
Through the seeding grass,
And the tall corn.

What calleth the wind,
Passing by—
The shepherd-wind?
Far and near
He laugheth low,
And the red poppies
Lift their heads
And toss i' the sun.
A thousand thousand blooms
Tost i' the air,
Banners of joy,
For 'tis the shepherd-wind
Passing by,
Singing and laughing low
Through the seeding grass
And the tall corn.

III.

THE WILD MARE.

(In Maremma.)

LIKE a breath that comes and goes
O'er the waveless waste
Of sleeping Ocean,
So sweeps across the plain
The herd of wild horses.
Like banners in the wind
Their flying tails,
Their streaming manes:

And like spume of the sea
Fang'd by breakers,
The white froth tossed from their blood-red nostrils.
Out from the midst of them
Dasheth a white mare,
White as a swan in the pride of her beauty :
And, like the whirlwind,
Following after,
A snorting stallion,
Swart as an Indian
Diver of coral !
Wild the gyrations,
The rush and the whirl ;
Loud the hot panting
Of the snow-white mare,
As swift upon her
The stallion gaineth :
Fierce the proud snorting
Of him, victorious :
And loud, swelling loud on the wind from the mountains,
The hoarse savage tumult of neighing and stamping
Where, wheeling, the herd of wild horses awaiteth—
Ears thrown back, tails thrashing their flanks or swept
    under—
The challenging scream of the conqueror-stallion.

IV.

THE WHITE PEACOCK.

HERE where the sunlight
Floodeth the garden,
Where the pomegranate
Reareth its glory
Of gorgeous blossom ;
Where the oleanders

Dream through the noontides ;
And, like surf o' the sea
Round cliffs of basalt,
The thick magnolias
In billowy masses
Front the sombre green of the ilexes :
Here where the heat lies
Pale blue in the hollows,
Where blue are the shadows
On the fronds of the cactus,
Where pale blue the gleaming
Of fir and cypress,
With the cones upon them
Amber or glowing
With virgin gold :
Here where the honey-flower
Makes the heat fragrant,
As though from the gardens
Of Gulistân,
Where the bulbul singeth
Through a mist of roses,
A breath were borne :
Here where the dream-flowers,
The cream-white poppies
Silently waver,
And where the Scirocco,
Faint in the hollows,
Foldeth his soft white wings in the sunlight,
And lieth sleeping
Deep in the heart of
A sea of white violets :
Here, as the breath, as the soul of this beauty
Moveth in silence, and dreamlike, and slowly,
White as a snow-drift in mountain valleys
When softly upon it the gold light lingers:

White as the foam o' the sea that is driven
O'er billows of azure agleam with sun-yellow:
Cream-white and soft as the breasts of a girl,
Moves the White Peacock, as though through the noon-
    tide
A dream of the moonlight were real for a moment.
Dim on the beautiful fan that he spreadeth,
Foldeth and spreadeth abroad in the sunlight,
Dim on the cream-white are blue adumbrations,
Shadows so pale in their delicate blueness
That visions they seem as of vanishing violets,
The fragrant white violets veinëd with azure,
Pale, pale as the breath of blue smoke in far woodlands.
Here, as the breath, as the soul of this beauty,
White as a cloud through the heats of the noontide
Moves the White Peacock.

v.

THE SWIMMER OF NEMI.

(The Lake of Nemi: September.)

WHITE through the azure,
The purple blueness,
Of Nemi's waters
The swimmer goeth.
Ivory-white, or wan white as roses
Yellowed and tanned by the suns of the Orient,
His strong limbs sever the violet hollows;
A shimmer of white fantastic motions
Wavering deep through the lake as he swimmeth.
Like gorse in the sunlight the gold of his yellow hair,
Yellow with sunshine and bright as with dew-drops,
Spray of the waters flung back as he tosseth
His head i' the sunlight in the midst of his laughter :

Red o'er his body, blossom-white mid the blueness,
And trailing behind him in glory of scarlet,
A branch of the red-berried ash of the mountains.
White as a moon-beam
Drifting athwart
The purple twilight,
The swimmer goeth—
Joyously laughing,
With o'er his shoulders,
Agleam in the sunshine
The trailing branch
With the scarlet berries.
Green are the leaves, and scarlet the berries,
White are the limbs of the swimmer beyond them,
Blue the deep heart of the still, brooding lakelet,
Pale-blue the hills in the haze of September,
The high Alban hills in their silence and beauty,
Purple the depths of the windless heaven
Curv'd like a flower o'er the waters of Nemi.

VI.

THE NAKED RIDER.

(*In the Volscians.*)

THROUGH the dark gorge
With its cliffs of basalt,
The rider comes.
The sunlight floodeth
The breast of the hill,
And all the mouth
Of the sullen pass
Is light with the foam of
A thousand blooms
Of the white narcissi,
With a waving sea

Of asphodels.
On a white horse,
A cream-white stallion
With blood-red nostrils
And wild dark eyes,
The naked rider
Laughs as he cometh,
And hails the sunlight breaking upon him.
Full breaks the flood
Of the yellow light
On the naked youth,
Glowing, as ivory
In the amber of moonrise
In the violet eves
Of August-tides.
Dark as the heart of a hill-lake his tresses,
Scarlet the crown of the poppies inwoven
I' the thick wavy hair that crowneth his whiteness,
Strong the white arms,
The broad heaving breast,
The tent thighs guiding
The mighty stallion.

Out from the gloom
Of the mountain valley,
Where cliffs of basalt
Make noontide twilight,
And where the grey bat
Swingeth his heavy wings,
And echo reverberates
The screams of the falcons :
Where nought else soundeth
Save the surge or the moaning
Of mountain-winds,
Or the long crash and rattle

Of falling stones
Spurned by the hill fox
Seeking his hollow lair :
Out from the gorge
Into the sunlight,
To the glowing world,
To the flowers and the birds
And the west wind laden
With the breaths of rosemary, basil, and thyme—
Comes the white rider,
The naked youth,
Glowing like ivory
In the yellow sunshine.
Beautiful, beautiful, this youth of the mountain,
Laughing low as he rideth
Forth to the sunlight,
The scarlet poppies agleam in his tresses
Dark as the thick-cluster'd grapes of the ivy ;
While over the foam
Of the sea of narcissi,
And high through the surf
Of the asphodels,
Trampleth, and snorteth
From his blood-red nostrils,
The cream-white stallion.

MATER DOLOROSA.

(*From* " EARTH'S VOICES," &c.)

SHE, brooding ever, dwells amidst the hills;
 Her kingdom is call'd Solitude; her name—
 More terrible than desolating flame—
Is Silence ; and her soul is Pain.

Day after day some weightier sorrow fills
   Her heart, and each new hour she knows
      The birth of further woes.
      And whoso, journeying, goes
Unto the land wherein she dwells for aye
Shall not come thence until have passed away
   For evermore the bright joy of his years.
   She giveth rest, but giveth it with tears,
      Tears that more bitter be
      Than drops of the Dead Sea :
But never gives she peace to any soul,
For how could she that rarest gift bestow
      Who well doth know
That though in dreams she can attain the goal,
   In dreams alone her steps can thither go :—
Solitude, Silence, Pain, for all who live
   Within the twilit realms that are her own,
   And even Rest to those who seek her throne,
      But these her gifts alone :
Peace hath she not and therefore cannot give.

SONG.

From "CHILDREN OF TO-MORROW."

LOVE in my heart : oh, heart of me, heart of me !
   Love is my tyrant, Love is supreme.
What if he passeth, oh, heart of me, heart of me !
   Love is a phantom, and Life is a dream !

What if he changeth, oh, heart of me, heart of me !
   Oh, can the waters be void of the wind ?
What if he wendeth afar and apart from me,
   What if he leave me to perish behind ?

What if he passeth, oh, heart of me, heart of me !
    A flame i' the dusk, a breath of Desire ?
Nay, my sweet Love is the heart and the soul of me,
    And I am the innermost heart of his fire !

Love in my heart : oh, heart of me, heart of me !
    Love is my tyrant, Love is supreme.
What if he passeth, oh, heart of me, heart of me !
    Love is a phantom, and Life is a dream !

ROSES.

From "A Fellowe and his Wife."

Roses, roses,
Yellow and red ;
A rose for the living,
A rose for the dead !
Who'll sip their dew ?
There are only a few
Of the yellow and red ;
Youth sells its roses
Ere youth is sped.

Roses, roses,
All for delight ;
What of the night ?
Hark, the tramp, tramp,
The scabbard's clamp,
The flaring lamp !
Where is the morning dew ?

Ah, only a few
Drank ere the yellow and red
Lay shrivelled, shrivelled,
Over the dead.

Roses, roses,
Buy, oh, buy.
The years fly,
'Tis the time of roses.
Here are posies
For one and all,
For lovers that sigh
And for lovers that die ;
And for love's pall
And burial !

Roses, roses, roses, buy, buy, oh, buy !
Why delay, why delay, roses also die.
Pink and yellow, blood-red, snow-white.
Roses for dayspring, roses for night !

Buy, buy, oh, my roses buy !
A kiss for a kiss, and a sigh for a sigh !

SIR GEORGE DOUGLAS.

From "POEMS OF A COUNTRY GENTLEMAN."

THE ANTIQUITY OF ART.

(PALEOLITHIC MAN.)

[Verses suggested by a celt, discovered in a "moss" in Teviot-
dale, and given to the writer.]

A SAVAGE, in a bleak world, on a waste,
  'Midst fir-tree-cover'd mountains, led his life:
The claws and fangs of mighty beasts he faced—
  A hunter, seeking food for child and wife.

And, on the smooth wall of his cavern lair,
  The image of a reindeer once he drew,—
Small, to the life, with faithful lines and fair,
  That all its antlers' branchings copied true.

Was this a savage? No! a Man. The dew
  Of pity touch'd him; the sweet brotherhood
Of Nature's general offspring well he knew :—
  Humane, he loved; ingenious, understood.

More :—the desires that kindling hearts inflame
  To leave dull rest, and court congenial woe—
The Love of Beauty, and the Thirst for Fame,
  Throbb'd faintly in that huntsman long ago !

And, friend, the self-same passion in his breast
That stirr'd, and wrought to permanence divine
One form of grace, most touchingly express'd,
Stirs in your heart to-day, and stirs in mine !

ELEGY ON THOMAS TOD STODDART, THE ANGLER-POET.

By Tweed, by Teviot's winding tide,
A form I knew is miss'd to-day !
The woods, the field, the rocks abide;
But he has pass'd away—

Where, pensive—straying without an aim—
As now, once more, these paths I trace
(Familiar haunts found still the same),
I seek him in his place !

For seldom—(whether Tweed ran strong,
Discolour'd, swoll'n with melting snows,
Awful with wrecks it bears along
'Twixt banks it overflows;

Whether, with summer-shrunken stream—
Where isles, before unknown, appear—
It sank in sloth, resign'd to dream)—
I fail'd to meet him here !

Indeed—by drought, fair skies, or flood—
So constant this his walk had been,
He seem'd, when met in fancy's mood,
The Genius of the scene ;

Or, even—with venerable beard,
  In his right hand a willow rod—
Late sighted where his name was fear'd,
  The very river-god !

His date was from that Golden Age
  When, sprung from Hercules and Mirth,
In manhood and poetic rage,
  Giants still dwelt on earth.

In mountain, water, field, and wood,
  Their might was felt—empowered, at will,
The broods of earth, the sky, the flood,
  To capture, tame, or kill.

Then, by the fair lake's margent clear,
  What nights were theirs ! how brave a feast !
Ranged all in order, peer by peer,
  Where he was not the least.

Methinks the moon was full by night
  When Madness, madder than before,
Drank deep, and kept till broad daylight
  That table in a roar !

But envying Time, with marksman's art,
  Waging dire war, slew, one by one,
Their race, large-limb'd and light of heart—
  Till he remain'd alone :

And lingering, lonely, very old,
  Saw baser times, and knew instead
Men in whose veins the blood ran cold,
  With hearts where mirth was dead.

Yet still his peaceful craft he plied,
   Haunting by river, lake, and rill—
With power to common men denied,
   Assiduous, angling still,

Till all in wonderment cried out,
   When he, at eve, his ploy forsook—
From head to heel, and round about,
   Hung with the spoils he took !

He dipt his fingers in the flood
   (I heard an ancient angler tell),
And, nibbling, straight the finny brood
   Swarm'd at the charmer's spell.

And sometimes, too, with childlike glee,
   In praise of stream and riverside,
He sang. A kindly man was he :
   And so, in time, he died.

And thus, by Teviot's rolling flood,
   His well-known form we miss to-day—
Gazing on river, field, and wood,
   Whence he has passed away !

Dear poet ! From that dead hand of thine,
   I (oh ! not rashly), born too late,
Claiming far kinship in the line,
   This legacy await :—

To others other gifts : to me,
   If I have praised thee here, at last,
Tho' ill, not unacceptably,
   Thy poet's pipe he pass'd !

Now, sleep !   Thy songs thou leavest with us :
   Thy story be it our task to tell;
But thee, we now departing, thus,
   Salute and bid " Farewell ! "

A NIGHT-PIECE.

WHEN saner men are sound a-bed,
   And beasts in woods and fields are still,
The lonely paths alone I tread,
   And wander on o'er dale and hill :

O'er waste and woodland, ford and fence,
   My onward course uncheck'd I steer,
Unseen—as walks the Pestilence,
   When damps infect the sorrowing year.

The screech-owl from her touchwood house
   Peeps forth, and chides me as I go,
That thus her fretful chicks I rouse,
   And through the echoing woods halloo.

For no latch clicks ; no footstep beats
   In tune to mine the loud highway,
Save his, whose face the night secretes—
   Whose craft abhors the eyes of day.

What goal have I to gain to-night ?
   Yon haunted tower, or yonder hill,
Which, on the utmost verge of sight,
   Cuts clear into the twilight still ?

Not these: a friendlier bourn I know,
  Five furlongs from the neighbouring town,
Where, o'er the broad champaign below,
  A bench-encircled beech looks down:—

A pleasant haunt when eves are long,
  And mild, and full of balm, in May;
When wordy elders round it throng,
  And children with the beech-mast play;

And lovers, lingering on till night—
  Still whispering with the whispering leaves—
Score on its bark the troth they plight,
  And many a trust the tree receives:

A pleasant spot when ponderers see
  The sweet old tale retold once more,
Mature Content and infant Glee—
  The simple life-play acted o'er.

But now—when Life is laid to sleep,
  And its unlantern'd watchman I;
Who hear alone the wheezing sheep,
  And, far away, the wild-duck's cry—

Now smile with more congenial air
  Forsaken seat and sombre tree;
Which smiled, with light and laughter there,
  For all the world but not for me.

The hour is mine:—on couch or straw,
  The scheming active myriads lie—
Clownish contempt with kingly awe,
  Like garments, for the time laid by.

Oh, then that pains of pride and power
  Might with the drear night pass away !
And brothers in the midnight hour
  Arise to brotherhood with day !

The hour is mine.   A charmer's hands,
  The finger'd branches o'er me pass ;
Whilst, rustling, in the woods expands
  The Spring's new life in leaves and grass ;

Till Sleep, from dreamland's confines pale—
  That lazy lover of soft sound—
Floats on the hawthorn-incensed gale,
  And weighs me, nerveless, to the ground ;

With silk-smooth arms about my neck,
  And cozening whispers in my ear—
As idle as the chattering beck,
  Which none but dreamers pause to hear ;—

Till, as from some insidious cup
  Inspired forbidden powers to wield,
Strange phantoms could I conjure up
  To move and mime in yon grey field.

Behold ! the shades of all those lives
  That fill'd the evening air with noise—
Grave husbands with their mild-faced wives,
  And grandsires crook'd, and girls and boys ;

Striplings and maidens, hand in hand,
  And babes — our life's small sweet spring
      flowers,—
Like strangers—in a far-off land
  Mindful of home and bygone hours—

Come back once more;—and, one by one,
  With wistful mein and eyes downcast—
Weak wraiths from world's without a sun—
  Still silently go trooping past.

So sad to see I scarce can stay
  For " By your leave," or, " With your leave,"
To take my stand beside the way
  And pluck the foremost by the sleeve.

" Now, gossip, whither, pray, so late ?—
  Hark ! though the noon of night be near,
Dawn yet shall burst his dungeon-gate—
  Where Doubt stands sentinel with Fear—

" And o'er old Ocean's labouring waste,
  O'er silent city, stretching plain,
Charged with dear hope, enjoin'd to haste,
  Shall ride, a messenger, amain—

" An angel—and like angels bright,
  Arm'd with the name that all revere,
Who hark and speed him on his flight
  To find and greet and help us here !

" When he, from yonder glimmering slope,
  Pausing his outworn steed to breathe,
Waves his plumed casque, and shouts us, " Hope !"
  Hope to the hearts that touch on death !

" Then straight, from signal-tower and hill,
  Our watchmen shall give on the cry;
Which, through the throng'd streets echoing still,
  Shall reach the hearts that faint and die ;—

" Till, with one voice, around, afar,
   Tongued like the forests, winds, and waves,
Choir upon choir shall hail the Star—
   The Morning Star that speaks and saves ! "

So, in the enthusiasm of my sleep,
   Moved by strong love and pity, I spake,
When, pierced with words like flames that leap,
   I started from the ground awake !

I stood alone.   That sorrowing train
   O'er the bleak world had ta'en its way—
Ne'er on my sight to rise again,
   Though life be blest with many a day.

JOHN DAVIDSON.

THE BATTLE OF BANNOCKBURN.

From "BRUCE."

SCENE—*The Gillies' Hill.   Men and women watching
the battle.*

A Young Friar. "St. Andrew and St. George!
    Fight on ! fight on !"
A whole year's storms let loose on one small lake
Prisoned among the mountains, rioting
Between the heathery slopes and rugged cliffs,
Dragging the water from its deepest lair,
Shaking it out like feathers on the blast ;
With shock on shock of thunder; shower on shower
Of jagged and sultry lightning; banners, crests,
Of rainbows torn and streaming, tossed and flung
From panting surge to surge ; where one strong sound,
Enduring with continuous piercing shriek
Whose pitch is ever heightened, still escapes
Wroth from the roaring whirl of elements;
Where mass and motion, flash and colour spin,
Wrapped and confounded in their blent array :
And this all raving on a summer morn,
With unseen larks beside the golden sun,
And merest blue above; with not a breeze
To fan the burdened rose-trees, or incense
With mimic rage the foamless rivulet,

That like a little child goes whispering
Along the woodland ways its happy thought
Were no more wild, grotesque, fantastical,
Uncouth, unnatural—and I would think　　　.
Impossible, but for the vision here—
Than is this clamorous and unsightly war,
Where swords and lances, shields and arrows, flash,
Whistle, and clang—splintered like icicles,
Eclipsed like moons, broken like reeds, like flames—
Lewd flames that lick themselves in burning lust—
With scorpion tongues lapping the lives of men;
Where axes cut to hearts worth all the oaks;
Where steel burns blue, and golden armours blaze—
One moment so, the next, a ruddier hue;
Where broidered banners rustle in the charge,
And deck the carnage out——A skeleton,
Ribboned and garlanded may sweetly suit
The morris-dancers for a May-pole now !—
Where hoofs of horses spatter brains of men,
And beat dull thunder from the shaking sod ;
Where yelling pibrochs, braying trumpets, drums,
And shouts, and shrieks, and groans, hoarse, shrill—a
　　roar
That shatters hearing—echo to the sky ;
Where myriad ruthless vessels, freighted full
Of proud rich blood—with images of God,
Their reasoning souls, deposed from their command—
By winds of cruel hate usurped and urged,
Are driven upon each other, split, and wrecked,
And foundered deep as hell.　The air is dark
With souls.　I cannot look—I cannot see.

　　　　　　　　　　　　　　　　　　[*Kneels.*

A Woman. The battle's lost before it's well begun.
Our men fall down in ranks like barley-rigs
Before a dense wet blast.

A Cripple.   Despair itself
Can only die before the English bows.
O that they could come at them ! Who are these
That skirt the marsh ?
 Woman.   My sight is weak. But see;
Here's an old fellow, trembling, muttering. Look
How he is strung; and what an eye he has !
 Cripple. Old sight sees well away. I warrant, now,
His is a perfect mirror of the fight.
You see well, father ?
 Old Man.   Ay. That's Edward Bruce ;
And none too soon. The feathered deaths speed
  thick
In jubilant choirs, flight after singing flight.
That tune must end ; the nest be harried. Ride,
Fiery Edward ! Yet our staunch hearts quail not.
Ah ! now the daze begins ! I know it well.
The cloth-yard shafts, like magic shuttles, weave
Athwart the warped air dazzling, dire dismay,
And the beholder's blood slinks to his heart
Like moles from daylight; all his sinews fade
To unsubstantial tinder. Ha ! spur ! spur !
There are ten thousand bowmen ! Gallop ! Charge !
Now, by the soul of Wallace, Edward Bruce,
The battle's balanced ! On your sword it hangs !
Look you; there's fighting ! Just a minute's fight !
Tug, strain ! Throe after throe ! Travail of war !
The birth—defeat and victory, those twins,
That in an instant breathe and die, and leave
So glorious and so dread a memory !—
The bowstring's cut ! What butchery to see !
They shear them down these English yeomen ! God !
It looks like child's play too ! And so it feels,
Now I remember me.—That's victory.
 Woman. But the knights, the knights !

Old Man. I see them. But our spearmen! Do you
     see!
This hill we stand on trembles with the shock:
They budge not, planted, founded in the soil.
Another charge! Now watch! Now see! Ugh!
     Ha!
Did one spear flicker? One limb waver? No!
These fellows there are fighting for their land!
The English army through its cumbrous bulk
Thrilled and astounded to the utmost rear,
Twists like a snake, and folds into itself,
Rank pushed through rank. Now are they hand to
     hand!
How short a front! How close! They're sewn
     together
With steel cross-stitches, halbert over sword,
Spear across lance, and death the purfled seam!
I never saw so fierce, so locked a fight!
That tireless brand that like a pliant flail
Threshes the lives from sheaves of Englishmen,
Know you who wields it? Douglas, who but he!
A noble meets him now. Clifford it is!
No bitterer foes seek out each other there.
Parried! That told! and that! Clifford, good-night!
And Douglas shouts to Randolf; Edward Bruce
Cheers on the Steward; while the king's voice rings
In every Scotch ear: such a narrow strait
Confines this firth of war!
     Young Friar.   God gives me strength
Again to gaze with eyes unseared. Jewels!
These must be jewels peering in the grass,
Cloven from helms, or on them: dead men's eyes
Scarce shine so bright. The banners dip and mount
Like masts at sea. The battle-field is slime,
A ruddy lather beaten up with blood!

Men slip; and horses, stuck with shafts like butts,
Sprawl, madly shrieking!   No, I cannot look!
[Exit.
Woman. Look here! look here, I say!   Who's this
   behind?
His horse sinks down—the brute is dead, I think.
His clothes are torn; his face with dust and sweat
Encrusted, baked, and cracked.   He speaks; he
   shouts;
And shouting runs this way.   He's mad, I think.
  Cripple. He's made his hearers mad.   Tents, blan-
   kets, poles,
Pitch-forks, and staves, and knives, brandished and
   spread
By women, children, grandsires!   What is this?

   [*Enter* CROMBE, *followed by a crowd bearing
    blankets for banners, and armed with staves,
    etc.*

Crombe. I rode all night to strike a blow to-day:
The noblest lady living bade me go:
Her kiss is on my lips and in my soul.
Come after me—yea, with your naked hands,
And conquer weapons!
[*Exeunt, shouting.*

THE REV. HABAKKUK McGRUTHER OF CAPE WRATH, IN 1879.

God save old Scotland!   Such a cry
  Comes raving north from Edinburgh.
It shakes the earth, and rends the sky,
  It thrills and fills true hearts with sorrow.

"There's no such place, by God's good grace,
   As smoky hell's dusk-flaming cavern?"
Ye fools, beware, or ye may share
   The hottest brew of Satan's tavern.

Ye surely know that Scotland's fate
   Controls the whole wide world's well-being;
And well ye know her godly state
   Depends on faith in sin's hell-feeing.
And would ye then, false-hearted men,
   From Scotland rape her dear damnation?
Take from her hell, then take as well
   From space the law of gravitation.

A battle-cry for every session
   In these wild-whirling, heaving last days:
"Discard for ever the Confession;
   Abolish, if you choose, the Fast-days;
Let Bible knowledge in school and college
   No more be taught—we'll say, 'All's well.'
'Twill scarcely grieve us, if you but leave us
   For Scotland's use, in Heaven's name, Hell."

IS LOVE WORTH LEARNING?

Is it worth the learning,
   This love they praise?
Pale lovers yearning
   For happy days,
For happy days and happier nights,
For waking dreams of dear delights?
   Is it worth the learning?

My heart is burning,
  It scorches me;
Is it worth the learning
  What this may be?
Why do I walk alone all day?
"She is in love," the maidens say.
  Is love worth learning?

Was it worth the learning?
  He kissed my hand.
Is love worth learning?
  I understand,
Though love may come and love may go,
It is the only thing to know:
  Love's worth the learning.

SELENE EDEN.

From "In a Music-Hall."

My dearest lovers know me not;
  I hide my life and soul from sight;
I conquer all whose blood is hot;
  My mystery is my mail of might.

I had a troupe who danced with me:
  I veiled myself from head to foot;
My girls were nude as they dared be;
  They sang a chorus, I was mute.

But now I fill the widest stage
  Alone, unveiled, without a song;
And still with mystery I engage
  The aching senses of the throng.

A dark-blue vest with stars of gold,
  My only diamond in my hair,
An Indian scarf about me rolled:
  That is the dress I always wear.

And first the sensuous music whets
  The lustful crowd; the dim-lit room
Recalls delights, recalls regrets;
  And then I enter in the gloom.

I glide, I trip, I run, I spin,
  Lapped in the lime-light's aureole.
Hushed are the voices, hushed the din,
  I see men's eyes like glowing coal.

My loosened scarf in odours drenched
  Showers keener hints of sensual bliss;
The music swoons, the light is quenched,
  Into the dark I blow a kiss.

Then, like a long wave rolling home,
  The music gathers speed and sound;
I, dancing, am the music's foam,
  And wilder, fleeter, higher bound,

And fling my feet above my head;
  The light grows, none aside may glance;
Crimson and amber, green and red,
  In blinding baths of these I dance.

And soft, and sweet, and calm, my face
Looks pure as unsunned chastity,
Even in the whirling triple pace:
That is my conquering mystery.

NOON.

From "FOR LOVERS."

. . . You gather as we pass along
Wheat-ears, and barley-ears, and tinted vetches;
Wild rose-buds that the nightingale's sweet song
Ne'er listen to full-blown, for—beauteous wretches!—
The sun's kiss that the scent rapes from their breasts
And opes their blushing bosoms, kills them too;
Bride-bed of gnats, woodbine, that hedges vests;
Forget-me-nots, scarce as your eyes so blue;
A lone spring primrose waning now in June
As Hesper pales when onward comes the moon;
And little earnest daisies, single-eyed,
That worship heaven with faces glorified.
With fairy fingers than the flowers more fragrant
This spoil of fields you link into a chain;
On shaggy rocks with groping foot and vagrant,
I search for berries and a hatful gain.
With berries crushed we make ourselves shame-faced;
With berries pierced you string a grassy thread;
Then with your flower-wove chain I gird your waist,
And wreathe your flower-outshining, golden head,
And on my knees fall down and worship Thee,
My berry-stained, flower-crownèd deity!
While from the very highest heaven of song,
And highest welkin-height a wing has measured,

Relays of larks their love-songs loud prolong
In surging notes that are in heaven treasured.
And then each quick descends from heaven's height;
His spirit swoons in such a high-pitched flight;
His serviceable wings, his tongue of fire,
His sun-enduring eyes wax faint and tire.
Where in the universe then must he wend?
Why, to that clime where languid poets use,
His mate's sweet bosom—she, his only muse,
As I to you my wearied spirit bend,
And drink deep draughts from those sweet fountains
    twin,
Your eyes, Castalia and Hippocrene.
  Within a pool, deep in a pebbly strand,
The purest of the diamonds that are strung
Upon the glen, a bracelet of the land,
We see the heavens as in a mirror hung.
Oh, then we wonder upon what great loom
The warp and woof of heaven's tent were wrought!
Who reared its poles and gave such spacious room,
Who hung its deathless lamps, their bright fire brought?
I wonder at your beauty's perfectness;
I wonder at the blueness of the sky;
I wonder at the sun's bright steadfastness;
I wonder at the breeze that wanders by;
I wonder at the larks constantly singing,
And at the proper motion of the stream;
I wonder at the still, green grass up-springing,
And what sweet wonder fills your sweet day-dream;
I hear the rolling music of the spheres,
Wondering, and wondering at the cloven dell;
 I wonder at the floating gossameres;
I see creation is a miracle.

LOVE AT FIRST SIGIIT.

From the Second Act of "Smith: A Tragedy."

A Garden.   Enter Magdalen *without seeing* Smith.

Smith (aside).   These plaited coils of hair, the
            golden lid
Of the rich casket where her live thoughts lie !
IIer cheek is tinged with sunset ?   IIas she eyes ?
IIer body sways : the crimson-blazoned west
Like organ-music surges through her blood.
My seeming aimless visit to the north—
The time—the circumstance !—I yield myself !
This is the woman whom my soul will love.
She moves this way, backward, to sit.   I'll speak.
Lady.
            (Magdalen *wheels round.*)
      Her eyes are living sapphires !
Magdalen.   What !
Smith.   I love you.
Magdalen.   Sir !
Smith.   I love you, lady.
Magdalen (about to go).   Sir I
Smith.   Lady, stay.
My body and my soul assembled here,
At war till now are wedded by your glance :
You make that man which chaos was before :
And this is love.   I dreaded love : I knew
It should with such a pang lay hold of me.
I am not mad although I tremble thus :
It is the inspiration of my love.
Fly not, repulse me not, and do not fear :
I would tear up my body with my hands,

And hide you in my heart did evil threat:
I am as tame to you as wild things are
To those that cherish them.　Be confident,
For I shall guard my dreams from harming you
As faithfully as time his vigil keeps.
　　Magdalen.　I do not fear.
　　Smith.　　　　　　　　　　Speak louder, speak again.
Like rose-leaves that enrich the greedy earth
The tremulous whispering bedews my heart.
Speak, speak !
　　Magdalen.　Who are you, sir?
　　Smith.　　　　　　　　　　　A mellow voice,
Falling like thistle-down, melting like snow,
Golden and searching as a sunny wine !
It bore a question.　Who am I ?　A man.
　　Magdalen (aside).　I think so, too.—What do you
　　　　want with me ?
　　Smith.　Our language is too worn, too much abused,
Jaded and over-spurred, wind-broken, lame—
The hackneyed roadster every bagman mounts !
I cannot tell you what I want with you,
Unless you understand the depth of this :
I want for you heroic happiness.
　　Magdalen.　How might I win this happiness?
　　Smith.　　　　　　　　　　　　Be mine :
I am the enemy of all the world :
Dare it with me : be mine.
　　Magdalen.　　　　　　　　I know you not.
I am engaged to one I do not love ;
My father swears that I must marry him :
It is a common misery, so stale
That I contemned it ; and I know you not :
But I have courage.　Let me think awhile.
　　Smith.　Think my thought ; be impatient as I am :
Obey your nature, not authority :

Because the world, enchanted by the sun,
The moon, the stars, with charms of time and space,
Of seasons, tides, of darkness and of light,
Weaves new enchantment everlastingly,
Whirled in a double spell of day and year,
A self-deluded sorcerer winding round,
Close to its smothered heart, coil after coil
Of magic zones, invisible as air—
Some, Cytherean belts; some, chains; and some,
Noisome and terrible as hooded snakes.
 Magdalen. What do you mean? What spells?
  what sorcery?
 Smith. The hydra-headed creeds; the sciences
That deem the thing is known when it is named;
And literature, thought's palace-prison fair;
Philosophy, the grand inquisitor
That racks ideas and is fooled with lies;
Society, the mud wherein we stand
Up to the eyes, whence if I drag you forth,
Saving your soul and mine, there shall ascend
A poisonous blast that may o'ertake our lives.
 Magdalen. I feel a meaning in your eloquence;
I see my poor thoughts made celestial,
Like faded women Jove hung in the sky.
Obey my nature, sir? How shall I know
The voice of nature from the thousand cries,
That clamour in my head like piteous birds,
Filling the air about a lonely isle
With ringing terror when the hunter comes.
 Smith. Shut out the storm and heed the still small
  voice.
 Magdalen. Have pity! Yet I think the woman's
  dream
Is given me—the strong deliverer
To pluck her from the dragon's jaws unharmed.

What can I say?   Rest still your eyes on mine,
And I shall dare to speak.   I love you, sir;
And I have loved you since I was a girl—
You, only you.   Good-bye.   Oh, in my life—
A miracle I think as this world goes—
I met the living image of my dream,
And was found worthy to be loved !   Good-bye.
I seem to see my daughter at my knees,
Listening with violet eyes of heaven-wide awe,
The virgin story I shall utter once
To her, only to her.
   Smith.   And so you go
To hell.
   Magdalen.   Ay, even so : my father's word
Is plighted to this man, and so is mine.
Perhaps that I may know this is no dream—
Sir, will you kiss me ?
     (*He folds her in his arms and kisses her.*)
Smith.   You are faint, my love.
Magdalen.   Oh, have pity, sir !
Smith.   I will have pity.
   (*Goes out, carrying her.*)

———

BACCHUS AND ARIADNE.

From "SCARAMOUCH IN NAXOS."

Ariadne. Here, by this sea, I waked—how long ago !
Here, by this sea, you found me.
   Bacchus.   Would you be
My bride again ?
   Ariadne.   O no ! each day, each hour
I am your bride ; and as the days and years

Gather behind us, every happiness—
And that is every minute of my life—
Doubles the joy of that which went before :
And yet the past is as a galaxy
Wherein no star excels the radiant throng.
   Bacchus. Not that fair hour when first you loved me?
   Ariadne.   No:
I have no memory.   I am striving now
To summon up the time when here you came,
And made me an immortal and your bride.
I might as well compel my thoughts to search
For some unnoted dream that I forgot
The moment after I had told you, love,
New wakened from the sleep I dreamed it in.
   Bacchus. But memory goes afoot—invalid here:
Love has a high-commanding minister,
Imagination ; and it serves alone
Beings who yield their moods and bow their minds
To its obedient masterdom : stout thought,
That trudges, blind and lame, the dusty way,
And memory, that casts its broken net
In Lethe's waves, keep not among your train—
Fit servants these for mortals.
   Ariadne.   So I do—
I banish them : but still there clings to me
Something of earth.
   Bacchus.   I love you best for that.
A goddess born is tame, secure of heaven,
And there is nothing to endow her with ;
But you derive divinity from me,
Yet keep the passionate heart that mortals have.—
Now, I am at the morn I found you here:
Come, Ariadne, leap into the past.
   Ariadne. I cannot.
   Bacchus.   See, thy flying traitor's sail !

Ariadne. No, no ! This night—this hour is in my
　　　blood.
The brine, the sea-pinks, and the soaring moon
Seem thoughts of mine which now I body forth ;
And these, and all the beauties of the world
Breathe of my love for you.
　　Bacchus.　　　　　　　　　I found you here
With crimson cheeks and nostrils wide, asleep ;
Your hair dishevelled, and your mantle torn.
　　Ariadne.　　　　　　　　　　　　No, no !
You cannot drive me back.　I see, indeed,
A picture of our meeting ; but not mine.
My fancy like a wayward messenger
Despatched to gather roses, on its wings
Bearing their scent, flies empty-handed home.
　　Bacchus. What picture, Ariadne?
　　Ariadne.　　　　　　　　　That we saw
In Athens, when we last alighted there.
Do you remember how it made us smile
Until we felt that love had painted it ;
And then we found it true and beautiful ?
　　Bacchus. Yes : and the poet.
　　Ariadne.　　　　　　Oh ! some mortals still
Love us, and deem us worthy of a song.
But for the subject of their art, I vow
They needs must know it better than myself
Who am the heroine : their feigning hangs
A veil before my fancy.—Come away :
Back where the water gurgles through the fern,
Dewing the feathery fronds, and hyacinths
Spread like a purple smoke far up the bank.

———

TRANSFORMATION SONG.

From the same.

THROUGH the air, through the air,
We are borne; from our hair
A spicy odour is shaken :
We sing as we sail ;
The strong trees quail,
And the dreaming doves awaken.
The pale screech owl
That, cheek by jowl,
Goes ravening with night,
Thinks day has come,
And hurries home
Half-starved, to shun the light.
An eagle above us screams;
But a star blows a silver horn,
And a faint far echo floats
From the depths of the lakes, and the streams
Warble the shadowy notes.
A young lark thinks it morn,
And sings through our flying crowd,
That seems to his eager soul
Like a low-hung dawning-cloud.
The bells of midnight toll ;
The night-flowers tell the hour ;
And the stately planets roll,
As we fly to our lady's bower.

FROM GRUB STREET.

RONDEAU.

My love, my wife, three months ago
  I joined the fight in London town.
I haven't conquered yet, you know,
And friends are few, and hope is low ;
  Far off I see the shining crown.

I'm daunted, dear ; but blow on blow
With ebbing force I strike, and so
I am not felled and trodden down,
        My love, my wife !

I wonder when the tide will flow,
Sir Oracle cease saying " No,"
    And Fortune smile away her frown.
    Well, while I swim I cannot drown ;
And while we sleep the harvests grow,
        My love, my wife.

ROUNDEL.

My darling boys, heaven help you both !
  Now in your happy time of toys
Am I to die?   How I am loth,
  My darling boys !

  My heart is strong for woes or joys ;
My soul and body keep their troth,
  One in a love no clasping cloys.

Why with me is the world so wroth ?
  What fiend at night my work destroys ?
Has fate against me sworn an oath,
  My darling boys ?

VILLANELLE.

ON her hand she leans her head,
  By the banks of the busy Clyde ;
Our two little boys are in bed.

The pitiful tears are shed ;
  She has nobody by her side ;
On her hand she leans her head.

I should be working ; instead
  I dream of my sorrowful bride,
And our two little boys in bed.

Were it well if we four were dead ?
  The grave at least is wide.
On her hand she leans her head.

She stares at the embers red ;
  She dashes the tears aside,
And kisses our boys in bed.

" God, give us our daily bread ;
  Nothing we ask beside."
On her hand she leans her head ;
  Our two little boys are in bed.

AUTHORS' NOTES.

The Song of Mrs. Jenny Geddes, p. 42.

See Chambers' *Annals of Scotland*, vol. ii. p. 103, year and date as in the text. The learned author says, on the authority of Wodrow, that the name of this mettlesome dame was not *Geddes*, but *Mean*. But, however this be, Fame has baptised her into Geddes, and with that appellation she must live through the ages, and will be famous as long as Scotland and Scotsmen are remembered.

The Confession of Annaple Gowdie, p. 100.

In this poem I have simply digested the substance of a somewhat miscellaneous and unprofitable reading of witch trials. Confessions of this sort were not at all uncommon, explain the fact as we may. The essential features of Annaple Gowdie's declaration will be found in the statements of the witches of Auldearn, as given by Mr. Chambers in his *Domestic Annals of Scotland*. There are one or two phrases in it which may require explanation. "Horse and hattock" was the expression used by witches when they mounted the broom or straw on which they were to ride through the air. "Withershins" means going contrary to the sun ; and it may be noted, as probably containing a deep symbolic idea, that the witch-rites were generally described as contrary to nature. To read the Bible upside down—to say prayers backward—to do anything withershins—these were the appropriate acts of devil-worship, according to this universal superstition. It was also common to give the good ladies nicknames, such as I have used here, taking them from Mr. Chambers. The "covin" was a group of thirteen—hence the devil's dozen, perhaps,—of whom the youngest was called "the maid," or favourite for the time. Generally, the maid was abundantly hated by her sisters.

The Rocky Mountains, p. 123.

These verses relate to the mountain regions at the sources of the Athabasca and the two Saskâtchewans, visited by the author in 1859. The "Siffleur," or Whistler, is the small animal known to naturalists as *Arctomys Pruinosus*, the Hoary Marmot. Its wildly plaintive music has a singular charm when heard amidst the stillness of the vast rock-solitudes.

The German Tower Keeper, p. 125.

Generally descriptive of the Margarethen Tower at Gotha.

The Mountain Fir, p. 127.

The scene is laid in the Aberdeenshire forest of Glen Tanar, on the eastern side of the wooded glen of the Allachie, a little above Altnafearn.

The Flitch of Dunmow, p. 138.

Under an old custom at Dunmow, in Essex, a flitch of bacon is publicly given to any wedded pair who will make oath that they have dwelt together without shadow of discord for the twelve months succeeding their marriage. In the present song, a husband and his wife, thus qualified, are supposed to be riding in procession to claim their reward.

February in the Pyrenees, p. 140.

Written in 1883, while walking in the beautiful valley of Asté, near Bagnères de Bigorre.

P. 147, line 25.

Fee.

Fee is deer, or stag—a common word in the old ballads.

P. 147, line 26.

Raches.

Raches are deerhounds.

P. 148, line 17.

Dreva's Laird.

The small estate of Dreva was for long an appanage of the Tweedies of Drummelzier. It was held usually by a younger son, and then probably by a cadet of the family. The Tweedies of Dreva do not appear to have been an improvement on the parent breed.   At the Justice Aire of Edinburgh, 1502-3, 4th February, John Tweedy of Drummelzier, Walter Tweedy in Hawmyris, and William Tweedy there, became surety for entry of Gilbert Tweedy [of Dreva] for slaughter of Edward Huntair of Polmude. Some thirty-three years later, January 26th, 1565-66, Adame Tweedy of Dravey was "delatit of the cutting of Robert Rammage's lugges, and demembering of him thereof." He pleaded the King and Queen's remission of November 30th, 1565—the "date of remission of the gudman of Drawayis." Nothing was done to him; William Tweedy of Drummelzier became, according to the usual formula, surety to satisfy parties.—*Pitcairn's Criminal Trials*, i. 474, 475.

P. 148, line 25.

They blew the mort on the Wormhill Head.

The *mort* was the notes blown on the horn at the death of the deer.

> "They hunted high, they hunted low,
>   By heathery hill and birken shaw;
>   They raised a buck on Rooken edge,
>   And blew the mort at fair Ealylawe."
>
> *The Death of Parcy Reed.*

P. 167, line 15.

The Sceptre oversways the banded peers.

Louis XI. began to crush the aristocracy of France, a process followed up by Richelieu and consummated by the Revolution.

P. 167, line 19.

Roscoff.

Mary Stuart, on coming to France to marry the Dauphin, landed at Roscoff.

P. 168, line 19.

Niagara.

Niagăra is the Indian, and proper, pronunciation of the word, corrupted, like many others, by Anglo-Saxon hurry, to Niagăra.

P. 169, line 5.

Concord's sage and Harvard's wit.

Ralph Waldo Emerson and Oliver Wendell Holmes.

P. 173, line 23.

Watcher with the hundred eyes.

The hundred-eyed Argus, slain by Hermes, in relief of Io.

P. 174, line 1.

One true wife.

Hypermnestra, who refused to slay her husband, as her sisters, being yoked under constraint, did theirs.— *V. Ovid, etc.*

P. 174, line 8.

Nauplius.

Nauplius, son of Poseidon and Amymone, gave his name to the seaport of Argolis.

Deities of Carthage, p. 176, l. 22.

The religion of Carthage, based on the old Phœnician worship, was mainly astronomical. It may be regarded as a link between the gloomier, if more lofty, abstractions of the East and the concrete artistic conceptions of Hellenic faith, several of which it had adopted. In another part of the play, allusion is made to the Carthaginian theory of the genesis of the world from air and fire.

P. 178, line 1.

Images.

The waxen busts of their ancestors set up in the *atrium* or forehall of the houses of noble Romans.

P. 249, line 15.

Kinaskit.

Kinaskit, as its inhabitants pronounce Kinnesswood, is a small village at the foot of the Lomond Hill and not far from Lochleven. In its neighbourhood is a small peat moss, from which the surrounding villages and farm-towns used to be supplied with fuel.

The Weird of Michael Scott, p. 282.

(Second Edition. Walter Scott.)

(*Michael the Scot: fl.* circa 1250.) Variants of the Michael Scott legends still exist in parts of the Scottish Southlands: betwixt Tweed and Forth, mainly in the remote districts of the shires of Selkirk, Peebles, and Roxburgh ; and, north of the Forth, here and there along the Fife coast. The most common is that which relates to the magician's power of changing into an animal any one who crossed him ; and it is upon this that Part I. of the ballad turns. That also is current which relates how Michael the Scot could win the soul from the body of any woman whom he loved. There are several versions of this uncanny kind of wooing : sometimes Michael Scott is said to have seduced the spirit from its tranced tenement, only to find himself eluded after all ; sometimes the maiden, unable to resist his spell, comes to him, but over the battlements, and so is killed ; again, just as she is about to yield she calls on Christ, and only a phantasmal image of her goes forth, though in the struggle her mortal body perishes (it was upon this version that Rossetti intended to write a poem ; his prose outline of it is given in his Collected Works) ; or, yet again, she comes at her wizard-lover's signal, but when he would embrace her a cross of fire intervenes, and, to save himself from sudden hell-flames which arise, he has perforce to bid her return in safety. I have in Part II. treated Michael Scott's allurement of Margaret's soul not wholly accordantly with any legendary account, yet in superficial conformity with that which most appealed to my imagination. Part III. (that which is given in this volume) is in treatment entirely imaginary, although, of course, the germinal idea—that of encountering at the point of death one's

own soul—is both old and wide-spread.   The Doppel-
gänger idea is a most impressive one in its crudest guise,
and I have endeavoured to heighten its imaginative
effect by making Michael Scott pronounce unwittingly a
dreadful doom upon his own soul.

Pp. 299, 300.

Song and *Roses*.

These two poems are not included in any of the
author's volumes of verse.   The first is from the romance,
Children of To-morrow; the second from the novel,
A Fellowe and His Wife, written in collaboration with
Blanche Willis Howard.

INDEX OF AUTHORS

AND THEIR

PRINCIPAL POETICAL PUBLICATIONS.

WILLIAM BELL SCOTT, born 1811, died 1890.

Poems (Ballads, Studies from Nature, Sonnets, etc.), 1875.
The writer states that in this volume he has collected the productions he wishes most to preserve, or at least the majority of these; having carefully revised them, so as to "place before the public his credentials to be considered a poet."

JAMES THOMSON ("B. V."), born 1834, died 1882.

"The City of Dreadful Night, and other Poems," April 1880. (First published in the *National Reformer*, then under the editorship of Charles Bradlaugh, in 1874.)
"Vane's Story, and other Poems," October 1880.
"A Voice from the Nile, and other Poems," 1884 (first published in the *Fortnightly Review*, November 1881).
Thomson's earliest poems were contributed to Tait's *Edinburgh Magazine*, the first of them, *The Fadeless Bower*, appearing in July 1858. *Sunday up the River*, afterwards incorporated in his earliest volume, first appeared in *Fraser's Magazine*, October 1869.

PROFESSOR JOHN STUART BLACKIE, born 1809.

"Lays and Legends of Ancient Greece, with other Poems," 1857.
Lyrical Poems," 1860.

"Musa Burschicosa: A Book of Songs for Students and University Men," 1869.
"War Songs of the Germans," 1870.
"Lays of the Highlands and Islands," 1872.
"Songs of Religion and Life," 1876.
(The two foregoing volumes are to some extent reprints of different portions of the volume of 1857.)
"Messis Vitæ: Gleanings of Song from a Happy Life," 1886.

DR. GEORGE MACDONALD, born 1824.

Poetical Works, 1893 (including "Within and Without," "The Disciple," "The Gospel Women," "A Book of Sonnets," "Organ Songs," "Violin Songs," "Songs of the Days and Nights," "A Book of Dreams," "Roadside Poems," "Parables," "A Threefold Cord," "Poems for Children," "Ballads," "Scots Songs and Ballads," etc.).
Exotics: translations from Novalis, Heine, etc., 1876.
"A Book of Strife, in the form of the Diary of an Old Soul," 1880.

DR. WALTER C. SMITH, born 1824.

"The Bishop's Walk, and the Bishop's Times," by "Orwell," 1861.
"Olrig Grange," 1872.
"Borland Hall," 1874.
"Hilda; among the Broken Gods," 1878.
"Raban; or Life-Splinters," 1881.
"North-Country Folk," 1883.
"Kildrostan," 1884.
"A Heretic, and other Poems," 1891.

EARL OF SOUTHESK; SIR JAMES CARNEGIE, K.T., born 1827.

"Jonas Fisher," 1875.
"Greenwood's Farewell, and other Poems," 1876.
"The Meda Maiden, and other Poems," 1877.
"The Burial of Isis, and other Poems," 1884 (comprising most of the poems contained in the two preceding volumes together with various new poems).

PROFESSOR JOHN VEITCH, LL.D., born 1829.

"Hillside Rhymes," 1872.
"The Tweed, and other Poems," 1875.
"Merlin, and other Poems," 1889.

GLOSSARY.

Abune, above.
Ae, one; only.
A-glee, a-squint.
Ahint, behind.
Aiblins, perhaps.
Aik, oak.
Airn, iron.
Aneth, beneath.
Ashet, trencher.
Aucht, eight.
Aucht, possession.
A-widdershin, adv. in a direction contrary to the course of the sun. (See Note to *Annaple Gowdie*.)
Awn, v. own.

Bailie, a burgh magistrate.
Bairn, child.
Barley-bree, liquor made from barley—whisky.
Bawbee, ha'penny.
Beass, beasts.
Begoud, begouth, pret. of v. to begin.
Ben, prep. within, in : n. the inner apartment of a house; *but and ben* (indecl.), the outer and inner rooms of a house.

Bent, coarse grass.
Bestial, a term used to comprise cattle, horses, sheep, or the brute creation generally.
Bethankit ! interj. expressive of ironical thanks.
Bethral, betheral, beadle (church officer).
Bewast, westward, westward of.
Bien, well-to-do.
Big, v. build.
Birken, birchen.
Birk-tree, the birch.
Blate, bashful.
Blinter, v. to shine feebly, or unsteadily; *Blintering*, weak-sighted.
Bole, boal, (architectural), a window furnished with a shutter.
Brae, a slope, hill-side.
Braw, n. adornment.
Bray, v. press; shove.
Breeks, breeches.
Broch, brough.
Buckie, a spiral shell; a shell-fish.
Bude, behoved.

Burn, a stream, streamlet.
Busk, v. attire, adorn.
But, vide *ben*.
But and, prep. besides (arch-aic and poetical).
Byke, wasps', or wild bees', nest.
Byre, cow-house.

Ca', *caw*, drive; call. Used by Dr. MacDonald for drive in the sense of to "lead" farm produce.
Caller, fresh.
Canna, n. cotton grass.
Canny, cautious; gentle.
Cantrip, n. a spell. Used by W. B. Scott as an adj. magic.
Canty, merry.
Carl, fellow.
Carline, old woman; witch.
Cauldrife, chilly.
Chanter, a small wind instru-ment akin to the bagpipe.
Chap, v. strike, clap.
Claik, "cackle."
Claucht, v. to snatch.
Clavers, idle talk.
Cleik, n. hook; v. to *cleik up*, snatch up.
Clud, cloud.
Coats, petticoats.
Cock, v. to throw up.
Contre, v. thwart, contradict.
Corby, raven; crow.
Corrie, a hollow in a hill (Gael.).
Couthie, snug.
Cowp, overturn.
Crack, adj. crack-brained.
Crack, v. chat.
Craig, (1) crag, (2) throat.
Craik, croak.
Cramoisie, crimson.

Cranreuch, hoar frost.
Creel, a fish-basket made to be carried on the back.
Crouse, brisk, bold. To *crack crouse*, "talk big", vaunt oneself of.
Cuddy, donkey.
Cuist, pret. of v. to cast.

Daff, v. romp.
Daffing, fun, gaiety.
Daft, silly, "out of one's mind."
Dargin', toiling (*darg*, a day's work).
Daunder, n. and v. stroll.
Daw, v. dawn.
Deidly (indeed ?).
Deval, v. cease.
Differ, difference.
Ding, strike, beat, overcome.
Dool, grief.
Douce, sedate, staid.
Dour, hard, stubborn, sullen.
Doutsum, hesitating.
Dowie, dull, sad.
Dree, endure.
Drook, v. drench.
Drookit, drenched.
Drouthy, dry, thirsty.
Drucken, drunken.
Drumlie, turbid.
Dub, pool.

Eldritch, weird.
Een, (1) evening; (2) pl. of *ee*, eye.

Fain, happy.
Fand, pret. of v. *find*, (1) to find, (2) to feel.
Fang, to "*lose the fang*," "*gang aff the fang*," (of a pump), to cease to yield water.

Fash, v. trouble; "*dinna fash
  your thoomb*," "don't
  trouble your head."
Fastern's Een, Shrove Tues-
  day.
Fell, adj. acute.
Feursday, Thursday.
Fire-flaucht, lightning.
Fisslin', rustling.
Flaught, n. flake.
Flaughter, flutter.
Fley, frighten.
Flinner, flinder, splinter.
Flite, v. scold.
Forbye, besides.
Fowk, folk.
Fyle, defile, soil.

Gangerel, stroller, "tramp."
Garten, *gartane*, n. garter.
Gash, at ease, "at home."
Gate, way.
Gaud, fishing-rod.
Gean, *guine*, the wild cherry.
Gif, if.
Gin, *gien*, if.
Girnel, granary, meal-chest.
Girse, grass.
Gley, bright.
Gleyt, squinting.
Gloamin-fa', the fall of even-
  ing.
Glower, v. stare, frown.
Goud, *gowd*, gold.
Gove, look stupidly.
Gravit, muffler.
Greet, *greit* (pret. *grat*), weep.
Gress, grass; "take the
  gress," wrestlers' phrase for
  being thrown.
Grilse, immature salmon.
Growf, stomach.
Gudeman, husband, head of
  a household.
Gurly, stormy.

Hag, bog.
Halflins, half-way.
Happit, covered, wrapped up.
Harl, n. heap
Haud, hold.
Haugh, a meadow by a river.
Hech ! interj.
Heize, *heeze*, lift up.
Heuk, hook, reaping-hook.
Hirple, v. limp.
Hiz, us.
Hoast, n. and v. cough.
Hope, glen.
Hotch, v. shrug.
Howff, a low tavern.
Hoy, v. to drive away.
Hyne, hence.

Ilk, *ilka*, every.
Intil, into.
Izzet, zig-zag; like the letter
  Z in shape (J. L. Robert-
  son).

Jalouse, v. surmise.
Jaw, a spirt of water.
Jee, v. to stir, to move to one
  side.
Jink, v. dodge, elude.
Jook, *jouk*, evade by ducking.

Kaim, n. and v. comb.
Keek, peep.
Kelpie, a water-sprite.
Kimmer, "gossip."
Kintra, *kintry*, country.
Kirk, church.
Kirkton, *kirk-town*, the; the
  village in which the parish
  church is situated.
Kittle, v. tickle.
Knowe, knoll.

Kyloe, a name given to cattle of the Highland breed.

Laich, laigh, adj. low.
Lamp, v. "the ground is said to *lamp* when covered with the cobwebs which appear after dew or slight frost." (Jamieson.)
(*Lane*), *his lane, her lane, him lane*, alone.
Langsyne, long ago.
Lave, the ; the rest.
Lee-lang, livelong.
Leeze me on, an exclamation expressive of joy or pride in anything.
Lichtly, v. slight.
Lichtsome, delightful.
Lift, the sky.
Link, v. to go arm-in-arm.
Limmer, "jade."
Lintie, the linnet.
Lippen to, lippin to, trust to.
Lo'e, love.
Loof, the palm of the hand.
Loot, pret. of v. to let.
Losh, interj. Lord !
Lout, v. to bow the body.
Low, lowe, flame.
Lowden, Lothian.
Lown, fool ; a term applied in not necessarily ill-natured contempt.
Lowne, tranquil.
Lowst, pret. of v. to *lowse*, to unyoke horses.
Lug, ear ; the handle of a vessel.

Mak' o't, the ; the mate or match of anything.
Miminy, dim. of *mim*, adj. prudish, demure.
Minnie, mother (familiar).

Mirk, dark.
Moss, a bog, a place where peats may be "cast," or dug.
Murle, moulder.
Murr, (1) to purr as a cat ; (2) a term applied to infants (Jamieson).
Mutch, a cap worn by elderly women.
Mynt, v. attempt.

Neb, beak of a bird ; slang term for the nose.
Neeps, turnips.
Neist, next.
Neive, fist.

Ocht, aught.
Owercome, n. the burden of a song.
Ook, week.

Parochine, parish.
Piece, "a piece," a piece of bread.
Pleuch, plough.
Pock, n. bag.
Pow, head.
Preen, pin.
Provost, Chief Magistrate of a Royal Burgh.
Pyot, the magpie.

Quhan, when (archaic spelling.
Quhat, what.
Quhilk, which.
Quhill, until.
Quey, a two-year-old cow.

Randy, n. a virago.
Rax, v. stretch.
Reck, smoke.

"*Reenge the ribs*," stir the fire.

Rig, ridge (of ploughed land).

Ripple, v. drizzle.

Rist, irreg. pret. of v. to rise (?).

Rive, v. tear.

Rock, a kind of sweetmeat.

Roup, a sale by auction.

Row, v. roll.

Rowst, v. a. to hasten (?); (*reist*, to become restive, Jamieson)

Ruck, rick.

Runkled, wrinkled.

Saul, soul.

Saut, salt.

Scale, disperse.

Scart, n. and v. scratch.

Scoog, shelter.

Scowther, scorch.

Screed, v. rend; n. (1) any loud shrill sound, (2) a homily.

Screich, v. shriek.

Serk, *sark*, shirt, or shift.

Shanks' naigie, "Shanks's mare."

Shearer, reaper.

Shill, shrill.

Shoo, v. to drive (beasts) in a particular direction by making this sound.

Shool, shovel.

Sic, *siccan*, such.

Siller, n. money, adj. silver.

Skaith, injury.

Skep, bee-hive.

Skelp, n. splinter, fragment; v. (1) to beat, (2) to move quickly on foot.

Skirl, v. shriek, shrill.

Skirt, v. from *skyre*, to take fright; sheer off (?).

Snash, "Billingsgate" (Jamieson).

Sneck, the latch of a door; a small bolt.

Snicher, v. titter; "laugh in one's sleeve."

Snipie-nebbit, having a nose like a snipe's bill.

Snod, adj. trim, v. to tidy.

Snood, a band by which a woman's hair is confined.

Snoove, to walk quickly and steadily onwards (J. L. Robertson).

Snowk, to scent like a dog.

Sonsie, good-humoured; well-favoured; plump.

Soom, swim.

Sorn, to obtrude oneself upon another for bed or board.

Sough, onomatopœic, denoting the *sighing* of the wind, or any similar sound.

Souter, shoemaker.

Spang, jump, bound.

Spean, wean.

Speel, climb.

Speir, inquire.

Spleet, *split-new*, brand new.

Splore, frolic.

Stap, v. (1) step, (2) thrust.

Staucher, stagger.

Steek, n. stitch, v. shut.

Steer, v. stir, disturb.

Stell, a sheep-fold.

Stey, adj. steep.

Stibble, stubble.

Stieve, firm, steady.

Stook, n. shock (of corn).

Stookit, set up in stooks.

Stour, *stoor*, n. loose dust, dust in motion.

Stown, stolen.

Strathspey, a dance; the music of the same.

Straucht, straight.

Swith, quickly.

Swither, v. hesitate, n. hesitation.

Syne, then.

Tack, lease.

Tane, the ; one of two.

Tent, heed ; *tenty*, watchful.

Thraw, n. and v. twist ; *thrawn*, cross-grained.

Thrawart, perverse.

Threave, two shocks—or four-and-twenty sheaves—of corn.

Til, to.

Tint, pret. of v. *tine*, to lose.

Tirl, twirl.

Toon, a town ; a hamlet ; a single dwelling.

Toon-en', "farm-place."

Toozie, *towsie*, rough-headed.

Towled, toiled.

Tram, shaft of a cart or carriage.

Trig, neat.

Tuik, pret. of take.

Twae, *twa*, two.

Twa-three, "two or three."

Tyke, dog.

Unco. adj. strange, abnormal, excessive ; adj. very, very much, particularly.

Wae, sorrowful.

Waesome, woful.

Waff, v. wave.

Wale, v. select, n. choice, "the pick."

Wame, belly (used by W. B. Scott for the breast).

Warlock, wizard.

Warstle, wrestle.

Wastlin, westerly.

Waucht, a large draught of any liquid.

Waukrife, wakeful.

Wean, child.

Weird, n. fate, destiny.

Weyds, weeds.

Whaup, curlew.

Whins, gorse.

Whummle, overturn.

Whush, a rushing noise, whish.

Winnock, window.

Wite, *wyte*, blame.

Wow, an interj. denoting surprise, grief, or gratification ; sometimes used merely to confer emphasis.

Wud, mad.

Wuss, wish.

Yerl, earl.

Yett, gate.

Yill, ale.

Yird, earth.

Yowes, ewes.

THE WALTER SCOTT PRESS, NEWCASTLE-ON-TYNE.

THE CANTERBURY POETS.

EDITED BY WILLIAM SHARP. 1/- VOLS., SQUARE 8VO.

| Cloth, Red Edges - 1s. | Red Roan, Gilt Edges, 2s. 6d. |
| Cloth, Uncut Edges - 1s. | Pad. Morocco, Gilt Edges - 5s. |

Christian Year.	Ballades and Rondeaus.
Coleridge.	Irish Minstrelsy.
Longfellow.	Milton's Paradise Lost.
Campbell.	Jacobite Ballads.
Shelley.	Australian Ballads.
Wordsworth.	Moore's Poems.
Blake.	Border Ballads.
Whittier.	Song-Tide.
Poe.	Odes of Horace.
Chatterton.	Ossian.
Burns. Poems.	Fairy Music.
Burns. Songs.	Southey.
Marlowe.	Chaucer.
Keats.	Golden Treasury.
Herbert.	Poems of Wild Life.
Victor Hugo.	Paradise Regained.
Cowper.	Crabbe.
Shakespeare: Songs, etc.	Dora Greenwell.
Emerson.	Goethe's Faust.
Sonnets of this Century.	American Sonnets.
Whitman.	Landor's Poems.
Scott. Marmion, etc.	Greek Anthology.
Scott. Lady of the Lake, etc.	Hunt and Hood.
Praed.	Humorous Poems.
Hogg.	Lytton's Plays.
Goldsmith.	Great Odes.
Mackay's Love Letters.	Gwen Meredith's Poems.
Spenser.	Imitation of Christ.
Children of the Poets.	Toby's Birthday Book.
Ben Jonson.	Painter-Poets.
Byron (2 Vols.).	Women-Poets.
Sonnets of Europe.	Love Lyrics.
Allan Ramsay.	American Humor. Verse.
Sydney Dobell.	Scottish Minor Poets.
Pope.	Cavalier Lyrists.
Heine.	German Ballads.
Beaumont and Fletcher.	Songs of Beranger.
Bowles, Lamb, etc.	Poems by Roden Noel.
Sea Music.	Songs of Freedom.
Early English Poetry.	Canadian Poems.
Herrick.	Modern Scottish Poets.

BOOKS OF FAIRY TALES.

Crown 8vo, Cloth Elegant, Price 3s. 6d. per vol.

ENGLISH FAIRY AND OTHER FOLK TALES.

Selected and Edited, with an Introduction,

By EDWIN SIDNEY HARTLAND.

With 12 Full-Page Illustrations by CHARLES E. BROCK.

SCOTTISH FAIRY AND FOLK TALES.

Selected and Edited, with an Introduction,

By SIR GEORGE DOUGLAS, BART.

With 12 Full-Page Illustrations by JAMES TORRANCE.

IRISH FAIRY AND FOLK TALES.

Selected and Edited, with an Introduction,

By W. B. YEATS.

With 12 Full-Page Illustrations by JAMES TORRANCE.

London: WALTER SCOTT, LTD., 24 Warwick Lane.

SCOTTISH POETS

ISSUED IN THE CANTERBURY POETS SERIES.

Each in Two Volumes, Cloth, Cut or Uncut, 1s. per Volume.

POEMS AND SONGS OF ROBERT BURNS. With a Prefatory Notice, Biographical and Critical, by JOSEPH SKIPSEY.

POEMS OF SIR WALTER SCOTT. With Prefatory Notice, Biographical and Critical, by WILLIAM SHARP.

Each in one Volume, Cloth, Cut or Uncut, 1s.

POEMS BY ALLAN RAMSAY. Selected and arranged, with a Biographical Sketch of the Poet, by J. LOGIE ROBERTSON.

POEMS OF JAMES HOGG, THE ETTRICK SHEPHERD. With Introduction by Mrs. GARDEN.

POEMS OF THOMAS CAMPBELL. With Prefatory Notice, Biographical and Critical, by JOHN HOGBEN.

JACOBITE SONGS AND BALLADS [Selected]. Edited, with Notes and Introductory Note, by G. S. MACQUOID.

BORDER BALLADS. Edited, with Introduction and Notes, by GRAHAM R. TOMSON.

POEMS OF OSSIAN. With an Introduction, Historical and Critical, by GEORGE EYRE-TODD.

POEMS OF THE SCOTTISH MINOR POETS, from the Age of Ramsay to David Gray. Selected and Edited by Sir G. DOUGLAS, Bart.

CONTEMPORARY SCOTTISH VERSE (including Selections from William Bell Scott, Professor Blackie, Lord Southesk, Hugh Haliburton, R. L. Stevenson, Andrew Lang, George MacDonald, John Davidson, etc.). Edited by Sir GEORGE DOUGLAS, Bart.

May also be had in the following Bindings:—Red Roan, gilt edges, 2s. 6d.; Padded Morocco, gilt edges, 5s.; Padded Calf, 6s.; and in Half-Morocco, gilt top, antique.

Also in SPECIAL CLOTH BINDING, with **Photogravure Frontispiece,** 2s. per Vol.

London: WALTER SCOTT, LIMITED, 24 Warwick Lane.

LIBRARY OF HUMOUR.

*Cloth Elegant, Large Crown 8vo.   Price 3/6
per volume.*

VOLUMES ALREADY ISSUED.

THE HUMOUR OF FRANCE. Translated, with an Introduction and Notes, by Elizabeth Lee. With numerous Illustrations by Paul Frénzeny.

THE HUMOUR OF GERMANY. Translated, with an Introduction and Notes, by Hans Müller-Casenov. With numerous Illustrations by C. E. Brock.

THE HUMOUR OF ITALY. Translated, with an Introduction and Notes, by A. Werner. With 50 Illustrations by Arturo Faldi.

THE HUMOUR OF AMERICA. Edited, with an Introduction and Notes, by J. Barr (of the *Detroit Free Press*). With numerous Illustrations by C. E. Brock.

VOLUMES IN PREPARATION.

THE HUMOUR OF HOLLAND. Translated, with an Introduction and Notes, by A. Werner. With numerous Illustrations by Dudley Hardy.

THE HUMOUR OF IRELAND. Selected by D. J. O'Donoghue. With numerous Illustrations by Oliver Paque.

THE HUMOUR OF RUSSIA. Translated, with Notes, by E. L. Boole, and an Introduction by Stepniak. With 50 Illustrations by Paul Frénzeny.

THE HUMOUR OF SPAIN. Translated, with an Introduction and Notes, by S. Taylor. With numerous Illustrations by H. R. Millar.

To be followed by volumes representative of ENGLAND, SCOTLAND, JAPAN, etc. The Series will be complete in about twelve volumes.

DRAMATIC ESSAYS.

EDITED BY

WILLIAM ARCHER AND ROBERT W. LOWE.

Three Vols., Crown 8vo, Cloth, Price 3/6 each.

Under the title of "Dramatic Essays" will be issued, in three volumes, such theatrical criticisms as seem to be of abiding interest.

THE FIRST SERIES will contain selections from the criticisms of LEIGH HUNT, both those published in 1807 (long out of print), and the admirable articles contributed more than twenty years later to *The Tatler*, and never republished.

THE SECOND SERIES will contain selections from the criticisms of WILLIAM HAZLITT. Hazlitt's Essays on Kean and his contemporaries have long been inaccessible, save to collectors.

THE THIRD SERIES will contain hitherto uncollected criticisms by JOHN FORSTER, GEORGE HENRY LEWES, and others, with selections from the writings of WILLIAM ROBSON (The Old Playgoer).

The Essays will be concisely but adequately annotated, and each volume will contain an Introduction by WILLIAM ARCHER, and an Engraved Portrait Frontispiece.

London : WALTER SCOTT, LIMITED, 24 Warwick Lane.

THE SCOTT LIBRARY.

Cloth, uncut edges, gilt top.   Price 1/6 per volume.

ALREADY ISSUED.

Romance of King Arthur.

Thoreau's Walden.

Thoreau's Week.

Thoreau's Essays.

Confessions of an English Opium-Eater.

Landor's Conversations.

Plutarch's Lives.

Browne's Religio Medici.

Essays and Letters of P. B. Shelley.

Prose Writings of Swift.

My Study Windows.

Lowell's Essays on the English Poets.

The Biglow Papers.

Great English Painters.

Lord Byron's Letters.

Essays by Leigh Hunt.

Longfellow's Prose.

Great Musical Composers

Marcus Aurelius.

Epictetus.

Seneca's Morals.

Whitman's Specimen Days in America.

Whitman's Democratic Vistas.

White's Natural History.

Captain Singleton.

Essays by Mazzini.

Prose Writings of Heine.

Reynolds' Discourses.

The Lover: Papers of Steele and Addison.

Burns's Letters.

Volsunga Saga.

Sartor Resartus.

Writings of Emerson.

Life of Lord Herbert.

THE SCOTT LIBRARY—*continued*.

English Prose.
The Pillars of Society.
Fairy and Folk Tales.
Essays of Dr. Johnson.
Essays of Wm. Hazlitt.
Landor's Pentameron, &c.
Poe's Tales and Essays
Vicar of Wakefield.
Political Orations.
Holmes's Autocrat.
Holmes's Poet.
Holmes's Professor.
Chesterfield's Letters.
Stories from Carleton.
Jane Eyre.
Elizabethan England.
Davis's Writings.
Spence's Anecdotes.
More's Utopia.
Sadi's Gulistan.
English Folk Tales.
Northern Studies.
Famous Reviews.
Aristotle's Ethics.
Landor's Aspasia.

Tacitus.
Essays of Elia.
Balzac.
De Musset's Comedies.
Darwin's Coral-Reefs.
Sheridan's Plays.
Our Village.
Humphrey's Clock, &c.
Tales from Wonderland.
Douglas Jerrold.
Rights of Woman.
Athenian Oracle.
Essays of Sainte-Beuve.
Selections from Plato.
Heine's Travel Sketches.
Maid of Orleans.
Sydney Smith.
The New Spirit.
Marvellous Adventures
(From the Morte d'Arthur.)
Helps's Essays.
Montaigne's Essays.
Luck of Barry Lyndon.
William Tell.
Carlyle's German Essays

London: WALTER SCOTT, LIMITED, 24 Warwick Lane.